FENN HALFLIN
AND THE
FEARZERO

FENN HALFLIN AND THE FEARZERO

Francesca Armour-Chelu

WALKER
BOOKS

First published in Great Britain 2016 by Walker Books Ltd
87 Vauxhall Walk, London SE11 5HJ

2 4 6 8 10 9 7 5 3 1

Text © 2016 Francesca Armour-Chelu
Map illustration © 2016 Francesca Armour-Chelu
Cover design © 2016 Richard Collingridge

This book has been typeset in Palantino

Printed and bound in Great Britain by Clays Ltd, St Ives plc

British Library Cataloguing in Publication Data: a catalogue record for
this book is available from the British Library

ISBN 978-1-4063-6312-8

www.walker.co.uk

For my parents, Ian and Angela
Much loved, much missed.

Into the living sea of waking dreams. – John Clare

Prologue

They'd never escape them. No one ever escaped.

Tomas knew that, but had refused to give up. He'd been on the run with Maya for two years now and the Terra Firma had never even got close. But that was before this storm had blown them off course. If only they could have got back to East Marsh, the Resistance would have hidden them deep in the almost impassable fenland, where the Terras would never find them. But it was too late for those thoughts now.

Sleeting rain stung like knives on his face and waves swamped the deck. His eyes were black-ringed and blood-shot, and his body clumsy with tiredness. To prevent from being swept overboard he'd lashed himself to the barge's wheel, steering blindly into the wall of water ahead. Tomas looked through the hatch to see if Maya was all right; she had been in no fit state to help so he'd made her get below deck.

A burst of lightning flashed on her face. Tendrils of damp hair clung to her pale forehead as she huddled on the bed, holding their new baby tight. He tried to smile encouragingly to her, but then he heard the other ship's engines growing louder.

Tomas untied himself from the wheel and cut the engine. He'd pushed the *Albatross* as hard as he could but now the hunt was over. He stumbled over to the cabin steps and staggered down, bolting the hatch behind him. The lamp was guttering out; they had to move quickly.

"Now!" he shouted.

As he reached for the baby, Maya's eye was caught by the glint at Tomas's neck: a chain with a small key on it, the gold grip shaped like an intricate knot of rope.

"The key!" she cried.

Tomas ripped the chain off and looked around wildly. The portholes were at sea level and sealed, so there was no way to get rid of it, and nowhere the Terras wouldn't look. Instead he looped the chain around the baby's head; if the baby was found they were done for anyway. Even if they weren't recognised, it was prohibited to give birth at sea. There were to be no more true Seaborns. Tears streamed down Maya's face and her hands were trembling as she covered the baby with desperate, heartbroken kisses.

"Everything will be all right," Tomas lied, as he brushed the tears from her lovely eyes; one green and one blue. Then he swaddled an otter skin around the baby, so tight it might think it was still being held and lifted a curtain to reveal a hidden cupboard under the bed. He slid the door open and behind that pushed another secret panel aside – a secret within a secret. Tomas laid the baby gently down. Then he closed the doors, dropped the curtain back and took Maya tightly in his arms. They lay trembling in the dark as the lightning strikes blazed electric blue in the cabin. With each flash the other ship's shadow grew larger, like the dorsal fin of an enormous shark.

Finally it pulled alongside them; the banging turbines reverberated in their bones, and the sour stench of diesel made their eyes water. The waves buffeting their boat stilled as the other ship absorbed the energy of the ocean, then all fell quiet. In the eerie silence, Tomas and Maya peeped through the porthole.

It was the *Warspite*, one of the Fearzero fleet; the only ships permitted on that tract of sea. Vast and brutal, it was more like a fortress than a ship. Sheets of iron, welded together with rivets the size of a man's clenched fist, soared up like a cliff. Lines of rust bled down the iron strakes. On the bow was the Terra Firma logo: a black triangle with the initials TF in the centre on a scarlet background. Ladders lined the sides and high up, winking in the night, lights began their descent. The Terras were coming.

There was a clatter as grappling lines were thrown onto the barge and scraped on the deck above, then came the vicious snarls of the Malmuts: Terra Firma dogs. Someone swore at the bolted hatch before striking it with a heavy blow. It was wrenched open.

Three huge Malmuts squeezed their sharp muzzles in through the gap and sniffed inquisitively. Scenting fear, the very thing they were bred to detect, the dogs skidded down the steps in a snarling frenzy; their claws slipping on wet treads and their fur claggy with sweat. The creatures crashed through the furniture unseeing; Malmuts could sniff a frightened human a mile away, but barely saw two feet in front of them. They scrabbled up against Maya and Tomas, growls curdling in their throats. Six Terras followed, dressed in grey uniforms, their faces completely covered by black masks that had narrow openings for the eyes and mouth with mesh behind them, to protect from the diseases Seaborns were said to carry. Across their bodies they wore a thick strap that held a gun and a short steel truncheon.

"What a stench!" came a muffled voice from behind the mask as the Terra pulled the Malmuts back, making them yelp in pain. Laughter followed.

"That's Seaborns for you," said another. "Filthy Jipseas and their stinking fish."

"Cockroaches!" another Terra spat. "Swarming back to land, spreading disease!"

He jabbed the end of his truncheon under Tomas's chin and lifted his head so he could see him better, then the Terra signalled to another who disappeared back onto the deck.

"I have a permit … Wait!" Tomas pleaded, buying time. The permit was fake of course, but Tomas held on to the hope that this might be a routine inspection. There was still a chance these Terras didn't know who they had caught. Without hesitation the Terra flicked his truncheon away from Tomas to Maya, striking her hard on the mouth. Blood spurted in an arc across her cheek, but she knew better than to cry out and gripped Tomas's arm to stop him trying to defend her. These days no one cared if a Seaborn was killed and tossed overboard; the only good Seaborn was a drowned Seaborn in the eyes of the Terra Firma.

A whistle sounded and Tomas and Maya were dragged up onto the deck. At the barge's bow end stood a lone figure. His long grey coat flapped at his ankles and a large, hooded cowl covered his face. He was gently tapping a truncheon in the palm of his hand, as if keeping time to music only he could hear. Tomas and Maya were pushed towards him.

"We have permits, sir," Tomas begged, pulling out the

papers from his pocket. He had paid highly for them on the black market; in a world without money, they had traded every piece of jewellery they owned.

But before the man even turned around, Maya knew who it was; she'd already spotted the gleam of the metal straps supporting his shattered legs.

Chilstone. Commander of the Terra Firma.

She let out a cry of fear; countless Seaborns had been drowned at Chilstone's command.

"Maya," Chilstone murmured quietly.

He pulled back his cowl, revealing a long, narrow face. He was delicately built, with soft skin so fishy-white and translucent that blue veins could be seen snaking at his temples. A fine web of lines was etched across his face, left like tidemarks from constant pain making him grimace and twitch uncontrollably. His large eyes were pale and gelatinous, like oysters, and he missed nothing as he looked Tomas and Maya over. Inhaling deeply to prepare himself, he took one shuffling step towards them, wincing as the steel gears implanted in his knees cranked open and took his weight.

He'd known what the price of saving his legs would be – that each time he moved the iron pegs embedded in his shin would rip at the muscles they anchored – but he never complained. Instead he thanked his suffering; Pain was his trusted counsellor, the confidant who never slept, muttering in his ear all night long, reminding him of the peril of clemency. When Pain succeeded in wrenching Chilstone from his troubled sleep, the nightmares played on. He saw himself in his mind's eye: on his hands and knees – what was left of them – crawling through the sinking Fearzero's twisted hull, dragging his shredded legs behind him like bloodied rags.

A Terra handed Chilstone the permits. He examined them, nodding to himself, then frowned, as if he'd just heard some sensible advice but was reluctant to take it. His fist clenched as he stared at the permit and the Terra backed away, well out of striking range. But Chilstone continued to inspect the forgery; the names were false of course, but it was useful to note the forger's style.

Then, without warning, Chilstone held the permits aloft and opened his fingers, letting the storm rip them into the waves. Tomas and Maya Demari had played no part in the assassination attempt against him, but they were leaders of the Resistance and without them it would crumble. All trace of the Demaris had to be obliterated. But Chilstone couldn't do it here; even weighted bodies had an irritating habit of washing ashore, such was the power of the sea and its brutal new currents. Chilstone didn't want to make martyrs of them, and make the Seaborns even more determined to fight back. He jerked his head towards a Terra.

Immediately Tomas and Maya were hauled up the ladders to the Fearzero, where Maya's screams became lost in the icy wind. The Malmuts were kicked back into their steel cage, which was hoisted up the Fearzero's side, leaving just one Terra on deck. He quickly painted a crude yellow scythe on the barge's bow.

I

A few hours later a rickety old tug was towing the *Albatross* across the mouth of a windswept estuary. The storm had faded now, leaving the sky a muddy grey.

It was remote: surrounded by boggy salt marsh where the wide green river flooded into the open sea. Once there had been a busy market town nestling in the valley, but now it lay deep beneath a broad expanse of water. It had been swallowed overnight when the coastal defences failed to stop the Great Rising and the sea had surged another three hundred feet, adding to the water that had already engulfed the low-lying lands. The colossal waves of the Great Rising robbed even more of the little land that was left and millions had drowned. Since then, only scraps of higher rocky land were left for survivors to live on – although not all survivors. Only those who could prove

Landborn ancestry, or obtain permits, had rights to land.

As far as the eye could see was salt bog and fenland; hundreds of miles of it smothered by a blanket of murky mist. East Marsh was a labyrinth of waterways and rivers, hidden by impenetrable reed beds. Thickets of groundsel bushes flecked with white flowers grew between the relics of old woodlands, where the branches of brine-dead trees clawed through the fog like a drowning man's fingers. The mists rarely cleared enough for anyone to do more than glimpse the silhouette of an immense Wall far inland, even though it was at least two hundred feet high by now. The Terra Firma were forging ahead with their building programme; it would take years but eventually the two ends of the Wall would meet and the East Isle it enclosed would be safe. Safe from the sea, safe from what was left of the Seaborn Resistance, but near to the marsh and its riches of peat that the Landborns needed for fuel and topsoil; land inside the walls might be safe from water, but it was barren and rocky.

The only high ground that remained here was East Point, the ridge of an old hill; now a spindly peninsula that curled around the estuary like half a horseshoe. On the very end stood an old squat shepherd's hut, surrounded by a scrubby garden of silverwort thistles and sea lupins, scorched so black by the sea winds it looked like there had been a fire. The owner was now at the helm of the tug, a man called Halflin.

If he had ever had another name, he had long forgotten it.

It was hard to guess his age; the mop of grizzled hair that reached his shoulders made him look older than his forty-three years, and his body was shattered by hard work and fear. His skin was still smooth, as if all the wrinkles had been swept away by the harsh winds, but deep, dark clefts ran from his nose to his mouth then down his chin. His mouth was a thin slit, as if made with the flick of a switchblade, and he never smiled. A semi-circle of beard grew around his chin in scraggy grey tufts like sea grass. After years of peering into salt spray his eyes were squinted, but because of this his hearing was sharp. As the tug slowly dragged the *Albatross* upriver, he thought he heard something over the sound of the engine.

In the warm shadows of the barge's cupboard, the baby had woken up. It hadn't cried at first, but now it felt a strange nagging feeling inside, something like pain. Hunger. The baby had tipped its face this way and that, searching for the comfort of its mother. Finding nothing, it had let out its first cry.

The tug was heading into the Sunkyard, which was built across one of the many rivers that flowed into the estuary. The Fearzeros were too big to come here – they would have run aground – so Halflin collected the condemned boats out at sea and towed them in. Here boats were sunk, although the Terra Firma never used that word, instead calling it "decommissioning". Just the threat of losing their boat was enough to keep most Seaborns obedient. As Halflin slowed the tug to navigate past the old church tower poking out of the water, the only other person in sight was one of the eel-catchers from the Sargasson tribe, drawing his horses through the frosty reed beds in the distance. It was unusual for them to come this far out, risking being seen by spies; the Terra Firma had made it a crime to take peat or wood reserved for Landborns.

He stared ahead doggedly, hoping the man wouldn't see him. The Sargassons didn't look kindly on Halflin working for the Terra Firma, and Halflin could never reveal why he didn't refuse them. He clung to the hope that if he did as he was ordered there was a chance he'd see his family again.

A new jetty flanked the harbour, where the doomed boats and barges were tethered like cattle waiting for slaughter. The Terra Firma had been especially busy lately, sweeping up the last of the Seaborn Resistance. This morning there had been four boats to destroy, each marked with the Terra Firma's yellow scythe, the symbol of death to show that a boat was to be scuttled. There was a beautiful houseboat, which would break Halflin's heart to sink, two fishing boats and now the old barge. One of the few perks of this hated job was that the Terra Firma usually turned a blind eye to

Halflin gleaning whatever he needed from the boats he scuttled. But he had been told to sink this one immediately, and on no account was he to salvage anything from it, so he took the *Albatross* straight to the Punchlock.

The Punchlock had been built in the tributary that had the strongest currents. There were two wooden gates opposite each other like a lock in a canal and over them a huge scaffold had been erected, like a hangman's gibbet, from which a tethering chain hung to keep boats in position. Beneath the waterline there was a lethal mechanism: two metal spikes, sharp enough to puncture the thickest hull. The tug boat would tow the condemned vessel inside the gates and automatically the spikes were winched out. Once at maximum tension they snapped inwards, like an animal trap, punching two giant holes in the vessel. Just as quickly the jaws would open again, leaving the boat free to sink. Within minutes it would be below water. It was easy; no messy explosives, no noise to disturb the peace. Water did the work of destroying the Seaborns' boats, an irony not lost on Halflin. The second gate would open and the current dragged the carcasses down into the flooded valley, where they were snared in the streets of the drowned town. At low tide, if the water was settled, it was possible to see the graveyard of hulks lodged between ruins of old houses and skeletons of trees where shoals of fish darted between slime-black branches.

The *Albatross* was in position. Halflin untied the tow line and steered the tug in the smooth curve around the Punchlock to go back to pick up the next boat. As soon as the second gate closed, the Punchlock spikes sprung shut on the bow of the *Albatross*, slicing cleanly through the wood. Then the spikes sprang out again in readiness for the next vessel.

Immediately water gushed in, filling the lower deck. For a few moments the barge remained balanced on the surface, but once the front cabin filled, it began to list. Maps and tide charts floated up, their ink bleeding away; cups and jugs drifted off their hooks. When the largest cabin was full, the *Albatross* abruptly tipped forward, nose first, and plummeted down through the thick green water towards the ocean bed. It fell quickly, like a kestrel diving to the ground.

As Halflin watched the stern disappear he was troubled again, thinking about the strange sound he'd heard just before the boat was sunk. Staring at the belching bubbles on the water's surface, he scratched his eyebrow with the callused stump that was left of his forefinger and slowed the tug.

Babies have a primordial instinct to hold their breath under water, and in this one's case it was remarkably strong. As the baby felt the cold rush of water, it gasped in shock, filling its lungs with air so it floated up inside the secret cupboard. The swirling current of water then drew the baby towards the gaping hole the spike had made. Instinctively the baby closed its throat, flailed its tiny arms and began to swim, out through the hole and up towards the light. In a few moments the baby was bobbing like an apple on the estuary's surface and it let out the air that had saved its life in a long, pitiful wail. Catching the sound for certain this time, Halflin lifted the flaps of his rabbit-skin cap from his ears, cut the tug's engine and looked back.

For a second he thought it was a dying seagull; there were plenty of those in the polluted waters. He narrowed his eyes and peered through the haze. Not a gull; a baby. What he'd taken to be a slick of oil was the black wet fur of otter skin around it.

"A bairn!" he cried.

He put a foot on the rail, readying to jump in, but stopped himself just in time, teetering on the deck. There'd be two dead bodies in the water if he did that; there was no way to climb back on the tug once overboard. Instead he ran to the stern and grabbed one of the landing nets, a wide round one on a long pole that he used to scoop up fish he caught with the line. Halflin balanced on the rail and peered into the water.

The baby was still there, but apart from bobbing in the rise and fall of the tug's wash, it was motionless. Halflin held the net out as far as he could, but the baby was being carried away from the tug by the suction of the *Albatross* as it slid towards the sunken town. Halflin grabbed another pole and as fast as his trembling hands could manage he lashed them together and dragged the net through the choppy water. After two tries, the baby at last slid in. It was face down.

Halflin hauled the net back onto the tug, trying not to bump it on the sides but still needing to be quick. His knees were weak with fear as he fell to the deck, pulling off the baby's freezing wet shift. It was a boy, no more than a few weeks old. Halflin parted its lips, hooked his little finger down its throat and pulled out a tangle of oily seaweed. The baby flopped lifelessly in his hands.

The wind was blowing lightly and the tug drifted on a slow current. Gulls wheeled through the rain-shadowed sky above but even they were silent for once, as if they too were listening out for life. There was no sound on the tug apart from the soft slop-slop-slop of water against the side and Halflin's own heavy, frightened breathing.

Halflin started frantically rubbing the baby's chest but still it lay motionless. He picked it up and stared into its tiny, crumpled face for a sign of hope, but it was as limp as a rag doll. He carefully laid it back down, took a deep breath, closed his mouth around the baby's tiny blue lips and breathed out. Like a balloon, the baby's chest lifted, expanded, and deflated. Halflin repeated this again and again, but it was too late. Each time the baby's chest swelled but flattened again immediately; there was no breath in it save that which Halflin blew there. Halflin felt his throat tighten with the loss of something he'd only just found.

"Don't be dead!" he whispered. He picked the baby up again and held it close against his thumping heart, cradling its head on his shoulder, willing it to live. "Don't be dead," he said again, almost angry now; he hadn't woken up this morning expecting his heart to be torn out again. He rocked the baby back and forth.

Suddenly the baby coughed, spluttering water all down itself and him, and opened its eyes. It began shivering and crying.

Halflin grabbed some old rags to dry it and peeled away the last strands of seaweed clinging to it. There was a key around its neck. His face grew ashen with fear as he recognised the design: the key of the Demari family. The symbol of the Resistance.

What idiot would put that around a baby's neck? Might as well tie a noose around it. Halflin scowled as he rubbed the baby's head dry. He didn't want any more to do with that lot; reckless fools, getting people's hopes up but never delivering. One thing Halflin knew was that you only defied the Terra Firma if you stood a chance of winning; all the Resistance had done was poke a tiger with a feather. Since the assassination attempt on Chilstone, he'd become even more vicious. Halflin ripped the chain off, and was about to toss it overboard when he had second thoughts. It wasn't his to throw away, and as angry as he was, he couldn't destroy something so precious, and once so full of hope.

Instead he stashed it deep in his pocket and pulled the scarf from his neck, carefully swaddling the baby. It was worse than he'd suspected: several toes were webbed. Halflin had seen this before; the deformity was once very rare but, over time, in a drenched world, more children were being born with the defect. It marked them clearly as being from Seaborn stock and it had to be undone. As Halflin had told his own wife when their youngest was born webbed, *better cut now than killed later.* A hot bolt of nausea thickened in the base of his throat as Halflin peered back out to sea. His forehead pricked with sweat as he scanned for the *Warspite*, but it was now a tiny speck in the distance. He let out the breath he hadn't realised he'd been holding.

Quickly Halflin put the baby into a wicker catch basket and lurched back to the wheel; he had to get the baby as far away from the Punchlock as possible. It was too early to stop work and he shouldn't do anything to draw attention to himself. He steered the tug towards shore, moored it, then ran with the basket to the workshop where he sorted through the loot gleaned from scuttled boats. He lit the lamp, turning it down low so it would burn all night and anyone passing would think he was at work. Halflin then carefully buttoned his reefer jacket over the baby to hide it and keep it warm. From a distance no one would think he was carrying anything, although they might wonder how an old man could get fat in times as lean as these.

Checking no one was nearby, Halflin hurried out, slipping into the gorse like a wily old fox. He was wise to be cautious; who knew who might be watching in these dark days? Terra Firma spies were everywhere.

It was nearly night time when he stumbled through the back door of his hut, clawing for breath. He quickly bolted the door behind him and closed the shutters to hide the light. Then he fumbled along the driftwood shelf, found a candle stub and lit it. The hazy light revealed two sparse rooms, separated by a threadbare sail sheet. In one room was an upturned crate next to a bed, which was made from a door laid on top of two old oil cans and covered with a sailcloth pad stuffed with bulrush seeds. In the larger room a second door bridged two crates to make a table, and next to an oil drum stove stood a wooden clinker boat cut in half – the bow pointing upwards – where Halflin could sit to smoke his pipe, protected from needling draughts. Plants hung from the ceiling to dry: marsh cinquefoil, red baneberry and gypsywort. Over the mantelpiece gaped a shark's jaw, its teeth glinting, and inside this perched a gull with a torn wing that Halflin had rescued. Now it eyed the bundle beadily and squawked for fish before flapping clumsily to the ground. Halflin shooed it away and shuffled over to the table. He propped the candle in a cup and shoved the dirty plates aside, then carefully laid the baby down and pulled off the scarf.

He took a penknife from his pocket, slid out the bright steel blade and lifted the baby's foot, noticing how the skin had pruned from being in the water. He quailed; Halflin was as tough as old leather but he'd never had the stomach for hurting any living creature. Even stoking up the stove he'd break the bark off each log to give the woodlice a chance to escape, singeing his fingertips as he plucked them from the flames. Folding the blade back into the handle he stared glumly at the baby wriggling helplessly on the table before him, but he knew he had to protect it. He gritted his teeth, pulled the knife out again and tested its sharpness on his thumb, drawing a thin line of blood across his own skin. A sharp blade would hurt less and the wounds would heal better. The Terras had got wise to this trick and looked for scars now; you had to be so neat.

He rummaged on the shelves and found the precious jar of honey he'd been saving. There was just enough. He stripped some leaves of dried woundwort into a cup and poured water on them, then held the blade in the candle flame for a moment, wiped it briskly on his cuff and tore two strips of cotton from his own shirt. He dipped the stub of his finger in the honey, put it in the baby's mouth and let the baby suck. Holding the baby's tiny foot in his rough hand he spread the offending toes out, stretching the wafer thin cobwebs of skin, like a frog's.

He made the first cut, biting his lip as he trimmed off the bits of extra flesh as though he was paring an apple and tossed the scraps of skin into the fire; there could be no evidence. Immediately the baby yelped in pain but Halflin put more honey in its mouth. He worked swiftly. The honey had barely dissolved on the baby's tongue before he gave it more again. Soon the toes were separated.

Halflin gently slid the damp woundwort leaves between the baby's toes, then cleaned the honey jar with the cotton rags and wound them around the baby's feet to heal the wounds. With the baby crying and shaking, he wrapped the remains of his shirt around it and laid it in an old box he had packed with sailcloth, then tugged a sweater from where it hung on a nail and tucked it around the baby. But it still wouldn't stop crying; it needed feeding. In the corner stood a wooden bucket of water where a pitcher of goat's milk was kept cold. That'd do.

Halflin filled a bottle with milk, cut the finger off an

ancient rubber glove, pierced this with the end of his knife and fitted it over the bottle neck, then squatted down by the stove to feed the baby. It sucked and mewed, then at last, worn out with crying, the baby blinked drowsily and fell asleep.

Halflin pulled on his only other shirt and flopped down in the clinker boat seat. He needed to think; a smoke would help. He fumbled in his pocket for his pipe and felt the cold of the chain. He took it out and held it aloft, staring as the key twisted back and forth, glinting in the firelight, then stuffed it away again. He tamped some dried yarrow into his pipe, lit the strands, and sucked hard several times to get it going. Damp smoke unfurled up into the rafters like a ribbon.

Halflin shook his head and frowned at the box and its contents. If he ever discovered a Seaborn hiding on a Sunkmarked boat, he was supposed to turn them in. How was he supposed to keep a crying baby hidden from the Terra Firma when he was collecting boats for them every day? He'd had some bad luck in his time, but this baby was the worst thing to ever happen to him. Even so, he'd pulled enough tar-smothered gulls from the oil-slickened sea to know that if you rescue something, then you're responsible for it. Only one person could help: Lundy. She lived deep in the treacherous marshes; the baby would be safe out there, for as long as she'd have him.

2

The boy Halflin found no more needed to be taught how to swim than a spider learns to spin. The first time he slid into the water he instinctively knew how to pack air into the many pockets of his lungs, like they were separate bundles he'd unwrap when needed. He could soon dive down for ten minutes or more before needing to come up for air.

This morning, deep in the dark green water, he was swimming directly above the hundreds of boats lying rotting in the ruins of the old town, their sterns sticking up through the wrecks of the stone houses. He dived down, weaving through the broken masts and rigging that lay tangled in the shattered hulls. When he arrived at the spot with the most recent wrecks he dived even deeper, down past bosuns' chairs and figureheads of beautiful women, wrenched off and lying broken on the old cobbled streets.

Bright shoals of mackerel flashed like silver daggers around him, swimming in and out of portholes and through the ripped bulkheads. He'd never been this deep before, but he felt happy in the gloom. He was never afraid, never feared drowning. Here he was away from prying eyes and felt free.

There was an old barge lying across the main gate of the sunken town. The hull of a smaller fishing boat had been crushed beneath it and the wooden struts stuck out like ribs. As he swam closer, he noticed how the two holes on either side of its bow looked exactly like the empty eye sockets in a skull and he shuddered. Suddenly an enormous black eel darted out of the nearest hole, straight for him, its teeth glinting like needles. It had to be twenty feet long at least. In all his life on East Point he'd never seen one so big. The eel came too quickly to dodge and clamped its vicious jaws around his leg. He jolted in shock and let out a stream of bubbles.

"Wake up!"

Halflin was shaking him awake. When he didn't move he gave him a sharp kick for good measure.

"Wake up, boy!"

Halflin never used the name he'd given the baby: Fenn, the name of the wetlands that had hidden him, a Landborn name, a name to hide behind. Maybe he thought by using it he would grow to care for him and he didn't want that; he didn't want to care about anything ever again.

"Geddup! Get dressed," Halflin barked.

Fenn slowly woke, rubbing sleep's glue from his eyes and blinking in confusion as Halflin threw his clothes at him. It was pitch black outside but Halflin had already rekindled the fire, and the room smelt of wood smoke and bacon fat. The oil lamp had been lit and its yellow glaze filled all but the darkest shadows in the corners of the kitchen where they slept on the bitterest winter nights. A forest of shadows shimmied across the whitewashed walls as Halflin's ropes of drying marsh plants swayed in the draught, and his bottles of ointments winked on the driftwood shelves. The old gull perched on the back of Halflin's smoking chair, preening its crooked wings and watching Halflin's every move in case of scraps.

Fenn groggily dragged himself out of bed. Normally he was awake first, feeding the pigs, collecting the eggs for breakfast, packing a bundle of food for Halflin to take out while he worked down at the Punchlock, and he scowled at having missed the opportunity for an early secret swim. He was forbidden to even go near the water and Halflin always kept him close to the hut, to look after the pigs or gather plants and herbs from the scrap of land behind, obscured by reeds. Halflin had always been terrified of anyone seeing him, but even though Fenn knew this and felt guilty disobeying, the pull of the water was too strong. He was like a moth to the flame; any time Halflin went to work, or before Halflin even woke up, Fenn would try to sneak out.

With nothing to get excited about, Fenn was slower than usual. He stretched and yawned widely at the thought of another day of being stuck inside, first mending nets while his grandad worked the Punchlock, then studying his one book saved from a barge by Halflin years before: a thick encyclopaedia covering every subject from Cadavers to Dragons. He peered over at the window; it had been glazed with twenty or more jars jammed tightly together on their sides, in which lay the chubby corpses of bristle-backed blowflies that had battered themselves to death trying to reach the sun. Through the shades of dappled turquoise glass, Fenn saw it was dark outside.

"It's still night!" he said, his voice thick with sleep as he pulled on one of Halflin's old Guernseys, greasy and blackened with dirt and oil. It stank of pipe smoke and fish and although Fenn was tall for his age it still hung halfway down his thighs. Fenn only ever had Halflin's cast-offs, hemmed up crudely, for even if Halflin had the means to barter for clothing the right size, it would have been too dangerous. Someone might guess about Fenn.

Fenn only ever went out before dawn or after dusk, so he was ghostly white, like one of the spills they used to light the fire, and never meeting another soul meant he had a shy, closed-off look in his eyes. Sometimes, after Halflin had finished for the day and if they'd got a bit more food than usual, he would stoke up the fire and tell stories. He'd tell Fenn about the mischief he'd got up to as a young boy or make up tales about his missing finger; like a squid had bitten it off, or he'd been picking his nose and it got stuck so his mum had to cut it off, and if Fenn looked up that right nostril really carefully … then Fenn would laugh so much there'd be tears in his eyes. When happy, Fenn's face would open up and if anyone had seen him they'd have said he was handsome. Although he was thin, he was wiry, strong and healthy. But Fenn didn't know what he looked like; there were no mirrors in the house, save a broken shard lodged on the shelf where Halflin shaved once a year – his birthday gift to himself. Fenn only ever saw bits of himself, a jigsaw face; a clear blue or green eye, an eyebrow there, a shock of soot-black hair.

"The *Panimengro*'s comin' today," Halflin reminded him gruffly. Every few months the *Panimengro* or one of the other Gleaners would moor up secretly in one of the tributaries, coming to trade whatever flotsam and jetsam they had scavenged from the oceans. Ever since Chilstone realised the Sargassons had been helping the Resistance, the Terra Firma had forbidden Gleaners to dock at East Marsh or anyone to trade with them. But Halflin had to take the risk; he needed too many things the marsh couldn't provide. He'd bundle up hare-meat, a flitch of bacon, eggs and medicinal herbs, swapping them for diesel, tools and parts for a generator he'd been trying to build – for what seemed like for ever to Fenn.

Halflin pierced a slab of bacon griddling on the stove and wrapped a slice of rice bread around it, squeezing it into a clump. He tossed it over and Fenn took a greedy bite.

"I forgot," Fenn mumbled through a mouthful of bread and hot fat. He waited until Halflin turned away again before ripping off the juicy rind and flipping it into the gull's beak. The gull guzzled it down with a happy squawk.

"Told yer before, bacon's too good fer the bird," Halflin grumbled, without turning around.

"What are we trading?"

"Meat. An' get us six dozen eggs from the store."

With that Halflin hitched three large hams up onto the rough table and rolled them in a thick layer of salt, then wrapped oily sailcloth around them, tying each with a length of twine. Fenn stared vacantly at him, slack-jawed and dopey. Halflin caught him looking.

"Stop faffin' about an' get on wi' it then! An' feed the animals while yer at it," he barked.

Fenn jumped up and quickly tugged his boots on. He

sometimes imagined what it would be like if his grandad wasn't so harsh. He guessed it must be because seeing him reminded Halflin of the day when Fenn's parents had drowned, but Halflin didn't like Fenn asking about the past. He stumbled over to the stone sink and cranked the pump's handle a couple of times until green water spat out of the copper piping. He splashed his face, rubbed it dry with his cuff, grabbed the bucket of pig swill then opened the front door.

Outside it was freezing and Fenn shivered as his breath puffed out in the cold air. A few raggedy stars still lingered in the sky, and a lank, briny fog had seeped up from the estuary and folded around the little stone house, making it hard to see more than a few feet. Fenn stumbled into the pigsty, emptied the swill bucket into the troughs, scratched the ears of the old sow who still missed her piglets, tossed the hens some marsh millet and filled the bucket with eggs from a fat earthenware crock, full of slippery water-glass to keep them fresh over winter. Back in the hut Halflin had already lined a crate with straw.

"Go see if it's docked," he said, without looking up.

"But it's too dark," Fenn moaned.

"Skeg fer lights then!" Halflin scolded, shaking his head wearily at Fenn's idleness.

Since he'd been old enough to climb a ladder up into

37

the roof space it had been Fenn's job to scan the "Whale's Acre" as Halflin called it. Every hour he had to look out for incoming boats: Fearzeros bringing boats to the Punchlock, Gleaners trading their sea harvests, and now and again the odd barge with Seaborns seeking refuge. When those came he'd help Halflin quickly bundle up whatever they could spare – a few eggs, a peck of rice – and leave it out on the marsh, beneath the red-berried Wayfaring tree. The Seaborns knew to look there, even if they never knew who left it. Fenn felt sorry for them; East Marsh was harsh, but so long as his grandad did what the Terra Firma told him, he wouldn't be rounded up and imprisoned in one of the dreaded Terra Firma Missions, where prisoners were forced to mine rock to build the Walls or to cut peat for fuel; destroying the marsh, inch by inch. Thousands of Seaborns had been swallowed up in this huge task and Fenn sometimes spotted one of the gigantic prison ships arriving in the distance with new labour for East Isle's Wall.

Fenn pushed the drying rack to one side to reveal a hidden trapdoor, slid it aside and clambered up into the loft. This was where he had to hide whenever a ship came to East Point, where he'd lie in wait until the ship departed. He crawled over to where Halflin had fixed up a telescope, which poked out of a secret spy hole made by lifting one of the hut's tiles. Beneath it was a small wooden platform with a couple of blankets, a bottle of water and some dry oats stored in a rat-proof tin, in case Fenn ever had to hide for longer than a few hours.

Fenn hated hiding away; his scars were invisible to the naked eye, but if discovered, they marked him as true Seaborn and Halflin was always reminding him that the Terra Firma believed anyone with the mutation hailed from pure Seaborn stock.

East Marsh was especially dangerous for Seaborns. Halflin had often told him how Chilstone had taken all the babies from East Marsh to punish the Sargassons for helping the Resistance. Fenn knew he would have been taken too, had Halflin not outwitted them. He loved hearing about their midnight flight to a woman called Lundy – who hid him until the raids were over – and the terrifying part where Halflin tricked the vicious Malmuts. It sounded so full of excitement and danger, and there wasn't a lot of either of those in Fenn's life. Nor would there ever be, as far as he could see, so long as his sole company was his grandad and a sad old sow.

With a heavy sigh, Fenn pressed his eye to the cold brass of the telescope and peered down the shaft. He found the *Panimengro* immediately, its lights twinkling, chugging steadily up one of the quieter tributaries that led inland.

They always moored out of sight; they weren't supposed to trade on East Marsh because Chilstone was choking all supplies to the Resistance – and anyone who helped it. Fenn had always dreamt of being out there on the sea, to feel so much space around him, and the ocean beneath him, to sail out to the horizon and discover what lay beyond.

The *Panimengro* was earlier than usual; dawn hadn't yet broken and the night sky was only just fading to the deepest indigo. Fenn yawned and stretched out lazily on the blanket. A sly idea sneaked into his head with a wink: if he said he hadn't seen it yet he could have a few minutes rest from chores, lolling in the cosy roof space. So instead of going straight back down he lay on his stomach, idly sweeping the telescope across the vast black ocean, seeing if there was anything else of interest. It was as he lingered on the faint point where the dark sea met the darker sky that he saw it; a huge patch of pure black looming on the horizon, as if an island had grown there overnight. He strained his eyes to see better; it was a Fearzero. But why was it in the dark like that, lights off, like it was skulking, waiting to pounce?

Fenn climbed back down the ladder.

"Grandad?"

"Yep?" Halflin said, barely looking up from packing the crate.

"There's a Fearzero, but its lights are off…"

The colour instantly drained from Halflin's face. He wrenched a telescope from his pocket and stumbled out of the door. He was back almost immediately, looking like he had aged ten years in as many seconds. The gull seemed to sense something was wrong and tried to fly into the eaves, screeching as it crashed into the drying rack and making leaves and dust rain down.

"Gimme them bags!" Halflin said weakly.

Halflin's voice was normally gruff, but it suddenly sounded thin and scared. Fenn looked anxiously at him. He always thought of Halflin in much the same way he did the old, gnarled oak tree growing by the house: ugly, tough and unrelenting, but always there. It frightened him to hear his shaky voice.

"Why?" Fenn asked, taking a tattered leather bag and a rucksack from the door and handing them to him.

"Nothin' on the tow line! No boats!" Halflin said, stuffing the bags with whatever came easiest to hand: a husk of rice bread, a pouch of scurvy grass, his leather gauntlets and a box of matches. Fenn looked at him blankly.

"Why's it here then?"

"Dunno, but we're not waitin' to find out. It's the *Warspite*…"

Fenn's heart beat faster. Halflin had always told him that if he ever saw the *Warspite*, hiding in the loft would not be enough; Fenn would have to run and never stop. Halflin scanned the room quickly, cursing himself; in the early days he'd always had a bag ready for flight, but as the years had come and gone he'd grown complacent. Now the moment was upon them he couldn't think straight. What would they need? He struggled to keep his voice level and calm.

"Get yerself a knife," he said.

Fenn rummaged in the tin where they kept the knives and passed the sharpest over, his hands trembling.

"Someone must've seen yer!" Halflin said, throwing the knife in Fenn's rucksack. "Have yer been sneakin' out?" he asked accusingly, before grabbing one of the hams and stuffing it in his bag.

"N–no," Fenn stammered.

Halflin put his head in his hands, marshalling his thoughts.

"Have ter get yer away from here," he muttered to himself.

"Where to?" Fenn asked. His voice was wobbly and he tried to keep it steady. *Had* someone seen him when he'd been swimming? He thought he'd always been so careful.

Halflin didn't seem to hear him. Instead he pushed past Fenn, stumbled over to the table and crouched down in the shadows, his fingers scrabbling at the wooden planks. Quickly he found a hole in the floorboard, stuck his finger in and pulled it, coughing and spluttering as the dust flew up. Fenn stared in bewilderment. In the whole of his thirteen years cooped up in the hut he'd never known it was there.

Halflin reached into a secret stash hole, lifted out another board and then an old tin box. He yanked the lid off. Inside was an old compass, a bag of jewellery and silver and an unopened bottle of the same liquid brown medicine he took when his back hurt more than usual – the stuff that made his speech slur and his eyelids droop. Reaching further in, he pulled out a wad of documents: fake sea-permits and ID cards. He rifled through them frantically, his hands shaking. At last he found what he was looking for: a sea-permit and ID card for Fenn, with false dates of birth, and a blank permit. As he groped in the dark, his fingers touched the cold gold key he'd taken from Fenn's neck, and for a split second he paused, wondering if he should take it. No; it was better left in the dark and forgotten. He forced the boards back into place, jammed the papers in the bag and shoved Fenn's rucksack at him.

"Where're we going?" Fenn asked as he hitched the bag onto his shoulder.

Halflin yanked back the heavy iron bolt across the door.

"Out the back! Less chance of being seen. Go!" he said, giving Fenn a push.

Across the doorway a spider had spun a web, its spokes

43

blanched with the frosty dew of morning and set rigid; *web across the door, a visit for sure*. Halflin glowered and angrily brushed the threads away; he knew who the visitor would be.

A veil of icy mist blocked their view of the path and it was impossible to see more than a foot ahead. Halflin grabbed a stick and tapped the ground in front of him like a blind man as he loped away from the hut.

"Keep up!" he growled, and for the first time in years took Fenn's hand in his own rough paw and yanked him down the flint path, the tip-tapping of his stick echoing across the estuary water.

3

The path led towards the marsh. It passed the ancient, wind-stunted oak, only just keeping anchor in the rocky ground, then snaked down through the gorse before dissolving into a muddy trail used more by wild creatures than humans. Fenn had never been into the marsh before, and despite his fear, felt a tremor of excitement. He glanced back over his shoulder, marvelling at how small his home suddenly seemed, silhouetted against the ashy moon.

"Where—?" Fenn began, but Halflin put his finger to his lips, signing for him to wait; marsh vapours had a knack of making sounds carry. They hurried on until the gorse gave way to an army of bulrushes, higher than either of them, their spiky seed heads thrusting into the lightening sky like spears. Whichever direction Fenn looked was the same, there seemed to be no path at all, but Halflin kept his eyes on the ground, taking them ever deeper into the dense reed beds; he knew that where the animals trod would be safe for them. Once they were completely concealed, Halflin nodded.

"Where are we going?" Fenn panted as he ran to keep up. For an old man Halflin was surprisingly fast, even though his breath was ragged and his forehead shone with sweat.

"Lundy," he said. Fenn was about to ask more but Halflin put his hand up. "Stop chelpin' an' save yer breath," he instructed. "It's a good way yet!"

They pushed on, away from the inky night and into the marsh's milky fog. The air was frosty and the reeds were bent with icy stalactites. As they stumbled through the blackthorn, knuckles of ice fell from its black prickles, stippling the water slopping at their feet. As Halflin and Fenn strode on, the clouds of their breath were lost against the white mist hanging over that part of the marsh. They had been running for nearly an hour when the ghostly shape of a ship's hulk loomed through the haze.

"Is that Lundy's?" Fenn asked, pushing forward. Halflin yanked him down to his knees.

"Could be Terras there," he whispered.

They crawled closer, peeping through the reeds, checking for movement, but save for the sudden startling of an avocet taking flight from the rushes, everywhere was still.

At Halflin's sign they broke cover and scampered across the open ground to the boat, peaty black clods kicking up from their heels as they ran.

When exactly the *Ionia* had been shipwrecked was long before living memory, but Halflin remembered playing on the wreck as a child. It was sixty feet long, painted black with pitch; probably a fishing smack washed up in the last Rising. The *Ionia* was just one of hundreds of vessels littering the marshes for up to twenty miles inland.

Over time the boat had settled, sinking deep into the oozy black mud, like a hen nestling down in straw. Old doors and broken pieces of wood leaned up against the sides under which Lundy stored wreckage gathered from the marsh. She had dragged all kinds of things back here: engine parts, scraps of twisted metal, a fridge door, empty paint cans, hubcaps and plastic chairs. Anything to recycle or barter; all now green with mildew.

A few yards from the *Ionia*, on the little hillocks of drier land, she'd grown vegetables, and on the last piece of high ground stood a neat pile of large, flat stones. Ragged robin and skullcap plants grew up against the weatherboards and lush moss caked the boat like a carpet of lime velvet, growing around the windows cut into the wood. A rich thicket of woundwort grew beneath the narrow steps that ran up the side of the boat to a door hacked out of the hull, halfway up.

The *Ionia* looked like part of the marsh itself, as if it had always been there and a hazy tranquillity hung over it, like a shroud. For a moment Halflin wondered if she'd died. It had been a year since he last came, bringing provisions she couldn't glean from the marsh: a bale of linen and paraffin for her lamps.

Halflin stealthily climbed the slime-green steps and listened tentatively at the door. When he was sure the place was deserted he beckoned to Fenn, who tiptoed up and followed him inside. Halflin crept under the curtain and into the boat.

"She must be out on the marsh," he said. "We'll get yer dry."

They were in a huge room, divided into compartments by hemp fishing nets that were woven with rags and shards of plastic. The whole place reeked of salty sweet leeks. Steam from damp cloths rose like ghosts in front of a pot-bellied stove, where a lid bounced on a pan of bubbling soup. Around the walls plants and roots were drying: water starwort, yellow pimpernel and seaholly. By the fire there was a rocking chair made from the barrel of a wheelbarrow strapped between two tyres, and on this curled a huge, one-eyed ginger tom cat with ears so torn they looked lacy. There was no sign of any other living thing. Never having been so close to a cat before, Fenn couldn't resist reaching out to stroke the dense orange fur. Unused to anyone but Lundy, the cat bushed up its fur in fear, then hissing angrily it lashed out, leaving four deep welts across Fenn's hand. Bright blobs of blood instantly beaded on his skin.

"Damn thing," Halflin muttered, toeing the animal brusquely out of the way. Snarling, the cat clawed up one of the nets, glowering at them, its frayed tail twitching viciously. Halflin yanked the scrap of cloth from his own neck and gently wrapped it around Fenn's wound.

"It were jus' scared. Don't meddle wi' creatures yer don't know, boy, an' yer won't get hurt!" Halflin murmured. As he tightened the knot there was a click of metal behind them and Fenn jumped; a bulky woman blocked the doorway, pointing the snout of a loaded harpoon at them.

"No!" Halflin cried, instantly placing himself between the harpoon's point and Fenn. Lundy squinted to see better.

"Halflin...?" She lowered the harpoon. "Thought you were thieves," she said. Lundy turned and whistled down the steps.

"Gelert!" she called.

An enormous wolfhound, which reached the same height as Fenn's shoulders, trotted up beside her. She clicked her fingers and the dog obediently slunk over to a goat-skin rug, where it lay down and stretched out, resting its head on massive paws as it gazed adoringly at Lundy. Fenn considered stroking its shaggy white fur as it padded by, but remembered the cat's reaction. Lundy looked Halflin up and down.

"Time's not been kind," she said, "but expect you could say the same of me."

She laughed creakily despite her eyes being full of pain, and poked Fenn with a witchy nail.

"He's grown!" she said, as Halflin stepped aside. "Tall, but skinny!"

Fenn stared. Lundy was like a female Halflin: the same weather-mottled skin, the same capable, mallet-like hands. Her goatskin dress was covered in mud and held together with rope, from which hung knives, scissors, a sack and a long-handled colander. Four liquorice-black eels were threaded on a hook on her belt. Over her head and shoulders she wore a woven grass mat, part hat, part cape, which covered her back, and made her look like a shapeless green mound; but it helped to hide her when she went scavenging or hunting in the marsh. Burweed was wound into the mat's peak, obscuring half her face, but through the dead fronds a pair of bright, black eyes peered out.

"Cat got your tongue, young man?" Lundy said sharply. Fenn shook his head and lifted the bandage to display the cat's claw marks.

"My hand," he said.

Lundy laughed and her expression softened. She put the safety catch on the harpoon, propped it in the corner and flopped the eels on the table. Then she looked them up and down, taking in their thinness, their soggy clothes, the way Halflin hunched protectively in front of Fenn, who was shivering despite the warmth of the stove.

"So what do you want here?" she said. "Again." She shot Halflin a guarded look.

"The *Warspite*'s back," Halflin said.

Wincing in pain, Lundy shuffled as quickly as she could to the window, her belt of knives and scissors clattering like a wind chime and the sour reek of marsh water wafting from her clothes as she moved. She scanned the hazy horizon before quickly slamming back the bolts of the shutters.

"Might not be after *him*," she said, lighting one of the paraffin lamps and filling the room with a greasy smell of burning. Halflin shook his head.

"Chilstone will never give up."

Gelert's gleaming white fur bristled and he growled at the name.

"Then why've you brought him here?" Lundy said.

"You hid him last time," Halflin said hopefully. Lundy shook her head in disbelief.

"It's one thing hiding a tiddly scrap of a baby, another

hiding *that*." She jerked her head in Fenn's direction.

"Jus' fer one night?" Halflin asked.

"No," she said.

"Till dusk?" he implored. Lundy ignored him.

For a second Halflin looked beaten but quickly rallied.

"Yer could get 'im to the Sargassons fer me."

"With the *Warspite* here? Haven't they suffered enough?"

Something about the set of her jaw made Fenn realise Lundy wasn't going to help, but Halflin wasn't ready to give up yet.

"Saw fresh wolf scat on the way here – the pack's near. What chance 'e got on the marsh?" Halflin persisted, intending to prick her conscience. He squinted through the shutter slats, calculating how long it would be before the morning mists rose. If they had to hide out in the reed beds they'd best be going now.

"Should've thought of that thirteen years ago," Lundy muttered.

Halflin gave her a sharp look to ward her off revealing any more and Lundy nodded almost imperceptibly, but Fenn caught the glance they exchanged. It was some secret code between old survivors.

"At least let 'im take the dog. Fer protection," Halflin begged.

"No," said Lundy, folding her arms. "He's all I've got."

She stared ahead stubbornly. "I did my bit, Halflin. You're not taking me or Gelert down with you." Her voice trembled with anger and fear.

Fenn noticed how much like a mirror image of each other they were: both scared, both tired of hiding. He knew she'd risked her life when she'd cared for him as a baby and Halflin risked his life every day. With a sharp pang of guilt he remembered all the times he'd snuck out to swim, recklessly putting his grandad at risk, thinking he'd get away with it. He wondered who had betrayed him. The Sargassons loathed Chilstone, so it couldn't have been one of them. There had always been spies on East Marsh though; they were the reason the *Panimengro* was so careful to moor in secret. That gave him an idea.

"What about the *Panimengro*?" He cried. "We could get out on her."

Halflin frowned, but Lundy's eyes brightened.

"He'll be safest off the marsh altogether," she said, nodding.

The light seemed to fade in Halflin's eyes as he gazed at Fenn. Lundy was right; the boy would never survive the marsh without him. Halflin had tried to prepare him for the time when he'd be alone, when Halflin died; to teach him which plants killed, which ones cured. But he still had so much work to do; the boy wasn't ready yet. And how would he eat? Fenn had no hunting skills; Halflin had never been able to take him into the marsh to teach him. All the fears Halflin had ever had for the boy, the nightmares that kept him from sleep and turned his hair white, fell like an arrow shower on him now. If Fenn didn't wander into a bog, the wolves prowling the marsh would catch his scent and hunt him down by nightfall without Gelert to keep them at bay. But out at sea on the *Panimengro*? Gleaners were hard work, and if a Terra Firma patrol caught up with them, there'd be no place for the boy to hide.

"It's time to tell him the truth," Lundy said quietly.

"About what?" asked Fenn, frowning.

Halflin knitted his brow; he had to make a decision and make it quickly. If he didn't get back to the Sunkyard before the Terra Firma got there, Chilstone would know for sure something was up, and thirteen years protecting the boy couldn't end with him drowning in mud or being torn apart by wild animals. Halflin refused to let that be his end. The *Panimengro* was the only option.

"There's summat yer shou' know," he started. "But we don't have much time, so listen up."

He took a deep, shuddery breath; there was no way to sugar this pill. Best say it straight. "Yer parents din't drown. Chilstone 'ad 'em murdered. They were leadin' the Resistance."

"Their names were Tomas and Maya Demari," Lundy

54

added, quickly pushing a chair beneath Fenn as he buckled in shock.

"An' yer were..."

Halflin faltered. How could he tell the boy he'd sunk his parents' boat and that he wasn't his grandfather?

"Yer were brought ter me ... ter look after," he finished.

Lundy gave him a sharp look but Halflin had clamped his jaw shut. If he had to tell the boy he was alone in the world, he'd do it in his own time, without spectators.

"When the *Warspite* came, thirteen year back, Chilstone din't jus' take them Sargasson bairns fer revenge – he were after *yer*. Somehow he knew about yer, came searchin'. He's still searchin', cos of who yer be. So I kept yer hid."

"Why didn't you tell me before?" Fenn asked, guilt about sneaking out making his voice thick and dark.

Halflin knocked the stump of his finger sharply on Fenn's forehead.

"I din't lose this finger in a bloody squid's beak. I were forgin' papers for the Resistance. Chilstone's got ways of makin' folk spill their guts; used the Screw on me. I lost me finger, but kept me secrets."

Halflin glanced at Lundy to see whether she'd make him tell the whole truth but she'd shut her eyes to seal old horrors out.

"I did wha' I 'ad ter, boy. Reckoned if yer knew summat,

knew *anythin'* an' Chilstone found yer, he'd bleed it out of yer. Like 'e tried wi' me."

Lundy opened her eyes. He nodded to her, as if to say, *I'll tell him the rest when I'm ready*. Then he turned back to Fenn.

"Now it's different. Out there yer need ter know who yer be. How much yer matter; ter the Resistance – what's left of it – and ter Chilstone. They both wan' yer as bad as each other!"

Halflin shook his head at his failure to keep Fenn safe.

"Yer were always just a rumour ter the Resistance, a puff of hope," he said. "But looks like yer no secret no more, an' sure as night follows day, the Resistance will be comin' fer yer."

Halflin's eyes darkened with anger.

"Yer just a kid, but tha' won't matter ter them firebrands; ones blowin' up Fearzeros withou' first checkin' who's aboard. You'll make 'em a tidy mascot all right. An' Chilstone? The more the Resistance wan' yer, the more reason 'e 'as ter kill yer. Understand?"

Halflin stared at Fenn but he was in a daze and consumed by sudden new emotions, a violent desire for revenge. Furious tears welled in his eyes and his knuckles gleamed white as he bunched his fists. He wanted to make Chilstone suffer for everything he'd done.

"Tell him the rest, Halflin," Lundy murmured under her breath.

"We've gotta get goin'," Halflin said, dragging Fenn to his feet and pushing him towards the door where he hesitated: Lundy was an old friend, he didn't want to leave behind harsh words. "It were too much to ask yer," he mumbled.

As Halflin hustled him down the steps and around the back of the *Ionia*, Fenn looked back, but only Gelert came to the door, his tail wagging sadly as he watched them vanish into the reeds.

4

They ran back into the marsh, northwards this time, through sea lavender and samphire growing in huge bushy clumps, making the air heady with their sweet vinegary scents. The *Panimengro* had come into the tributary that ran around the southern edge of the estuary, curling inland for a mile or so before shallowing out into mudflats choked with eelgrass. Hidden all along that part of the river were mooring places, where Sargassons and Gleaners met to trade out of sight beneath the leafy water elders. Halflin pulled Fenn past a sign to a place called "Hill Farm", then on through a copse of dying trees and up to a higher mound from where he could look down across the rivers that weaved through the marshlands. After half an hour's hard running, Halflin stopped for breath, bent double, hands on his knees and sweat running down his neck. Fenn tried to help pull him up, but Halflin brushed him off; he didn't want the boy to think he was weak.

"Think the *Panimengro*'s still there?" Fenn asked.

"Better be or we're done fer," Halflin rasped, still clawing for breath. The mists were beginning to clear and they'd soon be visible to any Terras searching the marshlands.

"Who's the captain?" asked Fenn.

"A Sargasson ... called Viktor," Halflin replied, still straining to see where the *Panimengro* had moored. There was a jeering chatter overhead and he glanced skywards, grimacing as a single magpie flew across their path; *one for sorrow*. A bad omen. "He owes me from a long way back."

"Where're they headed?" asked Fenn.

"West Isle," Halflin replied, dragging Fenn by the sleeve as he lurched through the gorse bushes towards a strip of water gleaming in the distance.

The ground under their feet began to squelch as they got closer to the water, and the spiky reeds sliced Halflin's hands as he pushed past them into a lush crop of velvety bulrushes. He peered through the fuzzy heads swaying in the breeze and pointed.

"There!"

Fenn followed the line of his finger. Down on the water he could just make out the silhouette of a battered boat emerging through the lifting fog. They clambered down towards the mooring post. Apart from the distant oinking of the pigs on the hillside behind them, there wasn't a sound. They were still a hundred yards or so from the river when the boat's engine rattled into life, sputtering out a column of smoke from its stack.

"No!" Halflin gasped. He let go of Fenn's hand and lumbered through the reeds waving his arms wildly. The *Panimengro* was already pulling away from the water's edge.

"Shore ter ship!" he called desperately as he staggered through the treacly sludge that sucked him in deeper with each step. His breath rattled like a box of stones in his chest. "Shore ter ship!"

He dragged himself through the mire, grasping at reeds to pull himself along. At last he broke free and slopped out into the water, shouting until his voice was hoarse. Fenn followed close behind, yelling too.

The *Panimengro* slowed. On deck a figure materialised through the mist. The engine was cut. Another figure stepped forward and leant on the rail.

"Who's there?" a voice asked, suspiciously. They knew the punishment for mooring illegally and were ready to fight their way out if they had to.

"Halflin!"

For a few moments there was complete silence, then

there came more shuffling on deck. Halflin turned to Fenn.

"Let me talk, they're jittery," he whispered.

The *Panimengro* crew slowly punted the ship towards the bank. Fenn could now see it was wooden, so thickly coated with bitumen that the joints between the strafes were completely obscured. It was an old steam drifter, a little over eighty feet, with a rickety funnel in the middle, and two masts with a patched sail fluttering off the back one. When they were about ten feet from Halflin, Fenn heard a sudden rushing sound and out of nowhere a stout gangplank crashed down into the mud.

While the crew stared silently from the deck, a man crossed over, listing slightly because one leg was shorter than the other, making the lamp he carried jolt with each step. He was lanky and a soaking wet sou'wester hung from his broad shoulders. His gun-metal hair was scraped into braids twining like ivy over his head, then snaking down into a plait that reached his hips.

"Kako Halflin," he said, ignoring Fenn.

"Viktor," said Halflin, nodding his head in respect. He managed to suppress his racked breathing and force a smile.

"You're late," Viktor said, narrowing his eyes as he scanned for the usual crate of food. "Not tradin' today?"

"Truth be told, nothin' much ter trade," Halflin lied. "Brung yer this though." He opened his bag and passed

Viktor the ham. Viktor hefted it in one hand to check the weight.

"That it?" he asked suspiciously, giving it a sniff before lobbing it back to one of his men.

"A gift." Halflin smiled. Viktor glowered mistrustfully.

"This one needs gettin' ter West Isle Marsh. Family business," Halflin continued casually. "Yer know me kin that way?"

Viktor nodded and cocked his head to one side. He turned to look at Fenn for the first time and lifted the lamp higher to cast a halo of light over him. A terrible scar ran down one side of Viktor's face, as if he'd been branded, and Fenn could just make out an F shape.

"Still a chavvy, won't be much use about ship," Viktor said, looking Fenn over critically. "What's it worth?" he demanded, aiming a spit into the reeds in a neat arc.

Halflin rummaged again in his bag and handed over the blank permit, gritting his teeth with impatience as Viktor held it up against the light to examine the watermark – the TF logo pressed into the very fibre of the paper. The muscles beneath his cheek twitched, making the scarlet scar flex like a serpent.

Without a permit no one was allowed at sea, and permits were solely Terra Firma issued. This forgery was completely clean of any name so could be sold to the highest bidder who needed a new identity. Hundreds of permits changed hands on the black market, the ink carefully scratched off the paper with the point of a scalpel, but it was dangerous to use them. A brand new blank permit like this was as rare as bees; it was worth vastly more than the *Panimengro*, but Viktor knew he might get more playing things cool.

"Worth more than yer boat an' cargo together," Halflin said impatiently, an ear cocked for any sound from the *Warspite*. He wondered if they had launched the patrol boat yet, but he was too far from the estuary mouth to see. In his mind's eye Halflin imagined Chilstone and the Terras arriving at the Punchlock and finding it deserted. He shuddered; it was forbidden to leave it unmanned.

"What's the nash?" Viktor smiled languidly. Halflin shrugged.

"No hurry, but yer want ter catch the tide, don't yer?" he replied craftily. "Yer best look slippy!"

"His ID ... permit?" Viktor asked.

Halflin huffed and dug deep inside the bag, pulling the other papers out and passing them over. Viktor scrutinised them carefully; nodding, holding them up to the light, one by one, checking each watermark. At last he stuffed both permits into the top of his jacket, thrust the ID back at Halflin and nodded curtly to Fenn. Then he gave Halflin a quick, strange glance – half smile, half scowl – and disappeared back up the gangplank.

Now alone, Fenn turned to Halflin, a quizzical look in his eyes.

It had come. The moment of truth. He was sending the boy away and he must never return. Halflin never wanted him back; it was too dangerous on East Marsh. It was more than the right time; it was the perfect moment to tell him he wasn't his grandfather and that they meant nothing to each other. Now was the time to say he was just an unlucky Sunkyard owner who saved a lucky child, kept him safe and hidden as best as he could, made him strong and healthy, taught him as much as he could to survive, but did not mollycoddle him nor weaken him with love. The time had come to cut him – like he'd cut his webbed toes thirteen years before. It would be for his own good.

Cut him loose. Cut him free. Cut him clean away for ever.

Say it! Halflin thought. *Say it!*

But he couldn't. His throat had turned to lead and his tongue seemed to shrivel in his mouth, shrinking from the words it had to speak. Onboard, the crew were preparing to cast off and whistled at them to hurry. Fenn looked at Halflin expectantly, but the moment had gone.

"Do we board?" he asked, searching Halflin's face for

answers. A sudden scatter of icy rain speckled the water and his teeth began chattering. He was frozen and exhausted. Halflin tucked the ID card in Fenn's shirt pocket and patted it to make sure it was safe.

"Grandad?"

"Warm enough? It'll be clap cold offshore," Halflin said gruffly. Something cracked in his voice. "Best ter keep warm."

Halflin shrugged off his heavy reefer jacket, hanging it on the twigs of Fenn's shoulders. It was damp from the marsh and weighed a tonne; Fenn's puny frame buckled beneath the load, but it was warm. As he dipped under its weight, he felt the truth dawn on him.

"You're not coming are you?"

Halflin concentrated on jamming the buttons through their holes.

"Pigs'll need feedin'." His voice had taken on a different tone; lighter than usual.

He squeezed the last button into its place and jerked his head towards the boat. "Viktor'll take yer to our kin. Won't take long; four weeks if the weather holds. Bit longer if yer hit storms."

"I'm not going without you!" Fenn said stubbornly. Halflin glared at him.

"You'll do as I tell yer!" he said, trying to keep the

shaking out of his voice. "Don't yer see? I've never left the Sunkyard, not fer one night, not in thirteen year. If I come wiv yer, Chilstone will smell a rat! Then they'll be lookin' fer an ol' man an' a kid. We'll stick ou' like a shark's fin. Yer safer alone."

Halflin managed to winch the sides of his mouth up to make an almost convincing smile.

"An' I'm safest stayin' put," he said, knowing that was what the boy needed to hear. "Anyhow, won' be for ever," he finished with a nod.

It would be for ever. Halflin would make sure of that.

For a moment Fenn looked like he was about to cry and for a second Halflin softened, but he shook it off as quickly as it had come. He took Fenn's shoulders firmly in his hands.

"Now don't go blubbin', it'll jus' make yer feel worse... Viktor's all right. Do as 'e tells yer," Halflin said, staring hard into Fenn's eyes. Fenn nodded, though his lips were quivering. The boat's engine suddenly snapped into life again and the *Panimengro* shuddered and rattled as the propeller turned.

"Spies are everywhere, throw 'em off the scent. Tell everyone yer fifteen! Best ter go older; folks will jus' think yer a runt. Don't forget wha' I told yer, but bury it! Bury it deep. Chilstone will hunt yer down and kill yer if 'e finds out, so trust no one an' nothin' ... 'cept yer instinct. Got it?"

With each instruction he roughly shook Fenn's shoulders.

Fenn nodded obediently and reached out to hug him, but Halflin held firm against affection; it helped no one. Instead he put his arm out, like a battering ram, and pressed the flat of his huge hand on Fenn's chest, as if trying to drive caution into his very heart. Before Fenn knew what was happening, Halflin had spun him on the spot towards the ship and pushed him along the gangplank.

Fenn felt a tremor of fear run up his legs and through his body. Beneath him the water glinted black as treacle and the sour-sweet smell of brine hit his nostrils. He was halfway across before he realised Halflin's hand was no longer on his back. He looked over his shoulder but Halflin was already hurrying up the rise in the direction of the hut. A hand grabbed Fenn's arm and the gangplank was yanked roughly away from underneath him. Fenn was on deck.

Immediately the *Panimengro* started surging up the river, steam panting from the funnel. The sun was coming up now and the mist was lifting quickly; the crew weren't wasting any time. Wild geese scattered from their hiding places, skipping across the river until the wind caught their wings, wrinkling the glossy amber water.

Viktor shoved Fenn towards the hatch to get below and out of sight; this wasn't the first time he'd smuggled someone off East Marsh, but Fenn ran back to the rail. It was freezing and the spiny cold gnawed into his skin, but he stayed, waiting for Halflin to turn and wave, feeling as if something was stuck in his throat, and however hard he swallowed it wouldn't go away. Instead Halflin hurried away without so much as a backwards glance, back to the hut where Chilstone would be coming for him.

As Fenn clutched the rail and felt the cold metal bite in his hands, he had the sudden sense that Halflin knew they'd never see each other again. His heart began pounding so hard it felt like it would crash through his ribs, and he shouted as loud as he could across the ever-increasing wash of water.

"Grandad!"

Although Halflin was already halfway up the hill, he still heard the boy cry out as clearly as he had heard him that first time, as a baby in the water. But he refused to turn around or stop; it would do no good for the boy to see him weeping. There was no place for tears in this world.

5

When Halflin used to go out to the Punchlock, Fenn would often climb up into the hiding place, just to scan East Marsh with the telescope for anything of interest. To the untrained eye there wasn't much to see, but Fenn knew every creature living on the marsh, all their comings and goings, and in particular he liked spying on his nearest neighbours: the Sargassons. They were a rare sighting, usually appearing after dusk to lay their eel traps, like ink blots in the haze, seeping out of the marsh mist itself. As Fenn turned away from the rail he realised that most of this crew were Sargasson too.

He stared wide-eyed, gaping at the crew. Some had sleek black hair knotted in complex weaves or in plaits that coiled like rope pots on top of their heads. Most were tall and moved quietly and carefully, never bumping into each other or dropping anything. For warmth they wore ganseys, tightly crocheted jumpers of twisted goat hair, but all their other clothes – trousers, shirts and jackets – were made from strips of soft eel skin, stained dull red and violet from marsh flowers and roots. Silently they got on with their work; carefully nudging the *Panimengro* up the tributary that led them out to sea, far away from where the Fearzero would have moored. Fenn was bursting to speak to them and had a million questions, but not one even acknowledged him. So it was true what Halflin said about Sargassons, he thought: they kept themselves to themselves and didn't like strangers. Viktor though, put his hand on Fenn's shoulder.

"Char?" he said. "Shala?"

Fenn looked at him blankly. Halflin knew enough Sargasson to trade, but Fenn had never heard the language before.

"Char?"

"Work," Viktor said, tugging him insistently away from the rail. "Shala?"

"Shala...?" Fenn stammered.

"Tu Shala? You understand?" Viktor snapped. Now Fenn nodded.

"Halflin's paid passage but you earn your scran," Viktor continued. He mimed eating before pushing his sharp fingers into Fenn's back, prodding him towards the hold in the centre of the deck.

"Stay down, out of sight," Viktor said, pointing towards the hatch. "In the day we've gotta clank you ... hide!" He patted his jacket pocket with the permits inside, then wagged his finger disapprovingly. "No risks! Halflin's papers are kushti but they're still fakes. Goes gami for us if we're caught with a fake. Worse than none at all. Chilstone always looking for boys your age..." For a second Viktor scrunched up his forehead as he peered hard at Fenn, then he shrugged away the thought.

The *Panimengro* had broken free from the calmer tributary and the water was starting to get choppier. A couple of the crew swapped smirks as Fenn swayed and stumbled over to the hatch. They'd only been at sea for a minute and he already felt unexpectedly unwell. He'd always longed to be on a boat, gazing through his telescope as the tug taxied out to the Fearzeros, fetching Sunkmarked boats to scuttle. After thirteen years of squelching around in the slobbery mud of the marsh, he often imagined the wonderful fresh feeling of the wind out at sea. But he'd never predicted his stomach would feel like it was being flipped upside down before being stuffed back up into his lungs, nor the strange, salty trickles of saliva in his mouth. He didn't even know this was how throwing up began. Halflin had taken such good care of him, he'd never once got sick. Suddenly sweat broke on his forehead and he pulled free from Viktor, rushed to the side and heaved up his breakfast. As he stared bemused into the water, the crew laughed again. Viktor followed and idly leant on the rail and peered over, looking at his spew in the waves. He slapped him roughly on the back.

"That's a waste. Supper's not till nightfall!" he remarked.

"What happened?" asked Fenn creakily. He was white and trembling.

"Bit of pani-puke. Don't fret it; you're a lubber but you'll get your sea-stimps soon," Viktor said, giving him another hard smack on the shoulder like it would help. He held out a tin flask full of water and nodded for him to take a swig, then he walked to the hatch and flipped it open, revealing a dark interior. Bent double, Fenn crept weakly down the ladder with Viktor following quickly after him, stepping on his fingers in his impatience.

At the bottom Viktor lit a hurricane lamp and hung it on a nail. The hold was large, practically the length of the boat itself. There were no portholes, but just enough light spilled from the lamp to show dozens of wooden crates against the wall, and a huge pile of what looked like rubbish heaped up at one end. The ceiling was low and despite the cold day it was stiflingly hot, with the fumes from the engine and the acrid stench of something dead. Viktor pointed to the crates in turn.

"Ever Mudlarked?" Fenn shook his head. "Been a Grubber? Tosher? Fish gold from mud?" Viktor asked. Fenn shook his head again. Viktor rolled his eyes at Fenn's uselessness. "You sort jetsam? Rubbish? Shala?"

Fenn nodded; he knew what jetsam was. He had always been good at sifting through the stuff Halflin brought back from the boats, sorting what they needed, what could be bartered.

"It's not hard," Viktor said and strode over to the rubbish pile. "The crates are for salvage to trade: plastic, wood, metal and tin. And you'll sometimes get a can that's full." Viktor bent down and picked up a tin and put it on a shelf stacked with other cans of many different shapes and sizes. "Nothing's wasted, so keep your yews sharp," Viktor said, pointing towards Fenn's eyes.

It was a huge pile: shotgun shells, rubber tubing, a broken table leg, the grill from a radiator. He pulled at a net in which a rotting turtle was trapped and recoiled at the stink. "Even this – it's foostie but valuable!"

He flipped a knife through the air towards Fenn.

"How long are we sailing for?" he asked, catching the knife. He had decided not to say he already had a knife; two knives were better than one.

"Maybe four weeks. Depends," said Viktor.

"On what?" Fenn asked looking around in dismay.

"The weather. The Slicks. Can't go through them: too much damage."

"Slicks?"

Viktor sighed.

"Halflin didn't tell you a lot."

"He told me all I needed to know," said Fenn defensively, but Viktor didn't rise to it.

"Not *all*, or you'd have no questions," he replied coolly. "Slicks are oil spills."

Fenn nodded gloomily, suddenly realising what he was in for.

"Where do I sleep?" he asked.

"We sleep on deck; you sleep down here. Make yourself a bed and doss over there. By the engine is tato." Viktor gave him a sharp look to see if he'd understood. "Warm!" he exclaimed with a rare smile, chaffing his hands together in case Fenn didn't understand. Then he walked over to a metal barrel in the corner and turned a lever on the side. Water the colour of tea trickled out of the spout into his cupped palm. "Pani nevi!" he said, nodding to Fenn as if he were simple-minded.

He scooped the water into his mouth, trying to reassure Fenn with an uneasy smile, but the water was from the river and filthy. With that, he wiped his sleeve across his chin then climbed back up the ladder. The hatch slammed shut behind him and Fenn was left in the reeking gloom.

Fenn stared back up at the steps, wondering if he'd ever see Halflin again. He swallowed hard, but still felt his cheeks begin to tingle with rising tears. Then he heard Halflin's voice – *don't go blubbin'* – and steeled himself for the task ahead. He gritted his teeth, opened his rucksack, found Halflin's gauntlets and put them on. It was like slipping his hands into a giant's gloves.

Gingerly he picked up the decomposing turtle and yanked it away from the net. He could hardly face touching it, but knew he needed the net to sleep in. After he'd managed to untangle it, he scooped out the flesh and slopped it into a lidded barrel to stop the smell. Then, with the tip of his blade, he ground a hole in the tail end of the shell, washed it out and hooked it up by the engine room to dry. He knew enough about curing bacon to do that much. Then he looped up the net to make a hammock, like Viktor suggested, and returned to the pile to start sorting.

There were plastic bottles with words on them that made no sense to him; bits of rubber shaped like feet with V-straps, which he guessed must be a type of shoe, several barnacle-coated metal discs, one with the word "Ford" in the middle, door handles, driftwood, netting, fishing tackle and an eyeless doll with "Made in China" imprinted on its back.

The day dragged on and on and the pile of rubbish never seemed to get any smaller, but one of the crates of plastic was already half full when the hatch opened again and a head appeared, silhouetted against the dusky sky. It was a woman, her face as tanned and wrinkled as a walnut shell. She brandished an iron ladle at him.

"Come up," she called. "Cap'n say it's time." Her voice was wheezy and cracked, like a pair of broken bellows, with a strange twang at its heart. When Fenn didn't move she stared crossly at him for a moment, then stuck out her tongue. "Well I ain't waitin' all night," she shouted, and disappeared.

Fenn scrambled up the steps onto the deck.

6

Despite Halflin's coat, Fenn was freezing. It was a breezeless night, but cloudless too and colder for that. He could hear the strains of thin, sweet music drifting above the gentle shushing of the sea. The crew had eaten already and were now singing and drinking, their laughter trailing across the deck. But Fenn didn't only shiver with cold; he'd spent most of his life holed up in two small rooms, always within sight of the hut or Halflin. He felt oddly light and unfettered, but in a helpless, frightening way, like he was drifting, unanchored.

Slowly, like a weathervane, he turned around and gasped. The vast indigo sky wheeled over him, dusted with sprays of tiny golden stars, and the sea rose and fell so gently it seemed to be almost breathing. Fenn felt he was riding on the back of an enormous, living thing. The horizon completely encircled him, no land to be seen. For as far as the eye could see there was only black water, sky and never-ending emptiness. The solitude suddenly made Fenn dizzy and he staggered slightly. Immediately the woman hooked her arm through his, like a shepherd's crook, to steady him and lead him towards the light and singing.

On the ship's deck there were two large crates and next to these a winch for the salvage and fishing nets, coils of rope, buckets, and pike poles to haul the flotsam out. Towards the front of the boat, by the pilot house, stood a thick, tall mast and Fenn could just make out the figure of someone high up in the lookout. The chart room and pilot house were painted a slug grey so they blended in at sea, and although the crew had quarters and a mess room they ate their meals out on deck, in the gap between the crates, over which a patched tarpaulin had been stretched. The crew warmed themselves around an oil can brazier, which sparkled brightly, making giants of their shadows.

"Sit!" the woman ordered, pushing him onto a huge coil of rope a little way from the rest of the crew. She went to the brazier where a pan was bubbling. While Fenn waited he listened to the men playing their music. In the flickering half-light he could just make out what they were holding: instruments that were all made from rubbish.

In the corner, the oldest Sargasson of all hunched over

a rusty oil drum gripped between his bandy legs, plucking taut strings on a fingerboard made from a small paddle, with tuning pegs of steel bolts and door keys. A younger man with a beard plaited tight into a dense mesh had a flattened can tucked under his chin, and he ran half a fishing rod across four strings anchored by the bent tines of a fork. A melancholy tune was made by a man blowing into the side of a piece of copper piping, with stops over the holes made of coins, ends of spoons and buttons, while a fourth strummed his thumbs across the only thing that wasn't rubbish: an old washboard. Fenn stared; he had never heard music other than the cries of the peewit and marsh warbler, or the croaks of the natterjack toads. Sargassons, so Halflin told him, learned an instrument before they even learned to catch eels, and they had beautiful voices. The men without instruments began to sing – a plaintive lament that unexpectedly broke into a joyful, upbeat chorus, with one of the men clapping spoons against his thigh to keep the tempo.

Over land drove a mighty sea surge,
With water came the fear.
Terra Firma built Walls to stop it,
Bringing sadness, far and near.
Take to the seas! Try not to drown!
Try your luck there! Keep your head down!

As the flood-tide swamped the land,
Deeper grew their hate,
Thousands homeless, millions starving,
This the Seaborns' fate.
Take to the seas!
Try not to drown!
Try your luck there! Keep your head down!

At the end of the song the entire crew erupted into laughter. The woman returned and handed Fenn a bowl of stew, then hopped up onto a barrel to sit and watch him. Fenn sniffed the bowl suspiciously, gingerly sticking out the end of his tongue to taste it. He took a mouthful and the flavour hit him like a firework exploding in his mouth. He had never eaten anything so delicious in his entire life; it made his head swim. Halflin's food had kept him strong and healthy, but it was basic – no flavour other than the salty water Halflin had boiled it in. But this food was layered, spicy and mellow, sharp and sweet. He felt like he was tasting colour after eating grey all his life and he wolfed it down.

"You like my gumbo?" the woman asked with a smile. "Grew the lady's fingers myself." She jabbed her thumb to where bushy plants grew in a few mossy tubs on the deck but Fenn was too busy gobbling to answer. "More?"

He nodded quickly and she fetched him another bowl.

"I'm Magpie," she said as she sat back down on the barrel, swinging her matchstick legs. Fenn could have wrapped his finger and thumb around her ankles she was so scrawny.

By lantern light her crescent eyes shone golden-green and her hair grew in long tortoiseshell-coloured spirals, blowing wildly around her head like seaweed. While she listened to the men singing and playing she nibbled a crust of bread, like a squirrel. After a few moments she sensed him staring at her and frowned.

"So, wha'chou staring at, child?" she asked at last. "Ain't you never sin a Cajun woman before...?"

Still befuddled and light-headed from breathing in the fresh sea air, eating the stew and listening to the music, he forgot himself and his manners.

"Are women normally as little as you?" he blurted out.

For a second she looked annoyed, then burst into laughter.

"So where you come from? A place with no women?"

"I haven't seen many," he said.

"What about your mam?"

"She was—" he began, then stopped himself. He didn't know this person – women could be spies too. "My mum and dad drowned," he said carefully. Magpie didn't bat an eyelid; people drowned in the sea surges all the time.

"So who was that old timer on the quayside?"

"My grandad," Fenn said, trying to push the thought of Halflin from his mind in case it started him off feeling tearful again.

Magpie nodded slowly as she looked him over, scrutinising his black, tufty hair, his peculiar eyes.

"So you Sargasson or Venetian…? Cos your hair say, 'Venetian' but your eyes say both; one blue, one green!"

"I'm…"

Fenn didn't know what to say or if he should say anything at all.

"I've always lived on East Point."

"So this your first time at sea?" she asked.

"I … I've never…" Fenn started, but his sentence dangled like the overhang of a cliff crumbling to nothing. Halflin said trust no one.

"It's my first time on a boat," he said at last.

Magpie laughed incredulously and slapped her knees.

"You kiddin'? You never go help your grandaddy fishin'?"

Fenn shook his head.

"You ever meet folks from elsewhere?"

Fenn shook his head again.

"What did your grandad tell you about Seaborns?"

Fenn sighed. He knew how to gut a pig, what wild plants to eat, which mushrooms caused agonizing death, how to tell north from where moss grew, but whenever he'd asked

Halflin about Landborns or Seaborns he'd always said the same thing: "Folk is folk; good 'n bad in both."

"My grandad was…" He was going to say overprotective, but that wasn't the right word. To be protective of something you had to love it first and Fenn wasn't sure Halflin loved him. It seemed more like a grudging determination to keep him alive. Suddenly, instead of finding words, thoughts of Halflin engulfed him like a wave and he couldn't breathe. Slippery as quicksilver, Magpie slid down next to him and put her hand on his shoulder, watching and waiting for the danger of him crying to pass. The tears quivered in his eyes but he blinked them back, focusing on one of the Sargassons as he passed by to take his shift in the lookout.

"You see Sargassons before?" Magpie asked, trying to distract him.

Fenn nodded.

"Course you did!" Magpie said, clucking her teeth at her own stupidity. "East Marsh is thick with them! But off the marsh you can tell a Sargasson from that fancy way they have. They come all the way from the Sargasso Sea. Most are eel-trappers, but some are scavs like Viktor. Allus roamin' the sea, like real Jipseas…"

Fenn pulled a face at the word. He'd often watched Halflin angrily scrub graffiti off a boat, later telling him, *They'll sink without that bleedin' word on it.*

But Magpie only laughed.

"Don't you look at me like you jus' smelt sour milk! Don't mean nuffin'. The Terra Firma might use it bad, but Jipsea's just a word for anyone the wrong side of the Walls. You know, sticks and stones," she said mockingly, giving his chin a teasing pinch. She nodded towards a man with bright red hair, blowing through the tube of copper piping.

"One with hair like a lit match? Scotian. From them islands they say a place called Can-Ada used to be, years ago. Fishermen; tough as 'gator skin. The tall one with hair black as a crow's wing, like yours? Venetian, from New Venice. Clever and canny traders – got fighting spirit too – but too hoity-toity for me. There are Moken and Badjoa too, from the Fareast Islands; practically fish they love that water so much…"

Fenn pointed to a huge man with a shock of blond hair, fixing one of the catch barrels with a colossal lump hammer.

"And him?"

"Caspian," she whispered, pulling a face. "So graspin'! Usually Mudlarks nowadays, allus sniffin' out where money's to be made. And then there's—" At this point she grandly pointed her two thumbs to herself— "Cajuns, from the Southern Islands, the place they called the Old Americas."

"I'll never remember them all," Fenn said.

"Don't try. Truth is Seaborn is less a race, more a way of

life. Nowadays you don't have to be born on water to make the grade, yer just have to live on water … or the marsh. Like yer grandaddy," she said with a bitter smile.

"Were you born on water?" Fenn asked timidly.

"My stock hails from swamps for sure, before they were swaller'd up by all this." She swung her arm in an arc to convey the vastness of the empty waters around them. "This ocean gettin' greedier every day, gobblin' up the last bits of earth. That's why Landborn don't wanna share, not that it's *theirs* to share. Plus they scared of our so-called diseases. Do I look like I got the plague to you?" she asked indignantly.

Fenn shook his head.

"Nope. Ain't no one born on water these days, too dangerous! They say last one was that Demari kid, and look what happen to him!" Magpie stuck out her bottom lip sadly.

"Demari?" Fenn asked, making his voice as light as a bubble.

Magpie shuffled nearer, lowering her voice until it was no more than a scratchy whisper.

"The Demari family led the Resistance. When Chilstone started stealin' the land and forcin' folk out, it was the Demaris who kicked off most. Like I say, Venetians are a fightin' sort. But some of the Resistance got crazy: blowing

85

up ships, blowing up Walls. Madness. The Walls will save us all."

Fenn nodded, trying to understand. He'd never thought of the Wall as a good thing before.

"Tomas Demari tried to calm things but Chilstone wanted blood. Rumour has it Tomas and Maya fled to her homeland, but Chilstone hunted them down and killed 'em before they got there. Some say their baby lived and Sargassons hid him in an eel trap when Chilstone came callin'. I wish that were the truth cos things would be different now if it were. But anyone with any sense know it's a figment. Chilstone's a cruel one..." Magpie shook herself as she shuddered. "Anyway, enough!"

She reached deep into her pocket, pulling out a crumpled felt hat, pinned all around with little oddments of shiny metal: a silver cross, a coin with a hole in it, a gold pen nib, half a brass hinge. She started pulling it into shape.

"How did you end up on the *Panimengro*?" Fenn said.

"I was trying for the Mainland because it was their Wall that took the hit and lots of Seaborns got inside. Thought I'd get in, lay low, find work. I work hard. But the ship I was on ran into trouble so we headed to West Isle instead. Got no further than the marshes though, but still got lucky; Viktor trades that way. Needed a cook, took me on."

"What's West Isle like? Is it safe there?" Fenn asked.

"Nowhere's safe!" Magpie clucked her tongue at Fenn's ignorance. "The Terras gotta hold of all of it. But West Landborn's s'posed to be more obligin'. Ain't so picky about who gets to live there." She plucked at a loose thread on her hat and bit it off.

"Land of hope and honey; they say it's easier to get a permit there cos they got more food than all the other isles put together. Orchards *drippin'* with apples!" At this thought Magpie hugged herself excitedly with a greedy glint in her eyes and smacked her lips.

"Still have to get over the Wall though, and Terras patrol 'em night 'n' day." Magpie shrugged sadly. "Nope, my papers weren't convincing no one. But yours...?" Magpie sucked her teeth approvingly and perked up. "Yours the best. Viktor say Halflin's the man! Viktor too. Smart as paint, that one; allus keeps to the safe routes." She jammed her hat down on her frizzy curls and tied a long woollen scarf around it to secure it.

"Do you speak French too?" Fenn asked.

"How'd you know 'bout Cajun French?" she exclaimed, clapping his shoulder.

"I had an encyclopaedia. Just the one though."

Magpie raised her eyebrows.

"Then you a learned child! Me, I never had no books, never learned my letters. An' French? Never knew none.

Chilstone banned all languages 'cept English, though Sargassons do as they please!"

She glanced surreptitiously at the rest of the crew and dropped her voice to a whisper. "Cos Sargassons the only one's puttin' up a fight now Venetians lost their sting."

Immediately Fenn leant in excitedly.

"You mean the Resistance is still going?" he asked.

But before she answered a low whistle sounded three times.

"Blackout!" Viktor hissed.

Without a word Magpie bounced up and grabbed a bucket, slopping water over the brazier fire, and throwing a wet blanket over the smoke. The boat began to turn a sharp course in the opposite direction to the one they'd been taking. She followed the men running along the deck putting out every light, even covering shiny metal objects. The engine was cut. Viktor sliced a finger across his neck. Everyone stopped talking and stood absolutely motionless.

"What's happening?" whispered Fenn in Magpie's ear. She put her finger to her lips, her eyes so wide with fright he could see the white around her pupils. She pointed out to sea. On the far horizon was the dark shape of a Fearzero, getting larger by the second.

Fenn watched as the men signed to each other. He understood what they were saying: Halflin went deaf in one ear when Fenn was six, and he immediately prepared the boy for a future when Fenn wouldn't be heard at all. *Were we seen?* one signed. Viktor grimaced and shrugged in reply. *Which one is it?* signed the Caspian. Viktor peered through his binoculars. *Warspite,* he signed back. Fenn felt his heart constrict as Chilstone's ship grew bigger and bigger. In front of it were beams of searchlights, sweeping the waves like a bright white broom.

As seconds passed in the black, eerie silence they peered anxiously into the sky. The sickle moon wasn't strong enough for their boat to be silhouetted, but since they'd cut the engine, they'd been drifting inexorably towards the path of the *Warspite*. Even if they weren't spotted, there was every chance they would be mown down under its steel bow. Viktor motioned to the Scotian, a burly man, who began to single-handedly winch the small lifeboat into the water. It would just about hold them all. The rest of the crew started to lower the survival barrels over the gunwale. The barrels could float alongside the dinghy, packed with enough food and water to last the crew three or four days. As quietly as possible the crew lifted down the oars and slipped them silently into the dinghy.

Viktor stared grimly at the Fearzero for a few moments more, then slowly raised his arm, the sign to abandon the *Panimengro*. But before he had a chance to drop it, the

Scotian had touched Viktor's arm and pointed. Before the lighted portholes of the starboard side of the Fearzero had not been visible, but now there was a faint glimmer, meaning the ship was turning away slightly. With baited breath, his heart thumping so loudly he was sure he could hear it, Fenn watched as more of the Fearzero's porthole lights slowly appeared. Still no one spoke, no one breathed a sigh of relief. Instead, crouching in the darkness, they waited and waited for what seemed like hours to Fenn, watching the monstrous ship turn completely until again no lights at all could be seen. At last they stood up, white and shaken.

"Were we off course, Cap'n?" the Caspian muttered.

Viktor shook his head.

"We're on the normal trail; see the Slick?" he flicked his head towards the ocean and Fenn glanced at the water. It hadn't taken long for the powerless boat to drift into the brown slurry of custard-thick sludge that they always kept in sight to navigate by.

"It's the Terras who are off route. Lookin' for something." He stared stonily at Fenn. "Or *someone*." He jerked his head towards Magpie. "Get him below," he barked and strode back to the pilot house to restart the boat.

7

The hatch closed over him and Fenn was plunged into darkness.

Someone. Viktor's word bounced around like a ball in Fenn's head for a long time after the dark closed around him. He was the *someone*. His mind was in turmoil; he'd woken that morning a nobody and now he was... Fenn stopped himself. He had to push his new-found knowledge deep down. Like Halflin said: bury it – for now at any rate.

He stumbled over to his makeshift hammock and climbed in. The stench of the flotsam and diesel, and a sudden pang of homesickness all crowded in. It was pitch black, but as clear as daylight Fenn saw Halflin trudging back up the hill. Something twisted painfully in his chest. He squeezed his eyes tighter to hold back the unhappiness but it was useless. Remembering Halflin's words wasn't going to help this time. A tear leaked out from under his eyelids and trickled down his cheek. He let out a sob.

There was a soft scurrying near by and something brushed his face. Instantly Fenn rolled out of his hammock, instinctively grabbing his rucksack to protect himself. He swung the bag wildly around and, as he did, heard something rattle. He felt inside and to his joy pulled out a small square box: Halflin's precious matches, but there were only a few. Carefully taking one out, he struck it, and while it sputtered in the damp air he just had enough time to find an empty tin. In this he dropped a strand of oily rope. As the match began to burn his fingers he lit the rope, sending off a hazy plume of choking smoke.

Fenn scanned the floor. He remembered Halflin's stories about king rats he'd encountered on the trawlers he used to work on in the old days – rats the size of small dogs. He could see nothing but something was scratching the beam above and he looked up. Next to a pulley for lifting the crates, a pair of red eyes stared down inquisitively. At first he thought it must be a cat, but as he crept closer, peering into the darkness, he could see it was shaped like a ferret, but with longer legs. It had pupils shaped like rectangular slits, a long snout, thick sandy fur, a fox-like tail and tiny ears like ormer shells, softly curved and delicate pink. It looked a bit like the otters Halflin used to rescue, washed up on the estuary banks, half dead and smothered with tarry oil.

If it had been a later volume of the encyclopaedia Halflin had found, Fenn would have known what a mongoose was and that it could squirt him with a foul scent. But he just understood that the creature was like him; afraid and alone.

"What are you?" he asked gently, clicking his fingers and whistling, but the more he tried to coax it, the further into the shadows it retreated, baring its teeth. Eventually it hissed at him and, as it turned back into the shadows, Fenn saw a ripple of ribs beneath its pelt; the animal was starving. He decided to save some of his breakfast for it. He felt happier; less alone. Curling himself into a tight ball, he fell asleep trying to work out what the little creature could be.

In the morning he woke to the hatch being opened again. It was Magpie. She put her finger to her lips.

"Cap'n says you ain't to come up no more," she whispered. "But he's sleepin' an' I got a treat for yer!"

Fenn scouted around for the creature he had decided to call "Not-an-otter" and found it in the rafters above him, still staring down, as if it had kept a bed side vigil. He clicked his fingers again and it pricked up its ears like a dog, but it wouldn't come nearer.

Fenn scuttled up and sat on deck with his feet dangling through the hatch. The night was fading and soon everyone would be awake.

"Rice 'n' coconut milk," Magpie said with a wink as she passed him a bowl.

Fenn started trying to pick out the tiny black bits, remembering Halflin telling him off for being too fussy about finding a few mouse droppings in the rice.

"Wha'chou doin' to my puddin'?" whispered Magpie incredulously.

"I don't like mouse dirt," Fenn replied.

"You soft 'n the head? That's vanilla! You pickin' out the best bit!" Magpie scolded, giving his ear a quick cuff. "Try it before you turn your nose up!"

Fenn tested a spoonful, letting the sweet warm grains spread over his tongue. It was delicious and he ate quickly, staring out over the empty, slate-coloured sea and the congealing clouds. Magpie paced up and down the whole time he ate, and when her back was turned he picked out a clump, squeezed the milk into the bowl and stowed it in his pocket for the Not-an-otter. The instant he finished eating she whisked the bowl away and hustled him below deck again.

Days and nights crawled by; the flotsam pile shrunk only to be refilled each night as the next load of rubbish was lowered down. To keep track of time Fenn unravelled some rope to make a simple calendar, just like Halflin had shown him, tying a knot for each day. On the fifth day, to break the tedium, Fenn started to try and tame the Not-an-otter every time he stopped for water. He'd already been leaving out any scraps he could spare to win its trust.

The *Panimengro* had to sail through the worst of the Slicks to avoid the patrolling Fearzeros and, on account of that, met no other Gleaners they could trade with. Soon rations got so tight Fenn didn't have enough food to spare for the Not-an-otter, but then he remembered the turtle flesh in the barrel. Holding a scarf across his face, he lifted the barrel lid and pulled off a piece, laid it carefully on a lower beam, then got back to work. Out of the corner of his eye he kept watch. Within a few minutes the Not-an-otter scampered across the beam and climbed down the rope. Fenn watched as it tentatively crept nearer, putting out one delicate paw after the other; its snout in the air, sniffing and twitching its long silver whiskers. When it was within a few feet it suddenly bounced along the beam, snatched the meat and scurried back into the shadows.

The next time Fenn stopped to drink, he put meat on the beam again, but nearer. Only a few moments passed before the Not-an-otter crept out, but now it didn't hesitate before thieving. Fenn did the same again, but this time worked a nail out of one of the crates and, using the iron-edged heel of his boot, hammered the meat to the beam. When the creature couldn't shift the meat it tore a small chunk off and, emboldened by Fenn's calm movements, stopped running back to the comfort of its den. It sat out the remainder of the day on the barrel top, twitching its nose for the next bit of food.

Fenn went through the whole process the next day and the day after. The Not-an-otter was constantly on the scrounge for food. In the evening, Fenn tucked a scrap of meat between the twines of his hammock, making sure the Not-an-otter could see what he was doing, then pretended to fall asleep. Through his half-closed eyes he watched the creature edge closer. The Not-an-otter ran and took the meat in its paws, but rather than scuttle away it clung on to the edge of the hammock and ate it there, watching Fenn carefully, sitting up like a squirrel with a nut. Fenn slowly sat up, pulled out another piece of meat and held it out in his palm. Now the Not-an-otter sniffed and crept along the edge of the hammock, made a dart for Fenn's hand, snatched the meat and scurried down Fenn's legs to eat it, sitting on Fenn's feet. Realising Fenn's feet were warmer than the rafters, the animal finally curled up in the end of the hammock like a cat on a bed, and was still asleep there in the morning.

They had set off in calm waters, but now bad weather tossed the boat around like a cork, making Fenn sicker than he thought possible. He longed to be back at home with Halflin, where even the most horrible tasks suddenly seemed appealing, if only because he would have done them with solid earth beneath his feet. Cleaning out the pigs, scraping up frozen dung on a snowy morning, even gutting the yearling he and Halflin had slaughtered together just before he fled. However grisly the task, each seemed like a pleasant, distant dream. Anything would be preferable to the relentless, stomach-churning pitch and fall of the waves. Every time Fenn staggered over to the bucket to puke, the Not-an-otter ran up and down the beams, chattering at him, its big eyes filled with worry.

On the fifteenth day the hatch opened unexpectedly in the middle of the afternoon, but instead of Magpie, Viktor glared down, his face tense and frowning. Clouds were broiling in the sky and a gale was raging above the boat.

"Grab your gear!" he shouted.

"Are we there?" Fenn asked, but Viktor had already disappeared.

Fenn wasn't leaving the Not-an-otter on its own; it had been half starved when he found it, and now its coat had grown sleek, and its tail fluffed out with a glossy curl at the tip. Fenn clucked and whistled, but the Not-an-otter was nowhere to be seen. He climbed up to the rafters, peering between the boxes of dried goods, whispering into the secret dusty places the Not-an-otter liked to prowl, coming out covered in cobwebs. But it was no good: it was nowhere to be seen. For a split second Fenn wondered if he'd poisoned it – the turtle meat had been pretty rancid – but he argued with himself that wild animals only eat things that are safe. On the other hand, was it truly wild any more? His thoughts were interrupted by Viktor calling again, even more angrily this time.

With a heavy heart Fenn hitched his rucksack on his shoulder and crawled up through the hatch, gratefully taking a deep lungful of air. The storm was on top of them; dark green waves rose up and closed around the *Panimengro*, and the charcoal-coloured sky splintered with lightning shaped like upside down trees in dazzling electric blues. Fenn staggered to the rail, clinging on for dear life. Magpie was waiting for him. She looked drawn and pale.

On the horizon were seven vast, strange structures looming out of the foaming spray of sea and surf. They were huge red boxes, hundreds of feet high and each stuck on four concrete supports that were splayed like stools narrowing near the top. The way their struts spread out made them look alive; like they were walking through the surf. Three of the boxes had lights coming from within, shining through the small uniform windows on every side, but the others looked desolate and uninhabited, with black holes where windows had once been. One of the boxes had been stripped bare of its outer casing of iron sheeting, leaving a skeleton of girders and pipes. All the structures were inter-linked by metal gangways and rope ladders, apart from one that stuck on its own. At the base of each strut, dozens of decaying boats and barges were moored and other vessels had been moored to these, and to those in turn, so that they spread out in web-like radials.

"What are they?" Fenn shouted over the wind to Magpie.

"The Shanties," she said. "Old sea forts, from before the last Rising." She pointed to the middle structures, "They kept the guns in those ones."

"What were they for?"

"I don't know. People allus fightin'."

"Who lives there?" Fenn asked.

"Seaborns without papers or Landborns who can't get legit. Anyone the wrong side of the Terra Firma ends up here … and a lot of orphans." She gave him a pitying look.

It was approaching night so fires had been lit across the Shanties and they were now close enough to see a few of the inhabitants huddled under tarpaulins and sheets of rusting corrugated iron, smoke billowing through chimneys of old piping and concrete sewage funnels. Between the gang-ways, interlacing the huts, was a mishmash of ropes and nets. The way the nets looped and swayed reminded Fenn of the old raggedy spiders' webs that draped between the rafters of the pigsties back at home.

"Why are we stopping here?" Fenn asked. Halflin had said he could trust Viktor, but Fenn didn't like the way Viktor couldn't meet his eye.

"There was a Terra Firma patrol boat back there," Viktor replied. "It's too dangerous with you aboard. Sorry."

Fenn looked at Magpie for more explanation, but she blinked back tears, unable to look at him directly or reply. The rest of the crew cast a glance his way but carried on working. Fenn faltered as he tried to grasp what was happening; they were dumping him. Dumping him on the Shanties. Viktor handed Fenn his sea-permit.

"If … when … another boat comes? Get on it!"

"But I'm s'posed to be going to West Isle!" Fenn yelled.

"Get on it; wherever it's going," Viktor repeated.

As the *Panimengro* steered down through a cut of water that led into the heart of the Shanties, people caught the sound of the motor and were crowding against the ropes that looped around the edge of the jetties, getting ready to jump aboard. Many of them were teenagers, kids not much older than Fenn, but with hollow cheeks and sharp features.

"Look lively and get your positions," Viktor commanded.

Seeing the crew arm themselves with pike poles, most of the kids climbed back over the rails. Sargassons had a reputation for being tough. You had to be to survive the marshes.

Magpie and one of the crew got the end of the gangplank ready, but they couldn't moor; it was too dangerous. Viktor pushed Fenn towards the bow of the boat and shouted at the crowd to keep back.

The rest of the crew gripped their pike poles harder and stood facing outwards. As the ship bumped against the ancient rubber tyres strung along the makeshift quay, a young woman, heavily pregnant, clambered clumsily over the rope and teetered on the edge of the jetty. She was beautiful, with a rope of white-blonde hair falling over her shoulders. She held out an angelic-looking boy, who looked pinched and malnourished.

"Take him!" she begged, holding the child aloft, his skinny legs dangling like sticks. The child was weeping and weakly clawing to stay with his mother. "I've got a permit!" she shouted. When they didn't respond, she took something shiny from her pocket and tossed it over the water. "Please!" she wailed, as a heavy gold bracelet clanged and skittered across the deck.

"Anyone boards, tip 'em," Viktor shouted over his shoulder.

"Please!" the woman shrieked again, throwing something else. A scatter of gemstones fell like a hailstone shower.

"Tip them!" Viktor repeated to the crew, loud enough so everyone heard. The woman wailed in despair, then spat at them. She heaved herself back over the rail, put her hand in her pocket and pulled out more jewellery; once she must have been rich, but wealth didn't guarantee safety in this world. She started hurling pieces at the crew, pelting their heads. Silver chains, bangles and brooches rained down on them.

"Take it!" She was screaming hysterically now. "It's no use to me!"

Suddenly a line was thrown onto the deck and a grappling hook splintered the wood. On the other end a bullish-looking man with shoulders like the stumps of tree trunks was pulling the line tight and a rake-thin boy got ready to shimmy over. The bosun quickly kicked the hook out of the wood and the line slithered back over the deck. The man began to swing the iron hook once more, like a lasso over his head. Seeing this, Viktor quickly yanked one of the distress-flares from its hook on the side of the pilot house and climbed up on the rail to fire it into the air. A plume of smoky flame shot up and the crowd instantly shrank back.

"You're gonna have to jump," Viktor shouted at Fenn. "It's too dangerous to lay the plank."

"I can't!" Fenn wailed, eyeing the distance between the ship and the jetty. If he missed he'd be killed for sure; sucked under by one of the vicious currents swirling around the legs of the forts or crushed between the *Panimengro* and the edge of the jetty.

"Jump or be pushed. Your choice," warned Viktor.

Reluctantly Fenn stepped up onto the rail and swung one leg over. As he did, Magpie pressed a package into his hand.

"Ain't much," she said, "but it'll keep you goin' a day or so."

Fenn stuffed it in his rucksack, took a deep breath and swung the other leg over. He was now on the wrong side of the rail, gripping on for dear life. It was a jump of only a few feet, but easy to misjudge. Some of the crowd jeered, encouraging him to fall in, telling him to get on with it.

"Now!" Viktor shouted, eyeing the crowd nervously. Fenn took a deep breath and stared down. The water was roiling into a muddy-white whirlpool as the *Panimengro* bumped back and forth. He sensed Viktor move out of the corner of his eye. Fenn refused to be pushed, he hurled himself with all his might off the ship's side.

He landed face down on the jetty. He just managed to push himself up onto his elbows and wipe the grit out of his eyes before he saw the *Panimengro* roaring into reverse, heading back to the open sea. Over the engine and the shouts of the desperate crowd now jostling around him, Fenn caught Viktor yelling one final, frantic warning: "Clank yourself, kid! Hide, and don't come out till dawn!"

8

The Shanties had a bad smell, a bad feeling, a bad everything. The barges and boats that had originally anchored at the forts had once been grand mansions of the sea, but now they were crushed by the weight of incoming vessels, and had snapped and splintered inwards, making them no more than derelict hovels. Some had been condemned with yellow Sunkmarks and Fenn guessed they must have escaped before they reached a Punchlock. Nailed up on the boats' sides were enamel signs with the black and red Terra Firma logo, under which were the words, "Resistance is Treason". Every sign had been vandalized, either scratched out completely or splattered with oil and clumps of tar.

Between the boats and barges were alleyways made from scrap metal, chewed-up car panels, tin drums, upended dinghies and plastic buoys. Anything that floated had been packed in to act as a bridge across the water. Walkways of broken pallets and wood ripped from the sides of boats had been nailed over it all to make the flooring. Above them, swathes of plastic or sail cloth were fixed to keep off the worst of the sea spray and were interspersed with sheets of rusty corrugated iron, as fragile as autumn leaves. Layers of muck from seagulls splattered every surface and made the sheeting sag, sometimes into dangerously bell-like globes that threatened to burst on the head of anyone walking below. People dodged around these the same way as people on land dodge around ladders.

Fenn hesitated, unsure of which way to go. He glanced back at the *Panimengro* but it was already far out at sea. As he walked down the jetty he realised that the crowd had bulked out with curious spectators and everyone was staring angrily at him.

Fenn tried to ignore them, but keeping a watchful eye, pushed through the rag-tag gathering. They obviously didn't want incomers but there was no one who looked like they'd have enough energy to harm him; they were desperate, pitiful souls. In the dusk, illuminated only by the light from the braziers, they looked like sea ghosts as they shuffled to see him better. Some of them were old timers who must have been on the Shanties since the beginning. Their clothes were tattered and threadbare, but weighted by salt from sea spray, which made the folds so rigid they rustled and shed white dust each time they moved. Their skin was also covered in a fine film of salt crystals, and their hair hung around their drawn faces in stiff, crusty locks.

"We ain't got room for more!" someone suddenly shouted.

"What d'yer want here?" yelled someone else.

Remembering Viktor's words, Fenn glanced up at the sky; it was a murky brown. The storm made it seem later than it was, but all the same he knew he wouldn't have long before night fell. A rickety wooden gangway sloped sharply upwards to the next platform and he headed straight for it, but it was too late. Some of the crowd were clumping in front of him, barring his way. They plucked at his clothes, and stroked his hair like he was an exotic specimen. Suddenly a man, sensing a newbie, pushed through them. He was wearing a filthy dark blue suit made from satin, and a rough sackcloth apron with what looked like a pattern of red roses all over it. His nose, a net of crimson veins, was flattened to one side, so one nostril was completely squashed inwards, and he kept flicking it open and sniffing. He grinned merrily at Fenn, showing a set of black teeth, bowed theatrically and grabbed Fenn's hand with both of his, which were calloused and caked in blood.

"Waggit!" he said shaking Fenn's hand vigorously. He slung his arm around Fenn's neck then, without warning, pulled down Fenn's bottom lip and pinched his front teeth, holding them tightly, between a grubby thumb and forefinger.

"Look!" Waggit spluttered, pointing out Fenn's straight white teeth to the crowd. "Look at the teeth on it! Ever see such a nice white set?"

Fenn tried to pull away but dozens of people were craning in to see.

"They *are* nice," a woman said, giving her neighbour a jab with her elbow.

"Too spick and span!" the other woman replied suspiciously. "Teeth like that? You Landborn?" she asked.

"Or a Terra spy!" shouted a man. An angry murmur rippled through the crowd.

But before Fenn could defend himself, a young boy – Waggit's apprentice – popped up right beside him, standing on tiptoes to gawp into his mouth.

"Now see these?" the old man said to the boy, going into lecture mode. "Worth a pretty penny they are. Get Old Pincher, could yer?" The child dug his hand deep into Waggit's capacious pocket and pulled out a long-handled pair of bloodied pliers.

"I'm presumin' you wanna sell?" Waggit enquired cheerily. Fenn jerked away from him in horror and shoved him off. Waggit looked mortally offended.

"No need ter be like that!" he exclaimed, before his face broke into a smile. "Oh, I *see*! You're alarmified by mine!" he said, tapping his own decaying teeth. "Don't be; I never *wear* the *wares*." He laughed. "I swap your nice young'uns … fer a bit of bread, an' I make you a lil wood set. They'll do you just as good fer a coup'ler years. While yer still growin'."

At this his young apprentice proudly opened up his jacket, revealing row on row of differently sized sets of teeth graded according to value, starting with polished wood and leading up to porcelain and silver sets. He strutted around the crowd hawking the wares, then took out a couple of sets, snapping them like a flamenco dancer with castanets to demonstrate the sturdy hinges. Waggit clapped Fenn on the back.

"When you get tooth rot you'll be comin' back ter see me anyway!" he said sympathetically. "Might as well get 'em sorted now! Trust me, you won't find no better jawsmith! Ain't I right?" He beamed at the audience. They nodded, smiling encouragingly at Fenn, showing their gappy mouths and pushing even closer.

Fenn felt like he was suffocating. With a sudden surge of energy he thrust his way through the sightseers, running towards a gangway that led upwards, away from the milling crowds.

"All right, suit yourself!" laughed Waggit, shouting after him amicably, "You'll be back when you haven't eaten for a week!"

Halfway across the gangway an old woman barred Fenn's way. She reached out to touch him, feeling his clothes to get a sense of where he was, her eyes too swollen to see properly. Sensing youth and speed she clutched him, digging her nails hard into his flesh and bringing her face close to his. Her breath wrapped around him rancidly.

"Need somewhere to stay?" she rasped, her eyes flickering blindly. She reached up and lightly patted his face with the tips of her fingers. "Ah! A young'un; nice an' ealthy."

She grinned; her rotten teeth rattling and wobbling in her mouth, barely anchored in her raw gums. On either side of her chin little margins of red showed where blood had trickled from her diseased mouth and dried. She was tugging Fenn towards a derelict drifter, barely afloat, when a younger man pulled her away by the turf of her hair and pushed her to one side. He was thin and his skin was knobbled with red-blue scurvy spots.

"Let him be, you old witch!" he hissed, shoving her aside and looping his wiry arm over Fenn's shoulders, steering him onwards, away from the crowd. "Watch who you talk to here," he said. "Blind Sally will fleece you as soon as look at you." Just then another man, shorter and with a shiny bald head decorated with tattoos of sea snakes, fell into step on Fenn's other side. For a few moments Fenn was squeezed between them, almost carried along by the pressure of their bodies. Then suddenly both were gone and he was standing alone. Something was different; he felt behind him and realised he didn't have his rucksack any more.

The men were already several metres ahead of him, melting into the crowd and the night air. Fenn was only just working out that he'd been hustled and was on the brink of shouting for help when the tattooed man shrieked out in pain. He'd dipped his hand in the rucksack to see what haul they'd got and now he dropped it, sucking his bleeding fingers. He swore furiously and kicked the bag across the gangway. Fenn didn't know what had happened, but he saw his chance, darted forwards and grabbed it back.

He hurtled through the rest of the crowd, using his rucksack as a kind of battering ram, and headed any way that seemed to go upwards. Once he was clear of the jawsmith's audience the Shanties' dwellers barely looked at him. He was just another skinny kid on the run from one of the Whippers, the closest thing the Shanties had to any kind of law and order.

He ran quickly, scampering between huge old barges smothered in barnacles and rotting tendrils of seaweed so thick he could barely see through. It was getting dark now and people were returning to their barges or wherever they called home. Now and then voices rang out, weirdly severed from their bodies in the rising night fog. Above him Fenn could hear the soft slapping of bare feet walking along the wet rafters and occasionally a thump, as someone landed on a lower beam. Handcarts squeaked and groaned as they were trundled about, pushed by emaciated people picking up whatever gleanings there were to be had.

Running along the maze of alleys, he suddenly found himself by a huge, vertical girder with bits of rope and netting tied to it. Going upwards seemed safer. Clambering nimbly onto the next level, he found fewer shelters there. Climbing up yet one more level he discovered it was practically uninhabited. Here the Shanties was just a mess of beams and girders.

The storm had abated now, but there was still a sharp wind. Way below, through the tangle of beams beneath him, Fenn could see the dark waves. Twenty feet above his head there was a small steel platform on which he caught the gleam of something bright yellow. High above that was the base of the lightless gun tower Magpie had pointed out from the *Panimengro*. Fenn looked around, exhausted now, hoping for somewhere to rest. Then his sharp eyes spotted a place just below the steel platform where two girders interconnected. It was a tiny ledge, but well hidden.

After a dangerous and slippery scramble up, he finally squeezed onto the ledge and lay there, slowly regaining his breath. He pulled the top of his rucksack open to find out what had made the thief drop it. Inside, two wide red eyes stared back at him. It was the Not-an-otter, curled into a tight ball, trembling with fear.

Fenn grinned in shocked delight. He would have liked to have stroked it, but the Not-an-otter had bared its teeth and was already scratching frantically at the cloth, trying to burrow away in fear. Fenn gently whistled, just the way he'd done in the hold, and the Not-an-otter stopped and pricked up its ears. The way it looked up at him with its clever, knowing eyes once again made him feel a bit less alone and afraid.

He unwrapped the bundle Magpie had given him and found a couple of pickled sardines covered in paper, a sticky clump of rice pasty and a yellow ball-like thing that smelt clean and tingly when he scratched the shiny, speckled surface with his nail. Maybe it was something to wash with, like the precious cakes of soap Halflin made from pressed lavender heads, wood ash and pig fat. He crumbled a few flakes of sardine into the rucksack and clucked softly to calm the Not-an-otter, then he ate a sardine, a mouthful of rice and a few strands of Halflin's scurvy grass. He wasn't sure how often to eat it but he didn't want to risk getting scurvy and losing his teeth like so many people had here. Then he carefully repacked the food and closed the rucksack. He hated shutting the animal away but the sky was darkening and they needed to find a safer place to sleep. There was nothing for it but to keep climbing as fast as he could.

9

Fenn looked upwards, assessing the best route. Against the blue-black night sky, the iron fort towered above him, red with rust, its windows blank and foreboding. Lights glimmered on the other forts, but this one looked deserted; there was a blind, cold look to it. At its base was a perfect circle: a hole or tunnel that must have been used for access. It was as dark as a cave and Fenn didn't fancy creeping up inside when he had only a few matches left. It would be colder out in the open, but he decided to make his bed on the platform just below the tower, where at least the girders were level. He made for the closest girder that went upwards, tearing off a piece of plastic sheeting as he passed by to use as some kind of cover.

Climbing up took a long time. It wasn't like the Shanties' alleys where a kind of road had been made. Here the girders didn't properly connect to each other and were slippery from the rain. When he finally reached the platform, he found it was enclosed by railings, to which someone had lashed a patchwork of broken grilles to try and cut out the biting wind. In one corner was a large yellow steel locker – the flash of colour he'd seen from below. There were bright red warning signs screwed into the door. Fenn guessed it must have once been used for safety equipment on a ship, brought up here to make a shelter. It was jammed between the girders to shield it from the buffeting winds and Fenn imagined it would be warm and cosy inside. He yanked at the door, but it was either too stiff or locked.

He rattled the door again. The panels clattered but it didn't sound hollow. He tried the handle but there was no shifting it. Carefully, so he didn't frighten the Not-an-otter, he took out his knife. He pushed the strong blade between the door and the frame and began to twist it back and forth. He'd only just started when there came a frantic thumping from the inside – someone beating their fist on the steel panel. He jumped backwards in shock.

"Go away!" hissed a creaky voice through the grille at the top of the door. It sounded like an old man. Fenn stood on tiptoe and spoke through the gaps, recoiling at the stench wafting out from the hole.

"I need somewhere to sleep," he pleaded. Silence. "Hello?"

he said more loudly, but still silence. He hammered on the door, thumping it hard with the side of his fist. "Hello?"

"Go away!"

Despairing, Fenn sunk his head against the door. He had to find somewhere, he was freezing and the night air was getting even colder. He warily put his face close to the grille again and whispered in the same coaxing voice he'd sometimes used to get the pigs to come back to the pens.

"I've got food."

"Shut up! They'll hear you!" came the voice.

Fenn peered around guardedly but most of the lights below had been put out now and he was sure no one had followed him.

"Go away and hide! While you can!" the old man pleaded.

An icy gust sliced across the platform and Fenn's teeth began chattering. He wrapped his arms around himself, clapping and stamping his feet to keep warm. Casting around to see if there was anywhere else he could shelter, Fenn saw a huge old oil barrel wedged tight against a single rail. Between it and the girder supporting it was a tiny space about a foot wide, like a small ditch underneath the curved side of the drum. Because he was so skinny, it would be just big enough for him to squeeze down into. There would be no shelter if it rained though, and the small piece of plastic sheeting wasn't really big enough.

He spied a rickety ladder against the railing with a maintenance shaft of sheet metal around it. Fenn grabbed the end of the sheet and pulled hard. It was so rusty it came away easily, but made a lot of noise as it banged against the girders. He dragged the iron sheet back to the oil drum and made a curved roof over his little trough. The ledge had no side and he was terrified of falling off, so he untied the strap from his rucksack, then tied one end around his waist and the other around one of the iron joists. Once he was secure, he held the rucksack against his chest and put his arms through the remaining strap, then pulled the sheeting over his head. He tucked his face beneath the collar of Halflin's Guernsey and breathed in the smell of oil and fish. The wind howled around him and rain started to patter down steadily.

Fenn had never felt so alone, and he was glad when the Not-an-otter wriggled inside the rucksack. Fenn tried to imagine it in there; curling its furry tail over its head in the dark warmth. By imagining how the Not-an-otter felt, he felt warmer himself. It was the same way he'd given the sow back home extra hay on freezing winter nights, so he could sleep easier, even when Halflin scolded him because the fodder had to last all winter. Fenn squeezed the rucksack closer to share some of his body heat. In a comfortless world, it felt better than nothing.

But he couldn't sleep. Instead he remembered the times

he'd grumbled about being cooped up, nagging to go out. He couldn't believe only a few weeks before he'd wanted to know about the world. Now he longed to be back home, falling asleep by the fire, listening to the soft shuffle of Halflin's feet as he moved around, always working. He was even homesick for the *Panimengro*, recalling all the good things: Magpie's delicious food and the twanging music. He even missed the stinking hold – at least it had been warm and dry.

Fenn clenched his teeth against tears until his whole jaw ached, consoling himself with the thought that at least things couldn't get any worse. Eventually he nodded off into an uneasy doze.

He was so exhausted he somehow slept until nearly dawn, but woke abruptly with a sharp stinging in his ankle. The plastic sheeting had stuck to his face like a shroud and he fought to be free. Pushing it to one side he shook himself awake and looked down at his ankle; a huge grey rat was sitting on his leg, staring at him with sly yellow eyes, its fur glistening with damp. So things could get worse! He kicked out and sent the animal squealing over the side of the ledge, then sat up, rubbing his ankle, sickened to feel his fingertips wet with blood.

It was then that he heard it.

Something was shuffling softly in the girders above. The

wind had dropped while he had slept, and there was just the noise of the waves below. It was so quiet that at first Fenn wasn't sure if he was imagining things, but then he heard the gentle scraping sound coming from the direction of the metal locker.

He looked up. Dark shapes were moving slowly in the girders, silently slipping downs towards the steel platform. Fenn couldn't work out what they were at first and had to squint to see clearly in the half-light. They were human in form, but didn't move like any human Fenn had ever seen; their arms and legs looked too long for their bodies. Most of them didn't have any hair, those that did had clumps growing around scaly bald patches and the thin, greasy threads of it stuck bedraggled to their sweat-wet necks. It was difficult to distinguish anyone from any other as their faces were covered in blue marks over every inch of skin, including their eyelids. The remains of clothes clung to their thin frames: tattered orange jackets and boiler suits shredded to ribbons that fluttered like kite tails behind them. Their sinuous movements made them look reptilian as they slithered downwards.

Fenn froze in fear. He looked over to the locker, gauging if he could get to it safely, then realised with a jolt that one of the creatures was already silently squatting on top of it, like a grasshopper. The scraping Fenn had heard came from a shard of metal the creature was using as it methodically worked around the top of the locker roof, slowly unscrewing every single screw. The others, three or four of them – it was difficult to see for sure – had arrived and were now crawling soundlessly over the locker like spiders. They each began to work at a weakness in a joint or a hinge. They hunted as a pack; one prying open the lock, another starting on the lowest hinges, a third easing a knife under a sheet of steel to prise it off. The last of the moonlight glinted on them. Their slender, blue-grey hands and spindly fingers glistened like snakeskin as they unpicked the seams of the tiny fortress. Soon the locker could barely be seen beneath their slowly writhing bodies.

Staring in disbelief, Fenn forgot to breathe and nearly fainted. In shallow breaths he quickly tried to pant some air into his constricted lungs. Immediately two of the creatures stopped and extended their bulbous heads. They turned their chalky eyes in his direction and his heart thumped so hard he could feel the wall of his ribcage being buffeted. He reached into the rucksack, keeping his breath as sound-less as possible. He couldn't take his eyes off them. He was mesmerised by their slow, graceful movements and felt cumbersome and heavy by comparison. His fingers felt the smooth handle of Viktor's knife and he grabbed it.

Fenn clenched the knife so hard it hurt, dizzy with terror,

unable to think straight. The faintest shimmer of dawn was on the horizon; soon he would be visible. So this was why Viktor had warned him to hide. He assessed his chances of outrunning them and getting back down to sea level. It was dangerous down there too, but safer than this.

The creatures had turned back to the task in hand and soon worked the door and sides free, detaching the yellow steel panels from the locker, making less noise than a banana skin being peeled. Inside, at the bottom of the locker, Fenn could see the old man, curled up fast asleep. He was a pitiful thing, dressed in layers of frayed cloth, his face covered in a thick layer of something like tar, his hair and beard in knotted dreadlocks that he'd wound around his neck like a scarf. He was snuggled deep down in filthy paper and cardboard, like a dormouse in a nest.

The creatures had their prize; the nest was ready to be raided. Quickly, moving as one, they reached in and grabbed the old man by the hair, pulling him up into a standing position. The old man opened his mouth to scream, but before any noise left him a fistful of cloth was stuffed in his mouth. His scrawny arms flailed uselessly as he tried to beat them off with his bony fists, but one of the creatures spooled out a length of cord and wound it around him. Within seconds he was trussed up, his arms and legs bound tight against his body – entirely cocooned, like a fly wrapped in spider silk. Out of nowhere, another rope suddenly dropped down and they tied it around his waist. The rope grew taut with the old man's weight as they hoisted him up through the air, bumping him through the girders. A few creatures followed, pawing their bounty possessively. Finally the bundle disappeared up into the black hole Fenn had noticed earlier. The ones that hadn't followed clustered around the old man's belongings, picking through them carefully, gleaning what they could.

Moving carefully and holding his breath, Fenn undid the strap securing him and hitched the rucksack onto his shoulder trying to silently edge out from the shelter. His movement must have woken the Not-an-otter, as it suddenly jumped roughly, making the rucksack slip. As Fenn lunged for the strap, the knife slid from his sweaty palm.

Time froze. He saw the knife and his own fingers grasping out for it as if he was watching himself in a dream. He saw the blade sparkle as it twisted, the slow somersault of the ebony handle over steel. He held his breath, waiting for the world to start spinning again.

Time unfroze. The blade clattered down against the first set of girders, bouncing from one to another, the sound of the last clatter still echoing as a new one started. Finally it bounced off the last girder and catapulted into the sea, disappearing for good.

Instantly the creatures stopped moving, their faces tense with concentration. Their eyes stared blindly as they turned in Fenn's direction, seeking out the stranger in their midst. The nearest one, a little taller than the rest, stood on tiptoe, tilting the hairless dome of his head to the breeze. Although barely recognisable as one, Fenn now realised the creature was a man. The man took a long, deep sniff, his nostrils flexing open as he drew in the scents of everything near: the sea, oil, rusty girders, rotting fish, the old man's stench. And Fenn – the sweet scent of fresh, young flesh. The man smiled slightly, rolled out his tongue and licked the air.

He took a step forward.

10

Fenn bolted towards the girder he'd climbed the previous evening. He threw himself onto it, clinging to the rusty wet sides, half sliding, half falling down towards the next girder that met it and then scrambling onto that. He jumped again until his feet found another beam, but he immediately slipped off and fell against a rotting fishing net. He grabbed hold of some wet rope but it fell apart in his hand and instead he sprawled on a jagged beam that stretched out into mid-air. For a split second he tried to get his bearings but then he heard noises above. They were coming for him. They had no need to be quiet now; the hunt was on.

He looked around in desperation. There was no quick or safe way down. One wrong move and he'd fall, smashing on the girders before hitting the decks and breaking every bone in his body. But if they got him, he guessed he was as good as dead anyway. The next beam was at least ten feet away; he shuffled back along the rafter holding on to the netting. He took a deep breath, two great strides, then took flight.

As he leapt he felt sure it was the last thing he was going to do in his life. He squeezed his eyes shut, blotting out the Shanties and all its secret horrors, and made himself think of something happy. He imagined Halflin giving him a thumbs up as he made his way back to the hut from the Punchlock, patting his bag to show he'd snared a rabbit for supper and they wouldn't be going to bed hungry for once. For a second he almost felt light and happy as he spun through the air but then reality smashed up against the soles of his feet with a jolting agony. He grabbed at some slimy rope and caught himself just before he fell. Swinging around, he looked back to try to see how many were chasing him. Against the silver dawn he could see more dropping out of the hole they'd winched the old man into. Several were now only a few feet above his head, reaching down for him. He felt long fingernails brush his hair.

Frantically, Fenn threw himself down again into some rigging below. It was a terrible mistake. His leg went straight through a hole in the netting and he lost precious seconds trying to disentangle himself. With sickening dread he realised he wasn't alone; two of them had jumped down onto the net after him. Without hesitating, they rotated like spiders until they were upside down, and crawled towards him. Half upside down himself, Fenn kicked out as hard as he could, catching the nearest one on the jaw. There was a horrible cracking sound and something small and black, no bigger than a pebble, spun past Fenn's face. It was a tooth. With a howl of rage the creature threw itself at Fenn and wrapped its bony fingers around his foot, dragging Fenn upwards, hand over hand, like a fisherman hauling in a catch.

Fenn kicked and jerked his legs with a strength he hadn't realised he possessed. He clamped his teeth around a strand of net for extra anchorage, held it as tightly as he could, then unhooked his free leg. He stomped the iron heel of his free boot against the creature's wrist and wriggled his other foot out of its boot. Then he let his body swing away, leaving the creature holding the empty boot, while Fenn dangled defencelessly a few feet below. Fenn looked down; thirty feet beneath him was a barge, canvas stretched over the deck. He calculated his chances; he might get lucky and just break a leg. They were almost on him...

The boot he'd left behind landed with a crack on his head. It tumbled across the net then dropped onto the canvas below, which instantly ripped open. If it was too rotten to take the weight of a boot, Fenn stood no chance. He still gripped the net with his teeth and hands, but just as he was preparing to let go, he heard a vicious snarling sound, like a dog makes when you try to take its bone. He looked up.

Perching precariously on the end of a girder jutting out opposite him was a boy not much older than Fenn. He was sawing at the tie lines of the rigging with a jagged piece of metal sharpened to a blade. In his other hand he held a thick, long stick, with two sharp spikes on the end of it, and he was stabbing this at Fenn's pursuers. When he drew blood from the nearest creature's arm, it grunted, sniffed and looked perplexed, then licked the trail of its own blood like a cat laps milk. For a few precious seconds the creature was distracted. Then the boy severed the last strands and the rigging fell away, with Fenn still clinging on. The two creatures screeched as they pitched down, smashing through the beams until they finally disappeared with a splash into the water below. As Fenn crashed against the girder the boy reached down, grabbed his collar and hoisted him up to the safety of a wider platform made from an old door.

"Follow me if you wanna live," he said, gulping hard as he spoke.

Up close he looked older than Fenn had expected, raddled and pinched. The boy's face twitched and his eyes were bulbous, like hard-boiled eggs, with darting pupils surrounded by filaments of blood vessels, taking in all dangers. He was stick thin, and wore a bright yellow oilskin that only fitted him because the hem had been stapled up.

On his feet were welly boots, so ancient that the rubber was cracking and splitting, and the soles had been tied with a rope to keep them from flapping. A plastic sheet was tied around his head with some baling twine, with the words "Smokeless Fuel" on it and a picture of some blazing coals. Stalactites of seagull dung dribbled down the sides.

Fenn hesitated for a second, looking down at where his boot had been lost.

"Quick!" the boy yelled as he swung under a girder. Fenn followed.

"Thank you!" Fenn just managed, but the boy was already off, dropping through the rigging and girders without hesitation, never pausing for breath. Fenn scrambled clumsily after him, cracking his head on beams, scraping his hands and cutting his bare foot on the raw edges of metal.

"They've got yer scent now. Gotta get off their patch!" the boy hollered over his shoulder. "Hurry!"

Together they scrambled down until they were deep in the alleyways again, but still the boy kept running, falling over his own legs as he galloped away. He headed off through a gap between two barges, using his spiked stick as a staff to speed himself along.

Dawn had broken and the Shanties were waking up. At this lowest level damp hung in the air like a blanket. Fumes of burning tar permeated the sky as fires were lit. In the alleyways between the barges, mantles of smog enveloped the gangplanks, only broken up by the silhouettes of people as they went about their business in the gloom, wading through piles of debris.

"Duck!" the boy shouted over his shoulder, bending double to keep low as they passed under beams that dripped with rusty seawater and reeked of stagnant fish.

"What were they?" Fenn gasped.

"Roustabouts!" the boy shouted.

Fenn was unable to make sense of the labyrinth of narrow streets. Tiny, half-starved children with filthy faces and hair in matted clumps wandered listlessly searching the ground for dropped scraps, or huddled in threes and fours with begging bowls at their feet. In other alleys, red lanterns dangled overhead as murky figures slipped soundlessly in or out of pokey windowless barges. As the boy ran ahead, Fenn noticed that everyone made way for him.

The boy slowed to a steady trot as they reached the decaying heart of the Shanties – the epicentre underneath the central fort. They passed the oldest-looking barge of all – which had a red cross on a white background painted on its side.

"You new here?" the boy asked.

Fenn nodded.

"You'll soon get the hang of it. That's the Mercy-Ship.

One of the first dolin' aid after the last Rising," the boy said as they ran by.

"Why's it still here?" Fenn asked.

"Stuck. Ran out of fuel. Sick 'ouse now. Captain's a saw-bone called Ancient." The boy nodded his head approvingly. "Good at stitchin' and choppin' is Ancient. Fast. Needs ter be. Can take a leg off in thirty seconds!"

In front of the ship and beneath the four concrete struts of the central fort was a platform, a kind of raft made from plastic barrels lashed together. In the centre stood a massive mast; at the top was a crow's nest with a hand-cranked siren. Above that a star-shaped finial of beaten copper shone like a Christmas tree decoration.

"What's that?" Fenn asked as they scurried past.

"Watchtower for the Peepers," the boy replied. Seeing Fenn's blank look, he continued, "Young'uns, who ain't got scurve-eye yet. On the squint for Fearzeros an' rogues."

"Rogues?"

"Waves. The big'uns."

Directly in front of the mast was a small square hole covered by a wire mesh grille, and flanking this were two long benches made of ornate cast iron. A couple of women nursing wailing infants filled one bench, their life's belongings strewn around them. The boy and Fenn fell on to the other bench exhausted. The boy swung his arm over Fenn's shoulders. For someone so scrawny his arms were as heavy as lead piping.

"We made it!" The boy grinned, swallowing hard. "I'm Gulper," he said, proudly jabbing his thumb towards his chest. He put his blood and grime-stained hand out and shook Fenn's hand. "You got funny lookin' eyes!" Gulper remarked cheerfully, peering curiously at Fenn's different coloured pupils. "When d'you get here?" he asked, his breath raking from his efforts.

"Last night." Fenn replied. "I'm Fenn."

"Last night?" Gulper asked suspiciously. "Where d'you sleep then?"

Fenn, still out of breath, pointed up into the shadowy network of rafters over his head. Gulper raised his eyebrows and let out a long, slow whistle through the holes where his teeth should have been. The few teeth that were left were black, like he'd been chewing coal.

"You..." Gulper tried to say, but couldn't get the word out. He took a gulp of air, making his eyes pop out, wider and shouted in a rush. "You mad? No one sleeps up in the Sticks! Lucky you weren't eaten alive!"

"A rat bit me." Fenn nodded.

"Vermin are the least of your problems up there! I'm talkin' about Roustabouts – or Roosters as I call 'em.' Call 'em wha' yer like, yer taste the same to them wha'ever."

A bleak peal of laughter spewed out of his mouth, making one of the babies cry out in fear.

"Used to feel sorry for them, before they got Coral."

"Coral…?" Fenn asked.

"My sister," Gulper said, momentarily frowning. "In the old days they worked the Rigs. Blind as bats and deaf as doorknobs they are. Guess that's why they do what they do, can't get no other livin'!"

"So how could they tell where I was?"

Gulper banged his stick hard on the iron struts of Fenn's bench. The hammering reverberated through Fenn's skin.

"Vibrations!" he said, then suddenly grabbed Fenn's arm and lifted it up, taking a deep, long sniff of his armpit. He nodded sagely, like a connoisseur of a fine wine. "Or maybe the stink?" He shrugged. "Who knows? Out at night sniffin' fer food. Nasty things!"

He tutted, like he was describing an everyday household pest, the way Halflin talked about the bloated mosquitoes that pestered the pigs on hot summer nights.

"You'd better use this," he said, untying his plastic hood and giving it to Fenn. "Don't wan' that gettin' any worse."

Fenn tied the plastic around his bare foot.

But before Fenn had finished tying it up, Gulper was up and off. Uninvited, Fenn limped after him; he was the only person here who'd shown him any kindness so far.

"Did they get Old Tizer then?" Gulper asked over his shoulder. "I sometimes wonder how he's doin'. Don't go up that way much these days, but when me an' Coral was kids he were all right to us, Old Tizer. Used to share his food an' that. People round 'ere were nicer, but there was more food then."

Fenn guessed he must mean the old man and felt a pang of shame. Old Tizer had probably been living there safely until Fenn had started crashing around.

A Waker-Upper passed by, hollering and rattling his stick on the portholes of a small tug, waking the occupants to get to Market in time. Gulper watched idly, then spat between the planks at his feet. He smiled reassuringly.

"They probably wouldn't bother wiv 'im. Skin an' bone!"

"We should go back!" Fenn blurted out.

"So they *did* take 'im?" Gulper asked.

Fenn bit his lip and looked back into the rigging.

"Then forget it. At least it was quick!" Gulper shrugged, scratching his armpit thoughtfully. "Go back if you want, I ain't comin'."

He gave Fenn a friendly punch, then ducked beneath a fallen mast and squeezed through a dank crawl space smothered in barnacles, where the water glugged up between two barges. Fenn hesitated for a moment and looked back up at the way he'd come, wondering what to do. In the distant gloom he could see people slipping in and out of the walk-ways above. He felt his heart constrict first with fear, then shame; he was too afraid to find out for certain what happened to Old Tizer. He turned to follow Gulper.

Crawling after him, Fenn noticed graffiti scrawled in different languages on the sides of the barges, but none of it meant anything to him. Eventually he caught up with Gulper, carefully edging his way around the skeleton of a dredger's hull. Next to it was the collapsing hulk of a huge barge, its stern still in the water but its bow submerged. On its side the faded shape of a gilded key was just discernible beneath a Sunkmark.

"Was that a Resistance boat?" Fenn asked as he hopped across the ribs of the old ship. Fenn realised they were now underneath the furthest fort, the one that stuck out on its own. Gulper nodded.

"Used to be strong here; Shanties were a good stop-over for Seaborns on the run. But after they tried to kill Chilstone..." Gulper stopped talking like he'd already said too much and narrowed his eyes. "Anyway it's all done now, innit? Careless talk ... don't want to give spies anythin' to snitch wiv."

He looked mistrustfully around him, his gaze eventually fixing on Fenn. He stared him square in the face for a moment.

"Yer know, I saved yer without askin' an' I'll kill yer just as quick if I find out yer spyin' for 'em. No hard feelings or nuffin' but that's just the way it is." He smiled genially.

"Course I'm not," Fenn said angrily, stepping back.

As they were talking the Not-an-otter had worked its way up the rucksack and suddenly squirmed its head out through the top. Gulper jumped back in shock.

"You got a rat in your bag!" he shouted, grabbing a little club hanging from his belt and raising it to strike.

"No!" Fenn shouted, his face ashy-white with anger. "It's not a rat! It's a Not-an-otter!" He pushed Gulper back.

"You've got some fight in yer then!" Gulper said admiringly. He leant in for a closer look and then said, "Definitely not a rat," as if Fenn had said it was. "What is it then?" The Not-an-otter and Gulper continued to stare at each other beadily.

"I don't know," said Fenn. "I've never seen one before either but…"

"But you let it live in your bag anyway?"

"I think it's thirsty," Fenn said, looking hopefully at Gulper. "So am I."

"Water costs here," Gulper snapped, but seeing the Not-an-otter stare so hard at him, he softened. "I can get some though."

He put out his hand to stroke it, but the animal bared its

135

teeth and flinched away. Gulper looked Fenn up and down then rubbed his hands together.

"Don't think spies keep pets... You can come up," he said after some consideration.

Fenn looked up at the iron fort high above. Barely visible through the swathes of sea mist, it looked like a floating island. On one of its concrete legs were iron struts, almost like staples, making a ladder and Gulper had already grabbed its sides. He hesitated; it looked a long way up and he didn't know Gulper, but then Gulper *had* saved his life. What more did he need to know?

"Don't know why you're stallin'..." Gulper said as he climbed upwards. "Safest place in the Shanties!"

11

Gulper climbed swiftly, unafraid and sure-footed. After fleeing from the Roustabouts, Fenn's legs were jelly-loose and he couldn't trust them. He clamped his hands on the struts but they had been rubbed smooth as satin and it was hard to get a grip. The iron was so cold that every time Fenn wrapped his fist around the bars it felt like he was being sliced to the bone. A couple of times he looked down by mistake and felt so dizzy at the sickening height that he had to stop climbing and hook a leg through the strut, taking deep yet un-nourishing breaths. As they approached the top, Fenn realised there was a steel platform beneath the fort, just like the one Tizer had lived on, and above it he saw the same kind of hole the Roustabouts had winched Tizer up through. He shuddered. Gulper reached down and helped him up.

The platform was small and seemed completely empty. Fenn was puzzled; why had they come up here? There was no way to go higher. But then Gulper took down a long wooden pole, which had been was concealed along the top of a girder. He raised it up through the hole above them until it touched against a hatch hidden in the dark. He jerked the pole up, thumping three times on the heavy metal hatch. From behind it whistled notes sounded; the first part of a song, Fenn thought. Gulper whistled back the remaining bar.

"There's always someone home. Gotta keep it guarded," Gulper explained. Fenn heard the sound of many bolts being drawn back and the hatch opened.

"Who is it?"

It was a girl's voice. The words clicked sharply without warmth, like her mouth was full of nails.

"Amber, it's me," Gulper called up.

There was a moment's silence, then a rickety wooden ladder came shooting down from the hatch, crashing onto the steel platform. Gulper bowed graciously.

"After you."

Amber stood at the top looking down at them with her arms folded across her skinny body, and as Fenn crawled through the hatch he couldn't help but stare, transfixed by her ugliness. Her tufty red hair was cut so badly that there were grazes all over her scalp, and she wore a stained hooded top, a pair of rolled up men's combat trousers and outsized hob-nailed boots. Her sullen face was covered in streaks of dirt. Her right ear lobe shone with a brass earring, roughly cut to look like a four-leafed clover.

"Newbie," Gulper said as he pushed Fenn up, following quickly behind.

"Sure he's safe?" Amber asked. Gulper nodded.

Amber looked unconvinced, staring frostily at Fenn as she slammed the hatch shut, slid the bolts across and hooked over an old piece of tarpaulin to stop the draughts. Meanwhile Gulper propped his spiked stick against a wall hanging with buckets, wire traps, nets and three seagulls hanging lifelessly from a nail.

Amber pushed aside some sacking. They were in a shadowy, low-ceilinged room, apparently windowless, although Fenn had seen windows from the outside. The walls were covered in bright red and yellow wallpaper, but when he peered closer, he realised it was made up of hundreds of plastic packets; a yellow "M" was emblazoned on a faded scarlet background and some of them bore the words "Happy Meal". Each had been opened out and pinned over the next, like tiles on a roof, but being so light they lifted and fell with every single draught, making a noise like a rattlesnake.

In the middle of the large room stood an oil drum with a square hacked out, on which a huge pot bubbled. The steam from this belched up into a massive upturned funnel that had a long loop of piping attached to the end of it, strung across the entire length of the fort and disappearing into a hole in the ceiling. To the right of the funnel there was another drum, cut in half and set on its side, in which embers were glowing, sending off a trickle of smoke. Above this hung a wooden laundry rack with what looked like dozens of stiff socks pegged on it with pieces of split wood. A metal grid was laid over the fire with something cooking and a pungent smell filled the room. Standing next to it was a girl, about nine years old, carefully turning several skewers laden with some kind of meat. Her thick black hair was tied in a snake-like plait that reached her waist, where it was looped onto a belt made of faded woven fabric that held a sarong in place. Her face was delicate, with long, almond-shaped eyes tilting upwards. Fenn wondered if she could be Chinese; his encyclopaedia had a bit about a place called China and pictures of the people who once lived there. She didn't even look up at their footfall.

As Fenn's eyes grew accustomed to the murkiness he realised there were others in the room and that in one corner tyres had been put together to make a chair, which had been raised on a few wooden pallets. A man was slumped on the chair, watching Fenn lazily, and next to him a woman with her head on his shoulder was snoring loudly. Amber clomped over to a corner, threw herself on the ground and picked up a book.

Gulper shoved Fenn nearer to the fire. As Fenn walked he felt the floor bounce slightly; this too had been covered with strips of tyres crudely stitched together to make a vast mat. It made the whole place even darker, but cosy.

"Dry off," Gulper ordered. "We'll see about gettin' yer another boot."

At the sound of his voice came a loud shriek and a flurry of movement from the woman in the chair.

"Thweetheart! You're back!"

She jumped down from the dais and ran to Gulper, squeezing him hard. Her dress was made out of bright red and white striped plastic and it crinkled and rustled as she moved. Her orange hair fluffed around her head like mashed swede and she had rubbed some kind of blue powder over the lids of her bright, sad eyes.

"Poor dear! Poor dear! You're half frothe to death!" she exclaimed, briskly rubbing Gulper's arms and shoulders.

"Teeth! Mrs Leach! Teeth!" said the man, now standing. "We have company!"

The woman let out a cry of embarrassed horror and clapped her hand over her mouth, then pulled out a set of shiny porcelain teeth from one of her pockets. She picked the fluff off, polished them up on her cuff, then clamped them in her mouth, champing on them until they settled.

"Sorry 'bout that darlin'!" she simpered. "Oh, I was worried about you. It's a grismal day to be out!" she said, turning back to Gulper, helping him get his wet things off like he was a toddler and flapping his coat to shake the damp off. She barely seemed to notice Fenn as she fussed.

Fenn edged closer to the embers, rubbing his hands in the heat while Gulper went over to the man and whispered in his ear. At last the man stepped slowly out of the shadows. He was wearing a kimono made from a patchwork of fine fur in different shades of drab brown, so long it dragged at the back like a coronation cloak. Over his bald patch he had combed a few strands of hair, twice as long as the rest to cover the soft pink scalp. He was slightly plump and with his scrubbed skin he had the look of a big baby. When he came into the light, Fenn noticed a little web of wrinkles fanned out from his deep-set, piggy eyes.

Fenn felt a shiver run down his back. It reminded him of the feeling he'd had once when he'd gone out to the woodshed, and without even seeing or hearing it, Fenn had known there was a rat in the rafters overhead, looking up in time to see its tail slither into the shadows. Gulper continued to whisper while the man listened attentively; now and then tilting back his head to look through gold-rimmed glasses perched in the dent of his puggy nose. When he did this, Fenn noticed he only seemed to have one cavernous nostril, a hole in the middle of his face. As Gulper spoke, the man gently stroked his top lip. His mouth was too pretty for a man; berry red, with a cupid's bow like it had been painted on. Eventually the man nodded.

"Yes, yes; just introduce us," he said, pouting.

"Fenn. Mr Leach. He's the boss round here," said Gulper grandly.

"Everyone calls me Nile," he corrected. "Pleased to meet you, Fenn."

He spoke aristocratically, each consonant falling sharply on Fenn's ear, the words too clear and well cut, compared to Halflin's husky drawl or Viktor's lilting sing-song voice. Nile put his hand out, palm down, as if he expected it to be kissed, but instead Fenn took his hand and shook it. Even doing that made his skin crawl and he let go quickly. For a split second a little sulky frown skitted over Nile's face, like he was about to have a tantrum, but he quickly recovered his composure and smiled, flashing a bright set of perfect, creamy white teeth the colour of pearls. After seeing Waggit's many sets, Fenn wondered if they were real.

"And this is Mrs Leach." He flicked a hand indifferently to the woman.

143

She narrowed her eyes as she looked Fenn up and down. "My Gulper found you then?" she asked pointedly, beaming at Gulper proudly. Nile paid no attention, now stalking around Fenn in a small circle, eyeing him curiously, like he was looking at an art exhibit.

"Newcomers are always welcome here, aren't they everyone?" he announced in a silky smooth voice. Amber didn't bother to look up from her book, but Fenn knew she was scrutinising his every move out of the corner of her eye; her book was upside down.

Another boy appeared, crawling out from under a blanket in a corner then standing and yawning. He looked a little older than Gulper; tall, with long frizzy dark hair coiled in tight ringlets and the deepest brown eyes Fenn had ever seen. Fenn remembered the Venetian on the *Panimengro*; this boy looked similar.

"I'm Fathom," he said, "and this is Milk." Behind him, lurking in the shadows was a boy who was Fathom's complete opposite, with pallid skin, faded eyes and hair the colour of straw, knotted in tight braids around his head, like basketwork. He was so white that he looked like he'd been dipped in bleach, and his veins were like blue ribbons beneath the surface of his skin. The boy stepped forward and lifted his forearm in front of his eyes to shield them from the firelight.

"Hello," Milk said, so timidly Fenn could scarcely hear

him. Fathom tilted his head towards the fire.

"Light hurts his eyes," he explained as Milk retreated to the shelter of the dark. "And that's Comfort," Fathom continued, pointing to the girl by the fire, who still didn't show any sign of acknowledging them.

"Deaf and dumb. But awfully good at cooking," Nile said in an exaggerated, stagey whisper.

"Who's hungry then?" Mrs Leach suddenly asked, daintily stepping towards a large metal table around which were more cable spools, tin drums and wooden crates. She fussed around, rearranging the cutlery, then took a silk flower out of her hair and put it in a bottle in the middle of the table. At last she sat down, gazing attentively at Nile.

"Take a pew." He smiled, offering a place next to him and looping a flabby arm over Fenn's shoulders as he sat down.

"So, where are you from and how did you get here, dear?" Mrs Leach asked. Fenn hesitated. He wasn't sure how much he should give away in front of Nile; every fibre in his body told him to steer clear of the man.

"I was down in a hold," Fenn said at last. "It was difficult to tell…"

Nile tutted.

"Let's start at the beginning," he said, ultra-patiently, like he was talking to a very young child. "Where is your home?"

"East Isle … well, East Marsh," Fenn admitted reluctantly.

Nile raised his eyebrows in surprise, then nodded thoughtfully. He pulled a tin toothpick from out of his pocket and wiped it clean on his sleeve.

"Still above water is it?" he asked.

"Yes," Fenn replied.

"I see. East Marsh; home of Sargassons and Terra Firma spies, or so they say," he added, peering at Fenn over the top of his glasses and beginning to clean his teeth.

"And bogtrotters!" Amber chimed in, looking up briefly from her book before studiously ignoring the proceedings again. Milk giggled from the shadows.

"Stop twistin' the hay, Amber," said Mrs Leach curtly.

"Bogtrotter is very offensive, Amber," Nile said. "There's more to those marshlands than meets the eye. They were once home of the Resistance. May it rest in peace!" he scoffed.

Fenn felt sick. It was as if Nile knew something, but he seemed more interested in what was dangling on the end of his toothpick than Fenn.

"And how old did you say you were?" he asked. Fenn flushed.

"Fifteen," he said, remembering Halflin's advice as he put on a deeper voice than normal.

Amber huffed and shot Fathom a knowing look. Nile stared coldly at her until she buried her head back in her book.

"Why are you here?" Mrs Leach asked; her eyes flicked

over to Nile, who frowned at her interruption, his eyes glittering. She busied herself folding the filthy grey napkins into grubby swans.

"The Gleaner I was on saw a Terra patrol," said Fenn.

Nile looked intrigued. "Unusual. They normally give us a wide berth."

"Why?" asked Fenn.

"Terras like to keep their boats clean and shiny so they steer far away from the Slicks round the Shanties." Grinned Gulper.

"But, in the end it doesn't matter how you got here; it's what you do *while* you're here." Nile smiled. "The Shanties are full of human flotsam and jetsam; people running from floods, ending up in the middle of the sea."

"Have you lived here long?" asked Fenn, looking around the room.

"Long enough to get comfortable," smirked Nile. "And you're welcome to stay."

"Thank you but I'm going to the marsh on West Isle; my grandad thought I'd be … safer there," Fenn stammered.

There was a resounding silence then all but Fathom burst out laughing, including Mrs Leach who held her loose teeth in as she giggled. Fenn felt his cheeks grow hot with embarrassment.

"And you ended up here? That was unfortunate! Well,

you'll be safe here if you follow the rules," Nile said, winking to his audience.

"What rules?" asked Fenn, puzzled, looking from Gulper to Nile, then to Fathom who, even though he'd only just met him, he felt he might be able to trust a bit more.

"Exactly! That's what we say! What rules?" Nile chortled, rubbing his hands together and drumming his neat, red-slippered feet on the floor in childish delight. He clasped his knees as he laughed. "So perceptive, Fenn, and you've only been on the Shanties one night!"

Fenn noticed a funny look flash across Gulper's face. He wasn't sure what that look meant, but he felt he ought to say something good about him.

"I wouldn't have made it if it weren't for Gulper. He saved me from Roustabouts." Gulper looked gratefully at Fenn, but Nile ignored the comment, rearranging his kimono as if it were made of precious silk, then clicking his fingers at Comfort to hurry up with the food. Desperate not to lose his moment in the spotlight, Gulper suddenly grabbed Fenn's rucksack.

"An' there's an animal, Mr Leach!"

"Is that so?" said Nile, tentatively poking his hand in Fenn's rucksack.

"No, don't..." began Fenn, but it was too late. Hearing the strange voices, the Not-an-otter flew out in a flurry of fur, jumping over Nile's shoulder and up onto the ledge just above his head, where it shrank into the shadows hissing and spitting. Mrs Leach screamed so wildly that her teeth popped out and fell clattering under the table. She clambered onto the crate, gathering her skirts around her and whimpering in fear. Gulper was instantly on his hands and knees, groping in the dark for her teeth.

"A rat! Gulper! Kill it!" she squawked.

Nile gathered the hem of his kimono up, displaying his hairless white legs and grabbed the nearest weapon; a spoon lying on the table. He stood up, peering into the gloom. Locating the Not-an-otter, he stepped towards it, jabbing the spoon forward like a rapier. Fenn jumped in front of him, knocking the table over.

"Stop it! It won't hurt!"

"Do thomething Mr Leath!" Mrs Leach sobbed, still tottering on top of the crate.

"Get out of the way!" Nile hissed at Fenn.

"It isn't a rat!" Fenn shouted.

With one hand stretched out to ward off Nile, he clucked and whistled, holding out his other arm to the Not-an-otter, still trembling in the shadows. For the first time ever, the Not-an-otter jumped into a human's clutch.

"What is it?" asked Nile suspiciously.

"I don't know," Fenn said, stroking its head. "But it's not

a rat and it's not an otter either."

"It's a mongoose," said Amber, surveying the commotion with a look of deep disdain. Nile pulled a face.

"That's no bird," he said sniffily.

"They're like otters but smaller," Amber sighed, rolling her eyes.

Reassured, Mrs Leach tentatively climbed down off the crate.

"I've nether theen anything like it."

"And when exactly was the last time *you* were on land, dear?" Nile asked her patronisingly.

Gulper rubbed Mrs Leach's teeth clean and handed them back to her. She clapped them back in and patted the moss of her hair back into shape.

"He's mine," Fenn said, curling his arms around the mongoose protectively. He opened the rucksack and the mongoose slipped back inside.

"Keep him out of my way. If you don't, we'll eat him," said Nile coldly. Mrs Leach nodded again.

"And don't expect no extra food for it neither," she said primly, eager to show her support of anything Nile said.

"How many times have I told you about double negatives Mrs Leach?" Nile sighed listlessly. "Comfort! Breakfast!" he barked over his shoulder.

Amber stowed her book away and trotted over to help

Comfort serve up. Comfort picked up the skewers and laid them on the plastic lid of a packing case, next to a mound of gritty-looking rice. She set the tray down on the table with a watering can filled with water. Nile pulled out a silver hip flask, embossed with a family crest and put it in front of him, unscrewing the silver cap. Clapping his hands, Nile summoned the other children to eat.

"Good haul, Gulper?"

Gulper grinned triumphantly as he dug deep in his pockets and drew out a fat dead rat, then from the other side two smaller ones. He dangled these by the tails for everyone to see then dropped them on the floor, wiping his bloodied hands down his front. Mrs Leach beamed at Nile.

"E's a clever lad, in't he?" Then to Fenn, "Think you could learn 'is trade?"

Fenn bit his lip. He hated rats.

"I could fish," he suggested.

"Slicks killed the fish round here," Fathom said.

"I'll learn yer rat-catching," Gulper mumbled reluctantly.

Mrs Leach peered at Fenn's foot still wrapped in the shreds of Gulper's hood.

"We'd best get 'im shod, Mr Leach," she said.

"*Shoed*, Mrs Leach. *Shod* is for horses."

"Whatever, we should give 'im a check."

Fenn thought he caught her give Nile a tiny wink, but he

was distracted as Gulper went over to a tin trunk and rummaged inside. Before he realised what was going on, Mrs Leach had pinned him from behind.

"Get off!" he shouted, but Nile had already grabbed his foot in a vice-like grip. He ripped off the remains of the plastic and wrenched his toes apart, scrutinising them through the lens of his glasses, like a master jeweller.

"Very tidy!" he said appreciatively as he dropped the foot.

Fenn angrily shook Mrs Leach away as Gulper tossed him a couple of boots to choose from.

"And that answers two mysteries: you're a true Seaborn, which isn't good news for you. But it means you can't be a spy, which is good news for us! The Shanties has more than enough of those."

A wide, tight-lipped smile split across Nile's face, smooth as a pebble.

"So you can stay. Train in one of the many arts we offer! Everyone earns their keep." He gestured graciously around the room and made a modest little bow. "It isn't much, but what we have, we share," he said humbly, splaying his lily white fingers over his heart in a gesture of compassion. "Friendship, food and a bed after an honest day's graft."

"Great!" Amber muttered. "Rations just went from one-seventh to one-eighth."

Fenn angrily shoved his foot into one of the boots.

"I won't be here long. I'm getting on the first boat I can." He stood up and stamped the boot twice to make sure it fitted. Amber shot him an incredulous look, then glanced at Fathom who was already shaking his head.

"Well, Fenn," said Nile, his voice soft and playful. "We all have our little dreams." Fenn looked around the table.

"There are hundreds of boats here! They must leave now and then, when people get permits…?" Fenn's voice trailed to nothing as he realised everyone was looking at him in disbelief. Nile leant forward conspiratorially and beckoned Fenn to lean in closer. In a soft voice that seemed to Fenn to flick out like a lizard's tongue, he explained.

"I think you'll find that while we may be at *sea*, the *last* thing you'll find is a *boat*. Well, not one that's seaworthy, anyway!" he said gently. "If there was, we'd all be on it! No; every Refuse-Ship ending up here has already been scuttled by the Terra Firma to stop it getting to land. Besides, there's no fuel for them."

"Refuse-Ship?" Fenn asked.

"Terras call 'em that cos they're full of refugees no one wants," Gulper explained. "So they're always refused."

"It means garbage too," Amber muttered angrily.

Nile clapped his hands together briskly, signalling the end of the discussion. "Enough. Tuck in. Work to do," he said.

Immediately the children grabbed at the meat, tearing

off hunks between their teeth. Fenn picked up the skewer in front of him. Although ravenous, he inspected it first, turning it around suspiciously. It looked like rabbit, except at the end... Fenn touched it gingerly. Yes, they were fangs. Halflin used to shoot the odd hare, but this was smaller. Maybe rabbit? They had big teeth like that but he didn't remember them being so pointy.

"Is this...?" he said as nonchalantly as possible, not wanting to sound rude.

"Rat," said Milk, through a mouthful, as if he'd said nothing more unusual than "rice". He pulled a whisker out of his teeth.

"Looks good," Fenn said; any food was better than none and he was famished. It tasted rich, a bit like rabbit, but stringier. No one else spoke as they gobbled in silence for the next few minutes.

"As you're obviously such a quick learner, Fenn, perhaps selling might suit you better than catching rats?" Nile said, finishing a skewer and tossing it aside. He wiped his mouth fastidiously and nodded to Amber. "Take him to market. He has an honest face, don't you think?"

"Why should I get lumbered with the newbie?" Amber groaned. Nile shot her a look.

"Just be careful," Mrs Leach said. "Don't want you getting snatched on your first day!"

"Snatched?" asked Fenn. Nile glared at Mrs Leach then turned to Fenn reassuringly.

"Amber will look after you. Nothing to worry about." Amber scowled moodily.

"Apart from *Amber*, that is!" Fathom quipped. He winked kindly at Fenn, but Fenn didn't take it in; exhaustion, a full stomach and the heat of the fire had caught up with him.

"Poor thing. You look done in," Mrs Leach said with what seemed like genuine kindness. "Bet you never slept a wink last night." Nile wafted a hand towards an alcove between two beams where a hammock made from thick plastic sheeting hung.

"Take that one. Gulper can move."

Gulper pulled a face, but quickly returned it to a smile the instant Nile looked his way.

"Thank you," Fenn said. "For the … for everything."

He stumbled over to the hammock, kicked his boots off and tumbled in. He let the mongoose out of the rucksack and it settled to sleep, stretched over his chest. He pulled Halflin's jacket tighter, drew the ragged blanket over his shoulders and closed his eyes, listening to the soft pattering of the Happy Meal packets flapping in the draughts and the wind moaning as it swirled around the fort's iron walls. This time sleep came instantly, like he'd fallen into a bottomless pit.

12

Bright, green-tinted sunlight sliced through the gaps in the packaging around the walls, and in each shaft of light minute specks of dust circled one another endlessly. Fenn had woken to the sound of metal on metal, that put his teeth on edge and pulled him sharply from his deep sleep. It was Comfort, poking the embers of the fire with a spoke from a wheel, dropping in little scraps of paper from a basket of torn shreds that she kept by her side. On these she carefully piled up a nest of tiny pieces of wood. She put her face close to the weak flames and blew, but too hard. A mass of ash puffed over her, turning her toffee-coloured skin white. Fenn smiled at her mishap, but she gave him a look Halflin would have said could turn milk sour.

At that moment a boot scraped on the rung of the ladder leading to the roof. It was Amber. She'd been tending Nile's

Water orchard that he'd built on the fort's roof when he first arrived at the Shanties. Plastic sheeting covered the entire area and was carefully pegged so that condensation ran down into tin drums. Over the top was a scaffold, from which hung Water trees – dozens of upturned umbrellas and buckets to collect the rainwater. As well as trading rat meat, it was the girls' job to harvest the water and mend any tears.

"Hello," Fenn said, trying a smile on Amber. She glared at him too.

"We've missed the morning trade," she snapped.

Amber stomped over to the wall and lifted one of the Happy Meal packets, partially revealing a window. She peered out over the sea. "See that: the sun's right up," she said.

Fenn called the mongoose down from the ledge where he was carefully licking his paws clean.

"He needs feeding first," Fenn said. Amber sighed and folded her arms while she waited and stared out over the ocean. Fenn felt around inside his rucksack and tried to find the little pack of sardines and rice from Magpie, but there was nothing left save a few strips of shredded cloth. The mongoose had eaten the lot, including the thing Fenn thought was soap. Amber pulled on a pair of heavy leather gloves and glanced over.

"What's his name?"

"Doesn't have one," Fenn replied.

"I had a dog once; wouldn't have just called it 'dog'."

"What was it called then?" Fenn asked. A strange, hurt look flitted over her face, then her jaw set hard again.

"I've waited long enough," Amber said, hoisting down the rack hanging above the smoky fire. It wasn't heavy with socks, as Fenn had thought earlier, but rats being smoked. She lifted a few dozen off, threading a sharp piece of wire through them until it was packed, then she did the same with a second piece of wire. As she did this, bits of charred meat fell off into the ash. Comfort quickly gathered them up and brought them over to feed the mongoose. The mongoose curled its tail in happiness as it scoffed down the meat.

"Is Comfort coming?" he asked, as Amber finished threading the last rat.

"She doesn't leave," Amber replied. "Someone has to stay to bolt the fort up or it'd be taken."

"She must get lonely," Fenn said.

"Tough," Amber retorted, but Fenn noticed how she still ruffled Comfort's head as she passed by.

Amber hiked the ends of the wires together to make a kind of choker and hung them around her neck. Then she put her coat on over the haul to protect it from being stolen or rained on. The coat was orange with silvery stripes across it, which shimmered in the slanting sunlight. Fenn was surprised to see the Terra Firma logo that someone had partially scratched off. No one on the marsh would have dared wear such a thing and he felt a flash of admiration at her nerve. As he grabbed his jacket, Amber passed him a hoop of rats.

"Round your neck," she instructed. He held it away from himself, grimacing at the yellow teeth sticking out from their charred skulls. Amber glared at him again.

"I'm fine," he lied as he hitched the hoop around his neck, shuddering at the way the crispy bodies crunched and rustled as they rubbed against each other. He whistled for the mongoose, which slipped into the safe darkness of his rucksack.

Amber grabbed a trade bag from the hook, unbolted the hatch and swung it open, then slid the ladder down. Just before she stepped out, Fenn noticed how she rubbed the little clover stud in her ear, as if for luck. He pulled his jacket over the top of the rats as she had done and climbed down after her. Above them, Comfort hauled the ladder back up and shut the hatch, snapping the bolts back hard.

"Keep up," Amber shouted. She was just as quick at as Gulper, practically sliding down the iron struts, and by the time Fenn reached the ground she was already a good distance ahead. He sped after her, the memory of Mrs Leach's warning snapping at his ankles.

The mist had lifted but it was no easier to make out the size and shape of the Shanties. Most of the alleys were murky tunnels that ran between boats so close to each other their top gunwales touched. Where the boats didn't quite touch, wood had been nailed between them to make another path running above the one at sea level, and this was used when the sea was choppier. Here and there, rickety ladders ran between these alleys; sometimes a barge blocked the way and over time a path had been tunnelled through, so Amber and Fenn had to walk through people's homes as they cooked or slept. Hurrying along, Fenn heard the bleating of goats and the excited clucking of a chicken letting the world know she'd laid an egg. Rheumy-eyed cats mewed at his feet and lines of sodden washing were spooled between the barges, bespattered by seagull muck. People huddled together on the decks of larger barges, pooling meagre scraps of kindling to make a fire, or sharing a pot to make soup in. Fenn realised that to be down in the Slimes, as Amber told him they were known, was the worst of all worlds to live in; there was no chance here of ever getting warm or dry. Along the way Amber yelled over her shoulder, explaining what to expect to trade for a brace of rats: four eggs, half a bag of rice or flour.

"Gulper came a different way," Fenn gasped, finally drawing level with her. He wondered if she'd deliberately taken a difficult route, to test him. She shrugged, pushing her way through some dripping fronds of seaweed and letting them slop back in Fenn's face.

"We never go the same way, in case someone tries to nick our stuff when we leave," she explained. They passed a barge where the portholes had rotted away, leaving huge splintered gaps in the side. Through the decaying wood Fenn could see a couple of young girls playing with two filthy little rag dolls made out of strands of rope.

"Giv'us!" they implored as Fenn and Amber ran past, stretching out their skinny arms. Fenn hesitated but Amber grabbed his arm and pulled him onwards.

"They looked like Comfort," Fenn said.

"There are loads of Moken here. Water Jipseas. The Terras confiscated their sea-permits first."

Fenn felt a wave of anger at the injustice of it all bubble up in his chest. What right did the Terra Firma have forcing innocent kids to live like this? He wondered if anyone on the Shanties had any energy to think of fighting it, but at that moment Amber pushed her way through another huge curtain of seaweed and let it fall back in Fenn's face again. He spluttered and coughed.

"Could you stop doing that please?" he said indignantly, but Amber acted like she hadn't heard him. Fenn wiped the green gunge from his face and tried to flick it away, but it wound around his hand instead.

"What about Gulper? Where's he from?"

"Born here. He had a sister but he never talks about her. Mrs Leach took him in."

"When?" asked Fenn, peeling the slime off his hand and getting it stuck on the other one.

"Before she met Nile … before I came."

Amber sighed heavily and picked up the pace, but Fenn didn't recognise the warning signs. The only entertainment back at home was talk: Halflin telling him about his day, using words to draw a picture of the world for Fenn who was always trapped inside. Halflin never minded questions so long as their answers weren't useful to Chilstone.

"And Fathom?" he asked. Amber was plainly ignoring him now, her eyes fixed on the ground. "Fathom?" he tried again. Still no answer. Then, "What about you?"

Amber stopped abruptly and whipped around to face him.

"Look," she said, and took a deep breath. She was almost laughing, but her eyes were hard and sharp, glinting like shards of flint in the sun. Her voice was brittle and clear as ice. "You may have had all the time in the world for chit-chat on the pretty little marsh with your grandad, collecting shells, chasing butterflies and having cosy suppers, but—"

She stopped short, like she'd run out of time for even this. "If we don't trade this lot before dusk, Nile will not be happy. And if Nile's not happy, we're out. If we come back empty-handed we get half rations. There are hundreds of kids who'd give their teeth *free* to Waggit just for one warm night in the fort. So shut up and move!" She jogged on again, dodging past a woman sloshing out the night's slops. Fenn only just managed to hop over the stinking brown mess.

The alleys were getting more crowded now as they approached the main square by the Mercy-Ship where the Market was held. Water-sellers hawked their wares in rusty tin cans and wood-sellers hobbled around, bent double under the weight of the damp flotsam wood that was loaded on their backs. Beggars and crawlers called out for scraps of food and women with bales of drying kelp, hanging from yokes over their necks, sang to attract custom. There was a pair of jugglers and a woman in a ragged dress walking a slack line tied across a huge gap in the bargeboards. The whole place felt decayed and dangerous.

At last Amber stopped in a narrow alley just off the main square and they set up in a free corner. She strutted back and forth, scowling at people passing by. From time to time she shouted aggressively, "Rats! Roast Rats!" No one looked her way. No one was buying.

By the Mercy-Ship mast a crowd had gathered and in their midst a woman was crying, a tattered black length of fishing net veiling her face. Ancient, the captain of the Mercy-Ship, was reciting a few quiet words, the hem of his straggly white beard lifting and dropping in the breeze. As Fenn watched, the wire grille from a hole was lifted up and a body, bound in cloth and weighted by a stitched-in stone, was held upright over it. Four more shrouded bodies were lined up crookedly against the flank of the Mercy-Ship. The crowd muscled in to watch, so Fenn couldn't see, but when a gap opened again one of the shrouded figures had gone.

"Is that a funeral?" he asked.

"It's a Seaborn tradition; *Bury me standing cos I've spent my life on my knees.*" Amber smiled bitterly. "And they sink faster that way," she finished pragmatically.

A group of young crawlers, who had crowded around the funeral hoping to get a bit of food, were shooed away by the congregation. They dispersed into the Market like hungry sticklebacks, trying to snatch food and steal little pieces of dropped kindling. One of them, a skinny little girl of about five years old with a smudged face, sidled up.

"Can you spare a bit? Got two hungry brothers, Miss."

"Tough," snapped Amber.

The beggar looked beseechingly at Fenn, her eyes large and watery in her haggard face. Her elbows and knees stuck out like joints on a twig. He pulled a rat off and handed it to her. She grabbed it, instantly running off without even thanking him. Amber turned on Fenn, so furious that spit flecked his face as she spoke.

"You idiot! We'll be hassled by crawlers all day now!"

"She was starving," Fenn retorted angrily.

"We all are!" Amber shouted. "Why do you think I look like this? I had to sell my hair just to get Comfort enough to eat! There hasn't been a single rice ship for two months! Too much water to cross and most of the Mercy-Ships get their supplies confiscated by the TF patrols anyway!"

"My grandad used to say a kindness comes back around," Fenn began. "He said—"

Amber snorted.

"He was wrong. Here it's dog-eat-dog. How's a crawler like that ever going to pay you back?" Fenn opened his mouth to answer but stopped.

"Quick learner. Yeah, right..." she muttered sulkily. "Normally this is a good spot, but I haven't sold one rat yet. You're obviously putting people off." She frowned and glanced along the alley.

"Tell you what," she said, "you're not going to sell anything anyway so you can stay here. I'll try down there for half an hour. If I can't find better than this, I'll come back and you move."

Fenn nodded. He was glad to have a break from her. Amber unhooked half the rats from Fenn's necklace and threaded them on her own. "I might as well have these, you'll never sell them," she said, and disappeared into the throngs of people.

Fenn let her go; he was sure selling couldn't be that hard.

"Fresh roast rats!" he called, but even he could barely hear himself over the hubbub of the Shanties.

"Fresh roast rats…!"

People milled by, glancing suspiciously at him from time to time, but no one stopped. Lots of kids were selling rat meat, dried or roasted strips of salted gull, bags of kelp. He thought hard; he needed to stand out from the crowd. A hook. Maybe he could pretend the mongoose caught the rats, make it a unique selling point? He opened up his rucksack and let the mongoose out. It scampered up his arm, blinking its eyes at the bright light, and sniffing the strange smells in the air.

"Fresh rat! Caught the natural way! Without traps!" He felt an idiot, but a woman stopped to stare at the mongoose. Fenn started getting it to perform little tricks: running up one leg, across his shoulder then down the other, going so fast you could barely see it. Two more women stopped to laugh; one of them offered a small bag of rice for three rats.

Fenn told some of Halflin's corny old jokes and the mongoose let himself be petted without baring its teeth, almost like it knew what Fenn wanted from him. A small crowd soon gathered. Someone gave the mongoose a nut and it managed to crack it open by repeatedly throwing it at the ground, making the assembled crowd roar with laughter. Within ten minutes, Fenn had traded every single rat; he had three bags of rice, half a dozen eggs and some coffee grounds. It was nearly time to show Amber up; he was looking forward to this. He whistled while he waited, swinging the empty hoop from one arm ostentatiously. He'd never felt smug before; it felt good.

He waited another ten minutes, twenty, thirty. Thirty minutes turned into an hour. By then the smug feeling had faded and his face and hands were numb from the cold. It slowly dawned on him that Amber wasn't coming back. The exuberance he had felt at selling all the rats faded. Now he was just scared and alone. He had no idea how to find his way back. It was impossible to see where the forts were once you were down at sea level and there were a multitude of passageways to get lost, robbed or murdered in. It had started to get dark.

He looked around for somewhere to get a good vantage point. Banked against the alley there was a fishing boat with a piece of net hanging over the side. He chivvied the mongoose to run up so that when it got as far as the netting its weight dragged it within reach of Fenn. He hauled it down, yanking hard on it to make sure it'd take his weight. When it held true he climbed up.

He reached the top, leant on the bow rail and peered over the marketplace and alleys, which splayed out like rays on a sundial. Amber was nowhere to be seen. As he let the mongoose back into his rucksack he noticed how some crawlers had spontaneously clumped at the base of the boat, peering up at him. Seeing as he had nothing left to give them anyway, Fenn stubbornly stared ahead and pretended he hadn't seen them.

"Oi! It's me!" a voice squeaked. Fenn looked out of the corner of his eye as he tied up the rucksack. It was the little girl he'd given the rat to earlier. She cocked her head to one side. "That ugly girl you were with? Thinks she's somethin' special?" The little girl spoke authoritatively, her eyes wide in her filthy, mud-streaked face. Fenn nodded. "Got 'erself in a spot."

"What?" asked Fenn, frowning.

"She's gettin' twocked." Fenn stared blankly. She tried again. "Twocked? Jacked? Pinched?" She looked at him like he was an idiot then yelled like he was deaf, "ROBBED!"

"Where?" Fenn gabbled, slithering back down the net as fast as he could.

"Down by the Bilge. Din't call a Whipper, ain't got nuffin' ter give 'im," the girl explained as she took Fenn's hand trustingly and lead him at a trot down through turning alleys. Finally she stopped and pointed down a dank lane, flanked either side by crumbling boats.

Fenn squinted into the smog, trying to see. At the far end, beyond dripping curtains of seaweed and wet washing, he caught a glimpse of the fluorescent stripe of Amber's jacket. She was standing with the blind old lady who had grabbed at Fenn on his first day.

"That's Blind Sally. Her boys work with her," the little girl whispered.

Sure enough, in the shadows beyond Amber, Fenn could see the two men who had stolen his rucksack when he first arrived.

"Amber!" Fenn shouted, trying to warn her.

She couldn't hear him. As Fenn sprinted towards her, he heard the little girl give a shrill whistle. At the same moment the men dived towards Amber and Sally grabbed her arms, pinning them by her sides. The bald one grabbed Amber's bag, but suddenly the gang of crawlers darted out from the surrounding alleys and mobbed them, scurrying between their legs, grabbing and nipping at their clothes like a shoal of fish. Swiping at the kids, the bald man tripped and fell head over heels in the slippery mud, dropping the bag. Fenn saw his chance. Skidding in the mud he made a swoop for the bag, slamming into Sally, knocking her over. She screeched loudly, clawing at the air and scratching his face. He struck out and, regaining his balance, grabbed the bag and yanked Amber to her feet. They flew back up the lane. The two men were still fighting the hordes of beggars, but they kept flocking around them like seagulls, kicking and punching back – giving as good as they got.

Fenn and Amber ran on through several more alleyways and up a level until they were sure they were in the clear, then they stopped to catch their breath. Fenn was doubled over with a stinging stitch in his side. He tried to take slow steady breaths like Halflin had once shown him, but the pain was making his eyes water. He wasn't going to cry in front of Amber of all people. Amber slumped against the side of a barge.

"She said she had a sack of flour to trade! *Flour!* Should have known it was too good to be true," Amber gasped. "How did you find me?"

Fenn had no breath to tell her about the beggar girl, but he was looking forward to speaking. After all, Amber had treated him like an idiot; it was high time she was told that she wasn't always right and that Halflin's advice about kindness coming back around had been good. The stitch was subsiding now and he straightened up. Amber was staring at him, waiting; her eyes larger than normal and grey as the sea surrounding them. She looked like a frightened ghost; white and scared, her lips trembling. And strangely she seemed much smaller.

In that second Fenn understood. This was the real Amber, beneath the sarcasm and angry showing-off. All that was just to make herself look bigger and scarier, trying to protect herself – like Lundy's vicious cat. Fenn realised he should have expected a few scratches from her; he should have let her get used to him first, before meddling with a creature he didn't know.

"Beginner's luck," he finally answered with a lopsided grin.

13

The sun had set and the sky had turned lavender-blue over the fort. Amber banged on the hatch with the pole and replied to the whistle with the same three notes Gulper had used. When she helped Fenn through, she shot Fathom a look which meant he left them alone for a few moments. They pulled the ladder up together and Fenn knelt down beside her, helping shunt the last bolts across the hatch. She couldn't look at him.

"Are you going to tell Nile?" she asked as she jammed a bolt in place.

"Course not," Fenn replied.

She nodded a "thank you", then stood up and glumly hung up her empty catch bag. But Fenn grabbed it back and slipped in a bag of rice; enough so her rations weren't docked. Amber flushed in confusion and tried to smile; for a second she almost looked pretty. Then without another word she disappeared into the main room.

At the table, Nile sat brooding while Mrs Leach cooked and fussed around, trying to make sure everything was perfect; anything to keep the peace. She was stirring a pot of sludgy green soup on the stove, her hand on her hip and a little garland of flowers set at a jaunty angle in her hair. She had a dreamy look in her eyes, as if she were somewhere else altogether, far, far away from the Shanties, but as Fenn passed by she noticed the long scratch down his cheek.

"You get a lash from a Whipper? We don't want no trouble here," she warned.

"N-no," Fenn stuttered, thinking fast. "It was the mongoose. An accident." Amber gave him another grateful look.

He took his place at the table and let the mongoose out of the rucksack. It was sleepy from being in the dark, and he laid it around Comfort's neck as she sat down. As soon as everyone was seated, he proudly laid the eggs, coffee and rice on the table. Quick as a flash, Nile picked up one of the eggs and dropped it in a jam jar of water. The egg bobbed around on top. Fenn pulled a face – he knew what this meant. He'd been conned; someone had traded rotten eggs for his rats.

But before Nile could start, Mrs Leach plucked it out.

"Still protein!" she said pragmatically. "You'll never taste it in a spiced dumpling." She beamed proudly at Gulper and

Fenn and ladled extra soup into their bowls. "A good day's work deserves a good meal!"

"Goody! Sludge again," Nile said sarcastically.

Mrs Leach's smile faded and she twiddled her finger around in her hair in embarrassment while the rest of them gobbled down the dingy soup in silence. Fenn felt a sudden pang of pity for her and an equal pang of anger at Nile. He lifted the mongoose off Comfort's neck where it had settled and began stroking it.

"Oh, that thing!" Mrs Leach shuddered. "It's so slipperty! And vicious too by the looks of things." She curled up like a cat against Nile who didn't bother to hide his distaste at her closeness. It didn't take them long to empty their bowls, licking them clean. Comfort cleared the table and wiped the bowls with a filthy rag, stacking them ready for the next meal. Water was too precious to waste on washing up.

"Who's up for Sevens then?" Fathom asked. Mrs Leach nodded happily and he pulled out a deck of cards made from cardboard, each one delicately hand-drawn. Fenn stared, bemused, as Fathom explained the cards, and how a "Knave" could be a "Jack" and "Aces" could be "high" or "low". Fenn blinked in confusion as Fathom flipped the cards on the table, trying to remember everything he'd just been told, feeling stupid compared to everyone else. The very second Fathom had dealt all the cards, Nile stood up abruptly, pushing away his unfinished bowl of soup.

"I'm done," he said, glaring at Mrs Leach.

They all fell silent as he strolled towards the ladder leading to his room, barking instructions over his shoulder.

"Put the candles out. Keep the noise down. Don't make a mess…"

With a final grumble he hitched up his kimono and slunk up the ladder, reminding Fenn of a large rat as he disappeared into the gloom.

Fathom gathered the cards back up and started dealing again, but a few minutes into the game Nile's whiney voice slithered like a cobra down from the room above.

"My bed's cold!"

Mrs Leach jumped up and scurried over to the oil drum, wrapped a rag around her hand and pulled a couple of large stones from the hot ashes underneath. She dropped them into a thick piece of sacking, which she swaddled up like a baby, and zig-zagged her way across the room, tottering up the ladder.

"Coming, honeykins," she cooed.

"Does she always do exactly what Mr Leach tells her?" Fenn whispered. "It's like she's his servant." Amber gave him a withering look.

"Wake up, Fenn. We're all his servants!"

As soon as Mrs Leach had gone and the hatch to the top

room had closed, they all relaxed. Fathom scooped up the cards and tucked them back in his pocket, smiling shiftily.

"It works every time! I only get them out to get *rid* of him," he explained to Fenn. "He doesn't like games he can't cheat at."

Amber laughed, but Gulper looked mortified. "You shouldn't speak bad of the boss."

Fathom gave him a shove. "Don't be such a suck-up. Let's play Truth or Dare!" he said.

"Remember what happened last time?" Gulper warned. Amber burst out laughing.

"Fathom dared me to swap Mrs Leach's teeth with a set he nicked from Waggit. She thought her head had shrunk! Seriously, it was hilarious!"

"It wasn't," said Gulper, pursing his lips.

"It was," whispered Fathom to Fenn. He plucked Mrs Leach's silk flower out of the bottle in the middle of the table and rested the bottle on its side.

"How do you play?" asked Fenn nervously. Fathom spun the bottle.

"Easy. If it points to you, you pick truth or dare."

Amber suddenly put her hand on the bottle, stilling it.

"Count me out," she said. "There's no dare I can do, not without getting on the wrong side of Nile."

Even though she had her head ducked down as she petted

the mongoose, Fenn noticed her eyes had the same glassy brittleness to them he had seen earlier when she'd mentioned her dog. He suddenly felt defensive of her and decided to try and make everyone forget the stupid game she obviously didn't want to play. He clucked the mongoose and let it sniff a little bit of rat meat that had fallen under the edge of the table. By dragging the little bit of meat up his arm and around his neck, he started to get the mongoose to run over his chest. Seeing this, Amber pulled out the loose cord from her jacket's hood and tied it to another little scrap of meat and dangled it in front of the mongoose. The mongoose sat up on its back quarters and boxed the meat playfully with its paws, like a kitten with a ball of string. They all giggled, even Comfort, bashfully hiding her pleasure behind her cupped hand.

"So we're not going to play?" Fathom said, obviously disappointed.

"Just one go then!" Fenn agreed reluctantly, spinning the bottle again. It finally came to a stop, pointing at Fathom.

"Truth," Fathom said.

Fenn hesitated; he couldn't think of anything. Then he remembered his question about Fathom that Amber had never answered.

"Are you Venetian?" he asked.

The others sighed. Fathom pointed mockingly at his coils of jet black hair.

"My mum and dad both came from New Venice, and their parents before them. So that'll be a yes." He laughed.

"Where's the rest of your family?" Fenn asked.

Amber shot him a look.

"It's s'posed to be just one go," she said hurriedly.

"Not sure," Fathom said quietly. "I've got a little sister. She'll be seven next month."

"Here?" asked Fenn. Fathom shook his head.

"We were trying to get to West Isle too. My parents had permits and ID cards for us all. We were on the convoy ships but there was a sea surge and I got separated from Neva and … ta-da! Here I am," he finished with a sad flourish.

"Can I play?" asked Milk, edging out from the shadows. Fenn nodded.

"Let Fenn spin again," Fathom said. "He wasted his last go."

Fenn spun the bottle and it landed on Milk.

"Truth," said Milk. He'd never asked for a dare once in all the times they'd played.

"How did you get here?"

"I was on a Show-Ship, with Nami." Milk answered.

Fenn looked puzzled.

"It's like a circus," Fathom explained as Milk heaved a deep sigh.

"But they dumped us," he whispered, his huge pale

eyes blinking with the indignant shock he'd never get over. "Set sail without us when there was a Sweep…"

Fenn frowned.

"A Terra Firma raid," Amber said. "To fill the Labour-Ships and Missions."

"To build the Walls?" Fenn asked.

"Everything. Walls, peat-cutting, mining. All to keep the Isles safe – so the Terra Firma keep power," Fathom explained. "But the raids aren't just about labour – it's nearly always boys they take."

"There're always rumours about sightings…" Amber started.

"Sightings of what?" Fenn interrupted.

"You mean who," Fathom said. "People won't accept the Resistance has gone for good. There's always talk about the Demari kid being saved or turning up after years of being hidden…"

"In an eel trap!" Amber scoffed. She licked her finger and dabbed it on the table for a few scraps of rat meat she'd missed.

"Or found living in luxury safe behind a Wall," Milk said.

"That's just TF propaganda," Fathom countered. "To make the Demaris look bad."

"That's right," Gulper said, putting on a voice full of airs and graces. "Ai've personally met the son of the Demaris several taimes, don't you know!" He reverted to his real voice. "An 'e looked differen' every time. One time he was so differen' he was a girl!"

"That was me!" Amber giggled. Gulper puffed in contempt.

"Gotta look a *bit* Venetian," he said, gazing at her red hair.

"How did Chilstone know it *was* a boy?" Fenn asked. Fathom shrugged.

"Who knows? It's all rumour anyway and the same rumour says it's a boy Chilstone's after."

"But why would anyone pretend to be him?" Fenn asked.

"Meal ticket. Chilstone's Sweep on East Marsh means there are always boys on the run, some end up on here." Fathom stared at his lap, locking one thumb over the other. "Say you get here; no food, nowhere to stay – like you. Do you starve…? Or say you're the last Demari? People will give you their last scrap of bread… You're safe … until your story doesn't add up or…" Only Fenn seemed to notice how Fathom ran dry.

"Or one of Chilstone's spies gets to hear," Amber butted in angrily. "Then there's a Sweep and everyone pays. Makes me sick. Doesn't matter *how* hungry you are, you don't pretend to be *him*! If I ever met anyone who pulled that stunt I'd … I'd…" She stopped, her jaw too clenched in fury to make words. Fathom glanced at her uneasily.

"Honestly, I admire you for not trying that one. You even

look the part!" she said to Fenn.

Fenn blanched, dizzied by the nearness of discovery, his neck and face suddenly clammy with sweat.

"Don't worry," Fathom said, misunderstanding Fenn's pallor. "There hasn't been a raid for ages. But when there is, we're on our own. Nile won't risk crossing the Terras. If he was found hiding boys they'd take him too."

Fenn bit his lip as he listened. He wanted to get off the talk of the last Demari, but something didn't add up.

"But why does he care about a kid? Why doesn't he just go after the Resistance? It was them that bombed the ship wasn't it?"

"Chilstone's virtually crushed the Resistance," Fathom answered. "But he wants revenge for another reason: his daughter. She was onboard the ship that day. It was his idea that she spend her birthday with him."

"Four years old," Amber added. "Enough to drive anyone mad."

"Chilstone had a head start," Gulper chimed in.

"Let's talk about something else," Amber said, shuddering.

"OK. Who was Nami?" asked Fenn. "There were more kids?"

Gulper nodded. "Nile and Mrs Leach have always taken in kids." An awkward silence fell. Fenn glanced at Comfort.

"And Comfort?" he asked.

"Found her when she was a tiddler. Brought her back fer Mrs Leach to look after. Missus keeps her locked in here; pretty kids get stolen to work for Landborn families," Gulper explained.

"Better than working on one of the Walls," Fathom added.

"Or being here," Amber said wistfully, giving Comfort's hair a stroke.

"So where's Nami now?"

Fenn looked at their faces uncertainly, but none of them would meet his eye or answer.

"Me and Coral was born on the Shanties," Gulper suddenly blurted out. "I ended up here just after..." He scrunched up his face at an unwanted memory before carrying on. "A Gleaner came. I could've worked – I work 'ard – but they din't want me, so I stowed away instead!" He stopped talking like that was the end of the story.

"What happened?" asked Fenn.

"Chucked me overboard! Had to swim fer it. A mile! Lucky it was summer and daytime!" He laughed; like nearly drowning was just a minor mishap.

Suddenly Nile banged on the roof above them and they heard his angry, muffled voice shouting at them to be quiet. They froze, but then Fathom started giggling and this set off a chain reaction. Even though everyone's stories were so horrible, Fenn could feel laughter bubbling up in him, like something coming up to boil that he couldn't stop. Seeing Fathom's shoulders shaking made it infinitely worse. Amber and Comfort were struggling too. Fenn desperately held his breath, bursting with the enchantment of unexpected happiness. Gulper was hissing at them all to be quiet, but this only made them worse. Finally they erupted into spurts of loud laughter, unable to contain it any longer. Gulper was mortified.

"He'll come down!"

But they couldn't stop now. It was only when Nile hammered on the floor upstairs and yelled that they'd all be out if they didn't stop that they sobered up. The fit of giggles subsided. Fenn's ribs ached. He realised that was the first time since he had left home that he had felt happy.

"Spin it again!" whispered Milk.

"No," hissed Gulper. But Fathom had already twisted the bottle so hard it spun for ages, winking in the candlelight. The mongoose's nose started twitching as it got ready to pounce on it. Amber watched.

"Whoever lands on it, gets to name the mongoose," she said, glancing at Fenn.

"OK, but nothing stupid," Fenn agreed reluctantly.

Suddenly the mongoose leapt out of Fenn's arms onto the bottle and tried to bite it. They all laughed. The bottle was pointing to Fathom. Fathom lifted the mongoose up and stroked it.

"You're all mine now!" he hissed in the mongoose's ear. "So what shall I call you? Honeykins? Twinkletoes?"

"No!" said Fenn earnestly, not realising he was being teased.

"Tiddles…?" Fathom laughed. At last Fenn smiled.

"What about Nipper?" Gulper suggested. Fenn laughed again.

"He's nibbled me once or twice."

Amber narrowed her eyes as she gazed at the mongoose, trying to recall a long lost memory.

"I know!" she said, banging the table with her hands. They all shushed her, pointing up at the ceiling. "How about … Tikki?" she whispered.

"Why Tikki?" asked Fenn, puzzled.

"I don't know… Think my mum told me a story once…" She tailed off and stared at the mongoose. "I'm pretty sure it was called Tikki…?"

"I like it," Fathom nodded.

"Me too," said Milk. "Suits him."

They all looked at Comfort, who was stroking the mongoose gently. She glanced up and smiled, before turning her attention back to it.

"Tikki it is then," said Amber with a happy smile, putting

Tikki into Fenn's arms. Fathom stared at him thoughtfully.

"You know, you act like you don't know your beam from your bilge, but you're a lot smarter than you look."

"What d'you mean?" asked Fenn.

"You asked all those questions about us, but didn't tell us one single thing about you."

There was nothing to do but shrug it off; he didn't want Fathom asking anything. Fenn guessed he'd be good at spotting lies, maybe good at telling them too.

"You all heard my interrogation when I arrived," Fenn said lightly.

"Well, I was going to ask if you lied about your age but I already know the answer," Amber said.

Fenn opened his mouth to protest, but Milk interrupted. "Nearly every boy lies about their age – rules them out of being the last Demari."

"So, do you really believe you can get off the Shanties and get to West Isle?" Amber asked.

Fenn nodded.

"I knew it!" She shook her head. "You *are* insane! If Gulper can't get a ride, how would you? At least Gulper and Fathom can handle a ship. Can you?"

"No, but I could learn. My grandad wouldn't give up on me, I won't on him," said Fenn defiantly.

"Did the Gleaner you came on let anyone onboard?"

Amber asked bluntly. Fenn shook his head bleakly. "Then there's your answer."

"Just think about surviving, Fenn; don't waste energy cooking up escape plans," said Fathom quietly, setting the bottle upright and dropping the flower back in.

Amber stretched, making a show of yawning. She picked up Comfort, who was already nodding off, and carried her to bed. Milk disappeared off to his corner like a wisp of pale smoke. Fathom raked the ashes over the fire to keep it going until morning, while Gulper nipped the candles out. Within a few minutes, they were all asleep. Only Fenn stayed awake, watching the faint glow under the stove's ashes.

As he listened to the sound of the waves below he thought about his friends' stories. So was this going to be his life? Dumped on the Shanties, working as a slave for the revolting Nile and always afraid he'd lose his place.

He wasn't going to live like that and nor should his friends. As sleep crept up on him, he was still dreaming of how they could escape; whether there were any ships he could patch up and where he could get bitumen, nails and sail cloth. It wasn't just to get back to Halflin or to East Marsh, it was what Fathom said about cooking up escape plans. He didn't want to just escape the Terra Firma, he wanted to fight them.

14

But escaping the Shanties stayed a dream. For the first few days Fenn went out with the others, trying to barter rats and water for anything they could lay their hands on. Then Gulper made good on his promise to train Fenn in rat-catching and, although Fenn hated killing, Tikki proved to have unexpected skills. Soon Fenn didn't need to do much of the work as Tikki was catching more than Gulper and Fathom put together. Fenn always split his rats equally though, because if any of them returned with empty sacks Nile made everyone's lives miserable; especially Mrs Leach's. Whenever Fenn was up in the Sticks, he'd stare out over the bleak horizon, scanning for ships, but the sea remained a defiantly empty sheet of green, disturbed only by the froth of waves. Each time he'd climb back down with a heavy heart, despairing of ever getting home.

Today had been a bad day. People weren't out bartering much as the rations had run to an all-time low. Milk had only managed to get a few sticks of firewood and Gulper had only picked up three runt rats. The others had nothing to show for themselves but sore feet. The weak winter sunshine that had warmed them a little that afternoon had now turned to drizzle, so the children had made their way back to the fort early to get on with evening tasks. Fathom was up on the roof making sure all the umbrellas were ready to catch the downpour, Fenn and Amber were mending the gull traps and Gulper and Milk were sharpening knives on a whetstone, grumbling about one of the other rat-catchers who they thought was stealing from their traps. Comfort and Mrs Leach were putting food on the table while Nile, as usual, was dozing in his chair.

As Fenn twisted the loops of wire into a slipknot, he thought he heard an odd noise in the distance, coming from the heart of the Shanties; a low moaning, getting louder by the second. The sound was swelling and falling as it ran up and down an octave in a wave of ugly notes. Amber's eyes widened and she jumped up.

"The siren!"

At that moment Fathom hurtled down the ladder from the orchard.

"Sweep!" he yelled.

Nile scrambled out of his chair, suddenly nimble.

"Out, boys, out! You know the rules!"

Fenn didn't have time to ask questions as Amber thrust his coat at him. He bundled Tikki into his jacket pocket and stumbled towards the hatch. Nile flapped at them frantically as he opened it.

"Get out! Quick!"

"Not Gulper?" Mrs Leach implored, wringing her hands.

"Go with him if you think he needs baby-sitting!" Nile snapped as he quickly lowered the ladder.

"I'll be all right, Mrs Leach," Gulper said as he clambered onto the first rung. "Don't worry."

They quickly descended, Fenn coming last. Outside the fort, the siren was wailing at a deafening pitch. The second Fenn's foot touched the platform below, Nile hoisted the ladder back up. For a split second Fenn saw Amber's anxious face peering down, then Nile slammed the hatch tightly shut, bolting it fast. As they scrambled down to the lower level Fenn looked out over the ocean; there were eight clusters of lights in all, coming in from every direction.

Down in the alleys people were spilling out of their barges. Everywhere was jammed with bodies trying to escape, carrying a few possessions on their backs or pushing carts, running helter-skelter towards the centre of the Shanties. Children were screaming and weeping; people fell and were trampled.

The elderly or infirm cowered in their boats. As the boys got to sea level they were instantly swept into the human torrent.

"Which way?" Fenn yelled, grabbing Fathom's arm to try and stop him being carried away. "The patrols are everywhere!"

But Fathom couldn't hear him over the noise and his eyes were full of blind panic. Fenn remembered Halflin saying he'd seen people drown because they'd frozen with fear and had been unable to do something as simple as put on a life jacket.

"STOP!" he shouted, yanking the others off the main alley, down under the bow of a tugboat and onto a crumbling jetty.

"We need to keep going; lose them in the alleys, we've done it before," Gulper gasped, straining to join the terrified mob hurtling down the gangways.

Fenn suddenly remembered how Halflin once told him about catching rabbits, when a few wheat fields still dotted East Marsh. During harvest the boys made a ring around the field and, as the older men scythed the corn in smaller and smaller circles, the rabbits became trapped in the middle. At the last moment, terrified, they would spring out, straight into the boys' waiting nets. From the way the patrols were encircling them, Fenn guessed the Terras were doing the same. He had to yell to be heard.

"We have to hide!"

"They search everywhere!" Milk cried.

"Everywhere?"

"Except the Bilge," Fathom shouted. "But that's way too dangerous – it's half underwater!"

"Then that's where we'll be safest," Fenn shouted back.

Suddenly the harsh shaft of a searchlight swung near them. There were shouts from somewhere further ahead and the crowds started running back along the alley. It had begun to rain hard now and people were skidding and slipping in the grime. From out at sea, powerful white beams of light swept over the tops of the Shanties. People who had taken refuge up in the Sticks scrambled back down to hide, some falling in their haste, bouncing off the girders and into the water.

They ran back across the alley with Fenn in the lead, shoving their way through the streams of people and climbing up onto the propeller of a small fishing boat, jumping over its deck to the other side and into a deserted alley. They crawled under the hull of a wooden salmon boat and clambered down onto a long punt that had been lodged across the water: the only bridge from this alley across to the Bilge. As Fenn stepped onto it, some of the decaying laths disintegrated under his weight. Gulper and Fathom followed, bouncing lightly across the outer edges that were less perished. Fenn looked back at Milk but he was standing rigid, drenched in the rain, his hair frizzing into a luminous halo around his head, like an angel's.

"C'mon!" Fenn shouted. Milk shook his head and took a step back.

"The Malmuts will get us!" he said, his face even whiter than normal.

Just then the beam of light tracked across the bridge and they heard distant snarls. Milk ducked back, terrified, trying to hide in the shadows, but it was impossible – the lights were too bright.

"Milk!" Fenn shouted again, but Milk had already bolted back the way they'd come. Fenn was just about to go after him when Fathom pulled him back into the dank shadows.

"It's too late," he said.

"We can't leave him behind," Fenn said, tugging to get away, but Fathom wouldn't let go. Suddenly they caught sight of a monstrous creature as it skidded into the entrance of their alley, snarling viciously. It stopped and put its snout in the air. Steam clouded from its sharp jaw. A Malmut had found them.

The boys dived behind the sodden ribs of a Skipjack, its torn sails flapping in ragged wisps. Beyond it an old drifter was slowly sliding into the sea; two thirds of it was already below water, its Sunkmarked stern propped up by the barge wedged underneath. The searchlight swept up and over the barge, skirting past them as they squeezed themselves back into the shadows. Fenn heard another Malmut growling somewhere nearby. Tikki poked his head out in fear and slithered out of Fenn's pocket, scampering up onto the drifter's deck.

"Up there!" Fenn whispered, following Tikki. Fathom climbed up too, pulling Gulper behind him. The slanted boards were covered with black gunky seaweed. As soon as they stood up, they slid the length of the deck, crashing into a pile of rubbish and seaweed blocking the cabin door, which Tikki was already scratching at in fright. The ship shook and made a deep groan, like an old man fighting off a nightmare in his sleep. They froze, terrified. A harsh voice sounded close by, then Fenn heard the sound of a Malmut's whine as it caught their scent.

Fenn grabbed Tikki and slung him around his neck, pulling the jetsam away from the cabin door and yanking it open. They squeezed through and scrambled down into a dingy galley where the water was already waist high. Clusters of purple and white mussels grew everywhere and barnacles smothered the stove. They shut the door, reached down into the murky water and pulled the rusty bolts across.

Fenn leant against the door and listened, his heart thumping. He heard the scrape of the Malmuts' claws as it jumped up against the drifter's stern, scrabbling to get aboard. Then another started barking excitedly, a terrible sound quite unlike the sharp, clean bark of normal dogs. Malmuts always sounded like they had something thick and hot and sticky in their throats; as if they were choking on blood. Fenn froze, holding his breath, and Tikki wrapped himself tighter around his neck. The footsteps were getting nearer.

"They can smell something," a Terra said. "Must be in there."

At the top of the door there was a vent with angled gaps in the metal. Fenn pulled himself up on the doorframe and peered through. On the quayside he could see the Terras: two heavily built men, with black masks completely covering their eyes and mouths. They were practically being dragged along by two enormous Malmuts which, when they lifted their muzzles to sniff, reached the men's shoulders. The dogs had dead-looking eyes, shrouded in cloudy white mucus. They only needed their noses and ears to see the world and as one caught Fenn's scent, its long fur bristled. The Malmut yanked at the leash and lunged towards the barge.

Fenn gently lowered himself down and backed away from the door, trying to stay calm, slowing his breathing to keep his fear cloaked. Outside the siren had stopped blaring, which meant the Terras had got to the Mercy-Ship, and apart from the water lapping against the boat, all they could hear was the sound of their stifled breath. Fenn wondered if they'd got lucky and the Terras had taken their search to the next barge.

He looked at the others with his finger on his lips as he strained to catch every sound; his heart thumping in his chest, slow and hard, like a funeral drum. In the far distance he could just make out Terras calling through loudhailers for people to give themselves up, and he wondered if they were the same men who'd just been outside. They waited for a few minutes longer as the water steadily rose around them, but they were going to have to get out soon. Fenn waded back to the door, trying to make no sound. He leant against it again, listening out. When he was certain the Terras had gone for good he put his fingers on the bolts to pull them back.

At that exact moment there was a huge crash as a Malmut slammed into the door on the other side, snarling and scrabbling to get in. The bolt shook. Fenn staggered back and Tikki fell screeching into the water. He grabbed Tikki, praying the bolt wouldn't shake itself open or snap. It was thick, but the ship was old and rusty and Malmuts were powerful creatures. A second Malmut crashed against the door, whining and snarling. The door bolts shuddered, and the old drifter made a kind of grunt, like someone taking a punch to the stomach. Quaking with the extra weight of the huge dogs, the ship shifted violently, sliding further down into the sea with a gurgling sound. Water began rushing up through the door on the other side of the cabin. Fenn tentatively peered through the grille again. The two Terra guards were almost within touching distance.

"Get the dogs off. It's going down!" one of them shouted. There was a sharp whistle, then a scraping sound as something crashed against the door. From around the Shanties came the deep bellow of the patrol ships' foghorns.

"Leave it," the taller of the two Terras said. "There goes the Recall."

He yanked off his mask to reveal something Fenn had not expected: a surprisingly ordinary face, crumpled, but not unkind.

"Shouldn't have to wear 'em unless we're in direct contact," he grumbled, wiping the beads of sweat from his forehead and flicking the mask dry.

The other Terra instantly copied and pulled off his mask too. He was just a boy. Fenn was so close he could make out the yellow fuzz of his first beard.

"Reckon one of the other platoons got him?"

"Hope so. Chilstone will make us pay for it if we go back empty-handed," the older one replied. Fenn could hear the fear in his voice.

"Why doesn't Chilstone just tell us what he looks like?"

the boy asked.

"Doesn't trust anyone with that. It could lead the Resistance to him. Our job's to cast the net and hope the Demari kid is in it."

"Chilstone's a madman; he's chasing a ghost." The older one shook his head at the boy's naivety.

"Don't you get it? The Resistance ain't finished till they've seen the body."

"I reckon the kid's dead already!" the young one said conspiratorially.

"I wish," the other replied bleakly. "I'm sick of raids, sick of the *Warspite*. I just want to get home to the wife an' kids. Why should I help get the Walls built if I never get to live inside them?"

He rattled the Malmuts' chains to bring them to heel, while the young one hammered his fist against the hull right by Fenn's head.

"It's going down. You're dead now, Jipsea scum!" he shouted, grinning at the other to see if he was impressed. The older one ignored his showing off and wearily pulled his mask back on. They stomped back towards the heart of the Shanties.

Fenn's heart was thumping so loudly now he could hardly breathe. They were hunting for him, exactly like they were when Chilstone took the Sargassons' babies.

The three boys waited for a few moments in the dark, listening to the sounds of the Terras retreating in the distance. As the freezing water rose higher around them, they began shivering and their teeth chattered. When he was sure the Terras were gone for good, Fenn gave the nod.

"Let's go!" he whispered. They waded over to the door and, with the tip of his boot, Fenn felt for the bolt under the water. He shunted it back as Fathom pulled back the top ones. Keeping an ear out for noise from outside, they gently pushed the door, but it didn't move. They gave it a shove but it still didn't move an inch. The water was up around their necks now, rising by the second.

"Harder!" Gulper said, beginning to panic. Fenn pushed his shoulder against the door and heaved as hard as he could. Still nothing happened.

"It's jammed," he said hopelessly.

The other two immediately heaved their shoulders against the door too, but it wouldn't budge. Instead the boat shook again and from deep inside there came the sound of splintering wood as the drifter's bow end filled with water and slowly began to rip away.

"We're trapped!" Fathom cried.

15

They pushed and kicked at the door but it was stuck. Gulper swam to the nearest porthole and felt around the edge of it. It was rusted solid and too small to get through even if they could kick the glass out.

"Milk was right! This was a stupid idea!"

"It wasn't stupid," Fathom said defensively. "They left us alone didn't they?"

"Yes! To drown on a sinking ship. Some escape plan!" Gulper yelled, pounding the door futilely with his fists. Fenn grabbed him by the shoulders and roughly dragged him around to face him.

"If water's coming in must be a hole down there!" he shouted, jerking his head towards where the water was deepest. Fathom stared at him in amazement as he realised Fenn's plan.

"It's too dangerous!" he cried. Ignoring him, Fenn jammed his knife between two of the grille slats in the door, wriggling it back and forth until they were wide enough apart so Tikki could squirm into the gap. Then he gave Tikki a kiss and pushed him through. He pulled off Halflin's jacket and sweater, passing them to Gulper.

"It'll be pitch black down there!" Gulper said.

Fenn began to gulp in air like a fish, in a series of quick little breaths as if he was packing the air into his lungs, making his skinny chest swell and his ribs ripple like a keyboard.

"Wait!" shouted Gulper, but without so much as a backwards glance Fenn slid silently into the dark water like an eel and disappeared from view.

Many of the objects in the lower cabin had stayed exactly where they settled the day the drifter started taking on water and the crew abandoned her. There was just enough light from the Terra searchlights streaming through the portholes for Fenn to see as he swam through; plates and glasses had fallen off the table and lay scattered on the floor, the iron bench the crew sat on was upturned and smothered with tiny rusticles making it look almost woolly. Map drawers hung out of their chest. A sou'wester floated up from a hook, seaweed tangling out of its pockets.

Ahead he could make out the silhouette of another door

and quickly headed for it. Its hinges had long rusted so it hung rigidly a few inches ajar, but Fenn was so skinny he could just edge through. He swam a few more feet into a corridor then pulled himself down a narrow iron ladder deep into the sleeping quarters of the lowest deck.

The light was dimmer here and he couldn't see beyond a few inches in front of his nose. Fenn pushed past barnacled bunk beds, their blankets lying in rotten heaps and crabs scuttling over the decomposing pillows. As he swam, the water shifted in his wake and the blankets disintegrated, fluttering around like volcanic ash.

Fenn swam into the pump room, where the floor had splintered as the boat began to break in two, and another wrenching sound came from the core of the drifter's hull. While he could still see a little he held his hand up in front of his face; the skin was still pinkish, which meant he wasn't running out of oxygen just yet. He felt around and found a gap between the broken boards. He pulled himself through and dived down, right into the murky guts of the ship, where the water was thick with particles of silt. His hands were his eyes now as he felt the ship's broken ribs to get his bearings. He reached the keel board and swam towards the bow end, searching for any sign of light.

Fenn was feeling faint now; he had been down several minutes already and it was harder to hold his breath with the water being so cold. It was tougher to feel too, as his heartbeat slowed down. He grubbed his way through the darkness, blindly groping in the empty coldness and praying his fingers wouldn't become numb and useless. Apart from the occasional fish sliding against his body, he felt like he was swimming through an enormous watery coffin; it was so dark and lonely.

He'd never been under so long before, and the pain of something heavy was balling up in his chest. He knew he had to concentrate on containing that ball of pain. He had to control it; it would be so easy to give in, to breathe in.

At the very second he thought the ball was going to burst inside him and he'd have to breathe, just as his willpower, along with his lungs, was about to cave in, he saw a faint glow ahead. A soft yellow light was streaming through a hole he knew had to be there. It gave him enough hope, and with that, enough strength to wrap his lungs one more time around the airless pain throbbing in his chest and thrust himself towards the light. Thrashing wildly he squeezed his skinny body through the tiny puncture in the ship's side, gashing his arms and legs, but the pain was nothing compared to the agony of no breath. With the last dregs of his energy he clawed his way up the side of the boat, shooting up to the surface.

He came up with a gasp directly under the ship's stern. The propeller was inches above his head, its four round blades like the leaves of an enormous rusted clover. He hoped it would bring them all good luck. Then he saw Tikki, waiting for him as though he had known the exact spot Fenn would come up. If Fenn wasn't still so scared, and had enough breath, he'd have laughed. Instead, bobbing in the water, he clung to the rivets in the side of the ship with his fingertips, snatching in air, checking the coast was clear. Apart from Tikki he was alone, and aside from the glugging water and distant yelps of the Malmuts, he couldn't hear a thing. He grabbed hold of the anchor chain and hung there for a few seconds more, trying to steady his convulsing breaths. Far from the pain in his chest stopping, it felt like his lungs were being whipped as the air started finding its way back into every black, airless gap. For a little while it was hard to breathe – even out of water – but he had to save his friends.

"Good boy, Tikki!" he managed at last, and Tikki ran around in a little circle of joy at hearing his voice.

He climbed the anchor chain like a rope swing, but by the time he'd hauled himself up onto the deck, the drifter was all but underwater. Tikki raced from one piece of rigging to another until he could watch from a safe place, well out of the water. Fenn waded down the deck to the cabin where Fathom and Gulper were still trapped. They were screaming and hammering frantically on the submerged door. Plunging his arms in the water, Fenn reached around until his hands hit a sail beam. It had fallen across the doorway and jammed behind the ladder running up the side of the cabin, like a bolt across a portcullis.

His teeth were chattering so hard in his head it hurt his jaw, and he was bent double with the pains in his chest shooting out like knives. He held his breath and ducked down under the water once more, sliding his shoulder under the beam. As he pushed upwards he couldn't feel a thing, but it took all his remaining strength to lift the beam free, and it was only as it clattered over the side of the deck that he felt a sharp, stinging pain in his neck. He wrenched at the door and it suddenly gave way; a vast rush of water surged over his head and he grabbed hold of the ladder to stop himself being swept overboard. Fathom and Gulper were carried out on the waves and crashed into him; Fathom grabbed Fenn's leg, and with his free arm caught hold of Gulper's coat before he was swept over the rails. The drifter shifted again: this time it was going down for good. Tikki ran down the rail, jumping to safety on the jetty.

As the initial rush of water rolled away towards the stern, they swam away. Fenn was too weak to swim so Fathom and Gulper dragged him onto the rotting boards of the jetty. They lay on their backs gasping for breath. From behind them came a deep sigh of rushing water inside the drifter as a final, huge wave belched up from the lower decks. The ship slithered from sight into the ocean, pulling down the barge it was resting on. For a few seconds the barge hovered in the water, then that too rolled over onto its side and, with a gurgling sound, the sea swallowed everything whole. All that was left of the two boats were the bubbles popping on the surface of the inky waves.

Gulper staggered to his feet, wiping the water out of his eyes.

"C'mon. They might come back!" He pulled Fathom to his feet, but Fenn didn't move. Just then the searchlights swept across the jetty again. Fathom and Gulper ducked down, dragging Fenn out of sight into the curtain of shadow beneath an old houseboat. They tried to prop him up, but he lolled sideways, his eyes rolling back in his head.

Fenn could vaguely hear his friends trying to help him, but it was like they were in another room and he couldn't answer. He suddenly felt so weak that he couldn't even lift his arm to pull himself up. Something warm and wet started tickling his neck. He was wondering what it could be, when everything went black.

Bright red blood was oozing out from Fenn's neck. Fathom quickly tore his shirt off and clamped it down hard on the wound, pressing his fist against the cloth.

"He's stopped breathing!" Fathom cried.

16

Fenn was barely conscious as Fathom and Gulper dragged him back through the alleys, but he could still hear the despairing cries of the survivors and families looking for their sons.

Chilstone had put out the order for the Terras to be as brutal as they wanted in their hunt for Fenn. Barges had been set on fire to flush people out who were then beaten or taken onto the waiting patrol ships. Even the Mercy-Ship had been set alight, the lookout mast ripped down and the siren destroyed. Once the fire had been brought under control, Ancient had tended to the wounded; but the cabins were full to bursting that night and he'd had to turn Fenn away. Instead, Fathom had made a bung of cloth and wedged it against Fenn's neck to try and stall the bleeding. Together he and Gulper had made a sling with their arms locked together and carried Fenn back to the fort. Amber and Mrs Leach helped winch him up to safety.

Amber didn't leave Fenn's bedside for nearly a week after the raid. She barely slept or ate. Even when Nile said there was no room for freeloaders in the fort and threatened to kick her out if she didn't go back to work, she stood her ground; they all did. With so few young men left on the Shanties after the Sweep, Nile needed them as much as they needed his fort, and knowing that gave them confidence to challenge him. Fathom threatened to leave if Amber was forced out, and even Gulper said Fenn needed someone to nurse him. Not only had Fenn got the bends from coming up from the dive too quickly, the cut in his neck had nicked an artery. If they had been five minutes longer carrying him back to the fort, if Amber had not been so swift stitching him up, Fenn wouldn't be here now, quarrelling with her about whether or not he was ready to go out rat-catching.

"What use will you be anyway?" she said, examining the jagged wound on his neck. She had a bowl of hot water in her lap, and was squeezing out a clump of seaweed for a poultice. As she looked down, Fenn noticed something glinting brightly behind her scarf: she'd been touching the little brass clover so much that it gleamed like gold.

"If a ship comes, I'll never see it stuck in here," Fenn said in frustration. He felt suffocated by her attention. He struggled up, knocking the bowl onto the floor, and Tikki jumped up from where he'd been sleeping on Fenn's legs. Amber sighed wearily and picked it up, shooing Tikki away from drinking the contents.

"You need to rest," she whispered. Nile had overheard Fenn talking this way already and didn't like it. She glanced over to see if he was paying any attention but he was busy giving himself a pedicure, his foot up by his chin, biting his toenails and spitting them onto the floor. Fenn lowered his voice.

"You mean wait here to be rounded up, like Milk?"

Amber involuntarily flinched. Milk had never returned but it was an unspoken rule that they didn't talk about anyone who went missing.

"I'm sorry but it's true," Fenn said, seeing her chin jut out the way it always did when she was determined not to cry. He felt under his hammock for his boots, frowning when he couldn't find them. "We've got to get off here."

"How?" she replied witheringly. Fenn pushed the blankets away and tried to get up.

"I'll find a way," he said.

"Even if by some miracle you did, then what?"

"I'll go back to East Marsh. Join the Resistance."

"The Resistance is dead," Amber said rattily. She'd heard enough of Fenn's ramblings when he'd been delirious.

"And you know that for sure," Fenn said.

Amber sighed angrily and slapped the poultice roughly on his neck, then wound a piece of clean rag tightly around it and tied a knot. She had been so gentle over the past week but now her fingers were sharp and business like. She might as well have been trussing up a piece of meat for roasting.

"All I know is you need to keep this clean."

Amber stood up and clumped over to the box under her hammock where she kept her precious books safe. She opened it and pulled out Fenn's boots. It was the only thing she'd been able to think of doing to stop him going out, but she'd learnt he was even more stubborn than her. She threw them over.

The boots were odd; one was the replacement for the one he lost in the rigging escaping from the Roustabouts, the other had been Halflin's boot before, stitched over with a patchwork of pigskin a dozen times and painted with tar to waterproof it – something Halflin always did this time of year, before the rains came. As he pulled them on, Fenn thought of Halflin, a knot of fear in his throat. If Chilstone was raiding the Shanties in his desperation to find him, Halflin was in more danger than he'd realised. His stomach twisted thinking of Halflin coming to more harm. He had to do *something*. Today.

Fenn stumbled out of bed, feeling light-headed and

dizzy, then hitched his coat on, wincing at the dull ache in his neck. A sharp breeze ruffled the packaging around the walls as Fathom came down from the orchard.

"You're up?" he said, pleased but surprised. "Going straight out to look for a boat?" he teased.

"What's that about a boat?" Nile frowned, strolling over to the stove, lifting up the tin can and sniffing the contents. Fathom quickly grabbed his catch bags and nets. He knew when Nile was looking for a fight.

"It's all very well dreaming of escape, Fenn, but meanwhile we have to live," Nile said, grimacing as he poured out some coffee. It was a pale yellow; they'd reused the grains too many times for them to have any flavour left now. "Gulper's been out since dawn. Earning his keep." He finished with a loaded look at Amber.

"No one's got anything to trade," she muttered, but still pulled her coat on and grabbed a spool of rats Comfort had prepared, looping it around her neck. She set off down the ladder.

Nile gestured to Comfort and she picked up the knife to cut him some rice bread. As she did, Nile adjusted the knife so that she cut a thicker slice and then from his pocket took out a date he'd managed to steal from somewhere. He pulled it apart and pressed the sticky layer onto the bread, like toffee jam.

Comfort dropped the knife to the floor with a clatter; she was afraid of Nile and it made her clumsy. She looked up at him with large worried eyes but Nile simply patted her on the head. Fenn frowned; in all the time he'd been there, he'd never seen Nile be nice to anyone unless he wanted something in return.

"Be careful what you wish for, dear," Nile said coldly. "Resistance fighters have a short life."

A flash of anger sparked in Fenn's chest.

"At least it's a life!" Fenn retorted sourly. "Not a slow death here!"

"Quite the little hero, aren't we?" Nile smirked as he watched Fenn angrily stuff his traps and leather gauntlets into his rucksack and whistle for Tikki. Tikki scampered across the room and bounced onto Fenn's shoulder. Fenn heaved the spiked poles and buckets onto his back. He felt dizzy and the pain was bad but he wasn't going to show it – not if Nile was watching.

As Fenn clambered down the ladder after Fathom, Nile peered down, lazily slurping the last dregs of his coffee. Comfort came and stood by his side, ready to refill his cup.

"Careful how you go, Fenn."

Fenn ignored him and Nile looked momentarily crest-fallen, like a disappointed parent. He shook his head sadly. "They never listen do they, Comfort?" He nudged her to draw the ladder back up and kicked the hatch door back in place.

It didn't take them long to get to the Sticks, the labyrinth Fenn had sheltered in on his first night. Hunting had proved slightly better here since the Terra raid and there were fewer people around, as they stayed inside, trying to keep warm. They met Gulper shuffling down a deserted alley, peering intently at the filth on the ground, his stick poised.

Suddenly the litter rustled and Gulper cocked his head. He stood stock still and stabbed his stick deep into the rubbish. There was a high-pitched squealing and he pulled out a skinny grey rat, squirming in pain on the end of the prongs. Tikki came out from under Fenn's jacket, sniffing the air inquisitively, and squeaked. Gulper heard it and grinned, flashing his mouthful of rotting teeth.

"First one I caught in a while!" He quickly put the rat out of its misery with the fat little club he kept on his belt. Grimacing, he prodded it with the end of his fingernail. "Even the rats are getting scraggy," he said, stuffing it deep in a pocket.

They spent the whole day hunting, but the rain had made the rats shelter in places they couldn't reach. Catching rats Gulper's way was useless; they were hiding on the barges keeping warm.

"Let's check the traps," said Fathom, shivering.

Every night they set the rat and gull traps, but there were normally slim pickings as they were often looted by someone else. On a day like today the Sticks would be especially slippery and dangerous. Gulper looked up glumly.

"You two get back," he said. Something about his look of dejection reminded Fenn of the way Halflin sometimes looked when he had to go and destroy another boat; tired and beaten.

"I'll go," Fenn offered. "Tikki will catch a couple up there." Gulper and Fathom looked doubtful.

"I'm fine," Fenn cut in. "Go and check on Amber. I'll meet you back at the fort."

The girders were so slimy and wet that every time he climbed up he slipped back, wrenching his neck. He could feel the scar throbbing but he kept going. The higher he climbed the windier it got, and the rain made it hard to see. He had to concentrate hard; one slip and he would plunge into the freezing, rolling sea and that would be that. The traps were set under the walkways between the forts, where the gulls liked to roost when they returned at nightfall. Fenn shuddered, remembering the Roustabouts, but he figured he had an hour or so before dusk fell and they left their lair.

There were just two gulls in the trap, one dead, one on its way out, exhausted from the battle with the line but still feebly flapping its large, oil-speckled wings. Its eyes were greying over the way they did when they were dying. Fenn carefully took a hessian square out of his pocket to wrap around the gull's head to stop it pecking him and pulled the drawstring tight. It was something he'd made to ease the next bit. Then he loosened the knot around its leg so it stopped panicking and gently held the gull's head in his left hand, before bringing its neck back sharply over his forearm. This wasn't the first gull he'd killed, but he still closed his eyes. He wondered how Halflin had ever managed to kill a pig he had raised and even given a name to.

He was putting the gulls in his catch bag when something far out at sea caught his eye. His heart skipped a beat. Out on the frothy horizon a ship was battling its way through the heavy waves, heading towards the Shanties. It was an ancient sailing barge, its tatty red sails glistening in the sleeting rain.

17

Fenn couldn't believe his luck; for once in his life he was in the right place at the right time.

He clambered back down to sea level. The barge was making for the far side of the Bilge on the northern side of the Shanties. It was a sodden evening; hardly anyone was about and those who were had their heads down against the downpour. Even more perfect timing: he might be the only one to have seen the boat.

Fenn didn't know of any mooring space in that part of the Shanties; as far as he knew it was just a slag heap of decaying boats, like the drifter they had escaped from. Hurrying down the alleyways, Fenn reached a crossroads and found himself facing the huge hulk of an old Venetian wreck, forgotten and decomposing in the water, smothered with a soft green mould-like moss. Its bow rail was all that remained above the waterline now, with gold letters picking out its name: the *Gloriana*.

There seemed to be no way past until he realised there was a rip in the boat where the wooden cladding had crumpled together, leaving a jagged, dark hole in the side of the main cabin. As Fenn crept inside the pitch-black hull he could see dozens of rats' eyes glimmering. Tikki was squirming excitedly in his pocket; Fenn quickly buttoned the pocket down so he stayed put. He stepped through another hole into the main cabin. The rats watched him carefully without fear until he pulled his jar and candle from his rucksack and lit it with one of Halflin's matches, then they scurried into their nests, squealing.

The cabin's interior had once been beautiful. Although the paint was blistering away, Fenn could still make out intricate murals of sea monsters and mythical creatures on the walls. Gold and red scrolls adorned the four panels that made up the ceiling, and on them were strange words, decorated with illuminated letters, which Fenn wished he could understand. All that remained by way of furnishing was the iron staircase leading to the upper decks, which must have been too heavy to move, and to one side of that a thick curtain still drooped, with deep vents in it where rain and sea spray had washed the fabric away. Through these tendrils, daylight was shining into the cabin in misty shafts, and Fenn realised there had to be another opening behind them. He picked his way cautiously across the rotting joists.

Crawling through a hole on the opposite side of the *Gloriana*'s bow, he dropped down onto a tiny, dank jetty, which was completely hidden from view and between another long line of broken-up boats. The water was channelled here and it was particularly choppy, slopping hard against the rotting vessels that surrounded it, slowly breaking them to pieces. He paused, getting his bearings and wondering why any ship would moor in such an inaccessible and secret place. The *Panimengro* had openly arrived at the Shanties and Amber had pointed out several places to Fenn to keep an eye on; places where ships had once often docked, always where the water was much calmer.

At the end of the jetty he caught sight of the red-sailed barge, which had just moored. On its side, in peeling paint, he could just make out the name: the *Salamander*. Quiet as a cat, he slunk against the *Gloriana*'s flank, keeping tight inside the fringe of her shadow.

The *Salamander* was unloved. Fishing nets lay strewn untidily on deck and the cabin windows were clogged with green mildew. There seemed to be a small crew: only three men in total, which was unusual for a fishing barge. Fenn guessed they were Scotians; they looked like some of Viktor's crew. Their bushy, red-gold hair was matted and their faces were sunburnt to the colour of lobster. They had clearly sailed from warmer waters.

Fenn struggled to contain his excitement. It was a fishing ship; fishing and salvage, he guessed. It would probably have a big hold where they could all hide, so long as it wasn't already packed to the brim with cargo or so empty that they'd be seen immediately.

Fenn decided to slip aboard and check it out before alerting the others. He waited while the crew secured the barge, learning from their shouted calls that the ratty-looking one with the scrappy beard was Owen, and that the larger, sloping-shouldered one was Logan. These two called the third man – who was the oldest – Captain; he was a burly man with a squashed face like he'd run hard into a wall. After a few minutes he left, passing within a whisker of Fenn, who was crouching in the shadows. The captain disappeared straight up into the hole in the *Gloriana* – the *Salamander* had obviously landed here before. As soon as the others' backs were turned, Fenn scampered to the barge and slipped aboard. He was just about to run over to the hold when Logan suddenly loped back along the deck. Fenn had no choice but to dive down the stairs.

Inside, the *Salamander* was in a sorry state, but that was good news, Fenn reckoned: a slovenly crew wouldn't be making inspections or be down in the hold setting rat traps every night. Fenn crept into a kitchen where he found a squalid mess; a pot of something sat on the stove with mould creeping over it, so thick and fluffy it looked like a pan of fur. Used plates had been dropped in a bucket of putrid water with food and dead maggots floating on the surface, and empty bottles of whisky lay broken on the floor. He waited a few moments to see which way Logan went, then suddenly heard his footsteps coming down the deck steps. Panicking, Fenn pushed open the next door and slipped behind it.

He found himself in a surprisingly neat little cabin, fitted out with small beds; basic, not the height of luxury, but better than anything he'd slept on in a long time. Judging from the size of the beds he realised this wasn't a fishing vessel at all – they weren't adult-sized. It looked like a convoy ship, similar to the one Fathom had talked about; shipping children to safety. Fenn wondered if any of the Shanties children would be lucky enough to get passage, recalling rumours that some were taken to foster parents behind the Walls. But if it was a convoy ship, why moor here, in secret? He listened as Logan thumped around in the kitchen for a bit, then he heard the sound of breaking glass, some swearing, and finally his footfall retreating back up the steps.

Suddenly his thoughts were interrupted by more voices directly above him: a woman's and a child's, then the sound of them getting closer. Fenn stumbled backwards in the dark and found himself against a cupboard door. He swiftly slid inside and shut it quietly behind him, just as the door to the cabin opened.

"You promise me he'll be safe?" the woman was asking. Her voice was thick with the sob she was trying to hold back.

Fenn peeped through a tiny crack in the door. It was the captain with the woman Fenn had seen on the dock the night he first arrived at the Shanties. Her young face was gaunt and she had a shrivelled, pinched look. Hunger had twisted her beauty to something ghoulish; her large eyes were now deep pits and her skin stretched yellow as parchment over her once fine features. Her head was shaved but a hint of golden hair remained. Like Amber, she must have bartered her hair for food. Holding her hand tightly was the little boy she'd tried to get aboard the *Panimengro*; his eyes were wide and frightened as he hid behind her skirts. In her other arm she carried a tiny bundle that was crying quietly; Fenn hadn't noticed the baby at first. It was obvious the three of them were starving. If she had no way of keeping them all fed, then getting the child passage on board a ship off the Shanties was his – their – only chance.

"He'll be right as rain," the captain said reassuringly. "There'll be lots of other kids for him to play with."

He had a gruff voice that sounded kind and comforting

to Fenn's ears; not like the delicate, fake voice Nile put on. He watched as the captain showed the woman where the child would sleep, when suddenly there was a commotion on deck and one of the men shouted for "Lord". Immediately the captain stomped up the steps, grumbling to himself.

As soon as he had gone, the woman felt the rough blanket and then the hard straw mattress. She smiled at the little boy and sat down on the bunk, then lifted him onto her lap and started whispering in his ear. She was close enough that Fenn could hear she was trying to stifle a sob locking up the muscles in her throat.

"This'll be where you sleep, my love. Look how cosy it is! You even have a little roof," she said, pointing to the bunk above his bed. Her voice had that sing-song tone adults use when they are frightened but trying to stay calm.

"What's that man called?" asked the child, his voice wispy and fragile from lack of energy.

"That's the captain," she said. "He's called Lord. But you must always call him 'Captain'. That's the way it is aboard a ship." The child nodded and laid his head against her arm. His mouth was wobbling as he tried not to cry.

"Chin up, sweetheart," she said. She patted the bed and plumped up the pillow as best she could. "Look – the captain has made it all snug for you."

She dipped her hand into her pocket and managed a smile for the boy, then pretending to be conspiratorial, she leant in.

"And see this...?" She opened her hand slowly, like a flower blossoming; a tiny stub of a pencil lay on her palm. "This is a pencil!" she announced, like it was a diamond. "I've been saving it for a special day. Like today!"

The boy stared at it and made himself smile, but Fenn could tell he was unconvinced.

"What do you do with it?" he asked.

"You draw with it," she said excitedly. "It was mine when I was little. Use it on the wood here, where it's nice and dry!" On the bottom of the bed above her she carefully drew something.

"You have to be careful not to break the black bit or it won't work, and you don't have a knife to sharpen it." The boy watched her drawing with large solemn eyes, taking in the rarity of the gift, then she handed him the pencil as if it were a gold nugget. He carefully stowed it in his pocket.

Lord hurried back down into the cabin and explained to the woman that they'd be back in six months, and if she got a permit she could come and join her child. The child would be on the Mainland; he would be safe there. Then Lord suddenly lumbered towards the cupboard where Fenn was hiding and slammed his hand hard on the door.

"The children keep their stuff in here, if they have anything."

The mother winked at the little boy, who touched his pocket furtively.

Fenn pressed himself flat against the back of the wooden cupboard feeling the rough grain in its surface and a knot bulging out. Suddenly it swung away from him to reveal a short passageway that lead to a small flight of wooden steps. Tikki must have sensed Fenn's fear and was making a low frightened whine in his pocket. Afraid he'd be heard, Fenn slipped silently down the passageway and gently closed the secret cupboard door behind him.

He was in a dank windowless hold, well beneath the water-line. Stagnant bilge water lapped around his feet. Tikki slipped loose from his pocket and ran up Fenn's arm, hissing gently. Behind him, Fenn heard Lord slap his fist on the cupboard door again before moving on. Fenn listened to their footsteps above: first the woman and child, plodding upwards, weak and worn out; then Lord, impatient, hurrying, his steel-capped boots clipping the edge of the stair-treads.

He waited patiently in the dark; the stench was unbearable. One minute, then two minutes passed. Fenn thought it would be safe now and opened his box of matches. Only three left. He lit one, cupping the flare so carefully that he nearly burnt himself. The flame flickered in the clammy air. Fenn shuddered.

The cabin was filled with rubbish. It was as wide as the show cabin he'd just been in but only three feet deep. Around the walls were narrow planks, like shelves just long enough for a child to lie on. Fenn counted thirty of them. At the end of each platform an iron hoop was hammered into the wall with a chain fixed to it. Here and there were smears of dried blood on the wall. In the centre of the room was a slop bucket just within reach of each platform. There was a sluice gulley blocked with human excrement. Fenn felt a bolt of nausea in his throat and a crawling sensation up his spine as he looked around. This was no convoy. This was a trafficking ship, trading children. The woman would never see her boy again. The match fizzed out in the damp air.

Scarcely breathing, his heart thumping, Fenn grabbed Tikki and pushed him back in his pocket. He had to get off the ship without being seen, or he might never leave it at all. He waited a few more minutes to make sure the coast was clear before climbing back up the steps and into the cupboard. Finally he came out into the little cabin. On the bed the blanket was rumpled from where the mother and child had sat and talked. Fenn leant down and looked at what she'd drawn: a miniscule picture of a happy stickman in a triangular boat, sailing under a big smiling sun, towards an island with a wall around it.

He tiptoed back into the dismal kitchen, still keeping an ear out for the sound of the men on deck, wondering how he was going to get past them. Slowly he crept back up the deck stairs and peeped out. Owen was standing at the stern end, untangling some rope from where it had caught on the fishing tackle, swearing and muttering under his breath. Logan was just a couple of feet from Fenn, with his back turned to him, tapping the blunt edge of a cleaver in his hand. He was leaning on the bow and seeing how far he could spit into the water.

Fenn would easily be seen if he tried to jump onto the jetty. He spied a wooden pail lying on its side, just within reach. He managed to stretch out and get his fingertips around the handle, pulling it a little nearer. It scraped slightly as he moved it and Logan looked over his shoulder. Fenn ducked back down. He left it a few seconds, then slowly peeped out again; Logan had resumed his spitting game.

He gently picked the pail up and swung it with all his might across the barge deck, away from the jetty. It clattered over the side and splashed into the water. Logan and Owen immediately ran around the side of the barge, shouting at the would-be intruder. Seizing his chance, Fenn ran and slipped back over the rail, racing back down the jetty to the *Gloriana*, ignoring the angry shouts behind him.

By the time Fenn got back to the fort it was already dark, the wind was picking up and the waves were foamy white. The Shanties were closing down for the night as people returned to their barges. Down in the alleys below Fenn could just make out the glimmer of a Lighter-Upper, carrying a long fishing pole with a burning wick that he used to light a few torches around the main square. Wisps of music drifted up as a crowd gathered by the Mercy-Ship to sing old songs; Ancient always lit a fire by the ship for anyone who had no other home to go to. Fenn scrambled up the last few metal rungs to the fort, banged on the hatch and waited for the whistle. But before it came the hatch was flung wide open and the ladder dropped down by Amber. Her eyes glittered in excitement.

"You're late!"

"You won't believe this…" he whispered, but she interrupted him, flapping her hands at him to make him shut up. Two bright red spots had blossomed on her cheeks.

"No. You won't believe *this*," she countered. "Nile's got us on a boat! And we're having a party!" She giggled. "With bacon!" Her face was pink with happiness as she waggled a rasher in front of his nose.

226

Before Fenn could respond, Nile yelled at Amber to close the hatch and come back into the main room. Fenn hooked the nets up on the wall, let Tikki up onto his shoulder, pulled the two gulls out of his rucksack and hung them up for plucking later on. He went into the living area.

It looked different from normal; there was a proper fire rather than just the charcoal embers to smoke the rats, and around the walls all the tallow lamps had been lit. The air was full of a wonderful smell that conjured up memories of the kitchen at home. As his eyes adjusted to the brightness, he saw Gulper and Fathom huddled excitedly by the fire, and Amber pushing in to get closer. He looked around for Comfort and found her lying on her stomach by Nile's feet as he chatted affably to another man, whose back was turned to Fenn. Comfort was meticulously packing her meagre belongings into a catch bag: a comb with only a few teeth left, a teaspoon sharpened to a knife, a raffia sleeping mat. On the other side of the man was Mrs Leach, sitting prettily, her hands neatly crossed on her knees. Her carpet-bag bulged by her feet; she'd already packed all her worldly goods and now she waited excitedly, like a child about to go on a birthday treat. Every now and then she smiled gratefully at Nile.

At the sound of his footfall, Mrs Leach turned to beam at Fenn. She was rosy-cheeked from the heat of the fire and the excitement of having guests, and she had drawn little wings on the outside of her eyes to make them look wider and bigger, using pieces of charcoal from the fire.

"Coo-ee!" she called, wiggling her fingertips at him like a little girl. Somehow she managed to make her face lift up when she wanted it to, like invisible hooks were attaching her skin to pulleys in the sky; it made her look younger but also waxy and stiff, like a ventriloquist's dummy.

Fenn watched as Nile dug his fist into a small hessian sack in his lap and pulled out a handful of ginger-coloured leaves. He crumbled them between his fingers and brought them up to his nose, inhaling deeply.

"Fenn! I was worried you'd miss the celebration!" he said over his shoulder, not looking in the slightest bit concerned. He turned to refill the stranger's jam jar from one of the three whisky bottles that stood under the stranger's chair.

"Fenn is our latest recruit but he's ever so keen to leave," Nile said with a sneer. "So he'll be very pleased to hear your news!"

The man turned and gave Fenn a friendly nod.

It was Lord.

18

Once, when Fenn was about nine, he hit Halflin really hard.

Halflin had been on the Punchlock all morning and, as always, left Fenn at home with strict instructions to hide if anyone came knocking. He had handed him a piece of slate and a chalk and told him to find out about a man called Chaucer, as he would test him when he got back. Fenn was soon so bored he decided to go and spy on Halflin.

He had crept up into the loft and trained the telescope over towards the Punchlock and found Halflin immediately. He watched Halflin destroy six boats that morning: two barges, two luggers, a houseboat and a drifter. Of course he knew that was what Halflin did for a living, but it's one thing hearing about something and another seeing it. By the time Halflin got back, Fenn was in a blind rage of injustice.

As Halflin came in through the door, he flew at him, punching and kicking.

Halflin had taken it. He hadn't given Fenn a clout or even shouted. He let him beat his fists against his chest and held him while angry sobs racked through his body. But when Fenn screamed that he should be more like the Sargassons, who didn't do any of the Terra Firma's dirty work, Halflin pushed him off angrily, then changed his mind and gripped Fenn's shoulders too hard while he told him a few home truths.

Sargassons didn't help or hinder the Terra Firma, he said. After the great Sweep when their children were taken, they'd learned to survive by keeping themselves to themselves and never showing their feelings to outsiders, knowing concealment kept them safe, like the very eels they hunted. As Halflin jabbed the stump of his finger hard into Fenn's chest, he explained that secrecy was what kept them both alive too. He said that there were only four ways animals avoided being killed: kill first, fight, run or hide. Halflin said that he for one could only manage the last; he didn't have the strength for fighting, nor the legs for running any more, and he'd never had the stomach for killing. Fenn could learn a thing or two from the Sargassons for sure, Halflin said; not flashing his emotions for all to see would be a start.

Fenn touched his chest now, feeling the very spot the

hard stub had bruised him years before, and knew he must hide his true feelings. His life, and the lives of his friends, depended on it. He snapped to attention, focusing on Lord's face.

"You've passage on my boat," Lord was saying. "And I hear you've got your own permit too? That's good; we'll want that. At least one we won't have to fake!"

Fenn hesitated, unsure what to say, and Mrs Leach chimed in.

"Didn't I say!" she said, jabbing Nile in the ribs. "He's speechless with joy!"

Nile swung an arm over the back of his chair and peered inquisitively at Fenn. His nose was practically twitching, like a ferret's.

"Thought you'd be full of questions. Aren't you wondering where we're going?" he teased.

"I … I just can't believe it," Fenn muttered. He'd never said anything truer.

"Lucky there's room for us all." Nile winked at Lord, "Lord's convoy ship is deceptively spacious."

"And you're getting off just in time too," Lord cut in. "Chilstone's fleet is less than fifty leagues west of here. More Sweeps are coming; they need extra labour. Repairs to the Mainland Wall have held up work on the West Isle's. Landborns are nervy and no wonder. West Isle marshes are swarming with Seaborns nowadays, trying to find ways to get in…"

Fenn glanced at the others. Amber wasn't listening and was still griddling the bacon with a great big soppy grin on her face. Fathom was scoffing the food down. None of them had eaten properly for weeks.

Comfort was sitting on the floor facing away from Lord and Nile, looking at Fenn intently; her mouth was pulled down at the corners and her eyes were brimming with tears. He guessed immediately that she suspected the same as him: that they might end up on the Mainland or behind one of the other Walls, but never as free citizens. They'd live out their lives slaving for others and lose every connection with the past that they'd ever had. Lord's silver tongue meant nothing to Comfort, instead she trusted her instinct.

Fathom called Fenn and Gulper over to get their share and Amber filled their plates.

Nile shook his head bleakly.

"Raids! Rationing! Roustabout attacks. The Shanties aren't what they used to be. It's certainly time for us to all move on," he said to the room at large. "And very generous of Lord to help us."

"It'll be fine sailing to have old friends like you and Mrs Leach with me," Lord said, clamping his hand down on Mrs Leach's knee and making her squeak with delight. "Although

I wonder how the little lady will cope on a rough barge." He held her hand and kissed it, making her simper at him.

While everyone discussed what routes they could take or how much stuff they could bring from the fort, Fenn nudged Fathom.

"It's a trick; it's not a convoy ship!" he whispered in his ear. Fathom didn't turn around at the news, but continued to watch Amber cooking.

"How d'you know?"

"I've just been inside it." Fathom shook his head.

"Why would Nile lie? He's going with us!"

"He must have a deal with Lord. Using us lot as his ticket out…"

Before Fenn could say more, Mrs Leach's powdered face was nestling between their shoulders; she pulled her arms tightly around their waists and squeezed them affectionately.

"An' wha' are my handsome boys whispering about now?" she asked, her eyes hazy and out of focus and a funny little wonky smile playing on her lips.

"Just saying how lovely you're looking tonight Mrs Leach," said Fathom quickly. Mrs Leach blushed, her cheeks dimpling with a shy smile. For a fleeting second, Fenn glimpsed how she must have looked once – the youth she was trying to recapture with her sticks of burnt wood and pots of blue powder. Mrs Leach made a pretty curtsey, lifting her crinkling plastic skirt graciously, and gave Fenn a sloppy wet kiss on his cheek. Emboldened and inspired by the compliment, she weaved her way back over to the two men, pulled her stool nearer to Lord, and started laughing too loudly at his every joke. If it was to make Nile jealous he didn't rise to it, but instead just looked her up and down condescendingly. After a few moments he said, wearily, "Oh, do please stop, Mrs Leach. You're embarrassing yourself." And Mrs Leach shrank back in herself, like a tortoise recoils into its shell. Fathom turned back to Fenn.

"I trust them; Lord and Nile go back years." He stood up and disappeared to where his belongings were kept.

In desperation, Fenn looked around at the others, wondering who would believe him. Gulper was staring adoringly at Nile; he'd never believe Nile could do wrong. But there was still Amber.

"When are we leaving?" Fenn asked Lord casually.

"Crack of dawn, if the weather settles," Lord answered. "Too dangerous to hang around any longer." He squinted through the smoke at Fenn as he spoke, and narrowed his eyes. "I'm sure I recognise you! Have we met?" Fenn shook his head. "Funny, you look familiar," Lord said genially. He shrugged and patted Comfort's head. "This pretty one will easily find foster parents on the Mainland!"

As the evening wore on and the fire was stoked up,

Lord and Nile got steadily sillier, revelling in their games of one-upmanship, bragging and tall stories. Mrs Leach gazed on her husband with slack-jawed admiration but finally, after too much laughter and too much food, Nile was sick. Fenn watched as she mopped him up. This was her servitude; taking his insults, looking after his every need, in exchange for the safety of his protection. She was a survivor and stronger than she looked; she hitched him up on her shoulder and half carried, half dragged him up the stairs, calling instructions to Fathom and Fenn to make sure Lord was comfortable for the night.

Lord's eyes were already starting to blink with tiredness as he slumped into his chair, now and then shifting to get out of the draught. Fenn's mind suddenly sharpened. He put another half a day's supply of wood on the fire at once.

"Let's get you warmer," he coaxed, as the fire sparkled and flurries of purple-blue flames flickered up like fireworks. He leant his shoulder up against the back of Lord's chair and gently eased it towards the fire. Exhausted from the endless sailing and drinking, Lord soon fell into a deep sleep. Fenn waited until Lord was snoring loudly, blowing little bubbles of spit with every breath, then he carefully pulled the laces out of his boots, tucking them in his own pocket. He slipped over to where Nile kept his boots and did the same to those.

As soon as everyone was asleep, Fenn pulled his

jacket on, gently lifted a sleeping Tikki and put him in his rucksack, then he scooped his little rope calendar and other possessions in too. Slipping silently through the room of sleeping bodies like a ghost, he went over to the tin drum where they salted and smoked the rats. He filled one pocket with a mix of ash and salt from the large crock, then took a fistful of hardened grease from the tray underneath the roasting rack. He tiptoed to the hatch and rubbed grease into the bolts and hinges. Once he was done, he crept up to Amber and put his hand over her mouth so she wouldn't yell out and wake the others. Amber struggled to sit up.

"What are you doing?" she spat, pushing him off. "And what's that on your hand?" She wiped her mouth furiously.

"We have to get away from here," Fenn whispered.

"What?"

"Lord's a trafficker. He's captain of a slave ship for children."

Lord stirred and scratched his belly in his sleep. Fenn patted down the air with his hands to make Amber quieten.

"I've been inside it…"

"When?" asked Amber suspiciously, her small eyes narrowing even more than usual.

"This afternoon. I saw it come in. I wanted to see if we could stow away," he whispered. Amber stared at him beadily.

"You mean if *you* could."

"No. I mean *we*," Fenn repeated firmly.

Amber scrutinised him. "We could just tell Nile."

"Can't you see what's going on? He's trading us, Amber. We're his ticket off the Shanties."

Amber bit her lip. Shaking her head, she pulled the cover tighter around her.

"That's what happened to your friend Nami, isn't it? And the other children that Fathom told me disappeared! Nile doesn't keep us here out of the goodness of his heart." Fenn stared hard at Amber. "This is a shopfront and we're the goods." For a few seconds Amber stared ahead blankly, then tears welled in her eyes.

"Have you told Fathom?" she asked.

"He doesn't want to know. You have to persuade him."

"I will." Amber nodded. "What about Gulper?"

Fenn shrugged. "Don't know if he'd leave, but I'd swear Comfort's guessed."

"So what's your plan?" asked Amber, climbing out of bed.

"To get off the Shanties. Tonight."

He nodded over to where Lord was still snoring.

"He's got an old sailing barge; they sailed it with just three of them. You said Fathom and Gulper could sail all right and I'm a fast learner. You take Comfort. I'll wake the others and catch you up."

Amber agreed, pulling on her coat.

Fenn got a lantern while she tiptoed to where Comfort was curled up like a cat in her hammock. Shaking her gently, Amber put her finger to her lips and quickly helped Comfort put on a pair of boots and some warm outside clothes. Meanwhile Fenn slipped over to the hatch and slowly slid the bolts back, lifting it open. They didn't make a sound, but a sliver of cold air streaked under the tarpaulin, making Lord stir in his sleep again.

"Quickly," Fenn whispered, beckoning them over, lowering the ladder gently. But it was too heavy for him to move quietly and despite it being slathered in grease too, it rattled and clanked as it fell downwards. Fenn just managed to grab it and cling on.

"Where's his boat moored?" Amber whispered.

"Know the *Gloriana*?"

Amber nodded.

"There's a hidden jetty behind her," he explained as he stepped down onto the ladder. "Red sail. She's called the *Salamander*."

He helped Comfort down through the trapdoor; a gusty wind caught them on the ladder and he encircled her with his arms as they climbed.

"Hurry," he said. "There are only a couple of hours before dawn."

19

It was the first time Comfort had been outside the fort for years and she was white with fear. Nile and Mrs Leach's plan must have always been that once she was big enough she'd go out and work until the time came for her to be traded; before she lost her appeal. But Comfort had always stayed so small that Mr Leach thought she was too fragile. Both of them must have been afraid she'd be snatched and their investment lost.

Comfort quivered like a leaf as Fenn guided her down to the lower level of the Shanties. The wind howled around them and the iron struts on the giant girder glinted like knives in the moonlight. Despite this, Fenn had to keep coaxing her to go quicker, afraid that the alarm would be raised before they got away. As soon as they reached the alleys, he grabbed her hand urgently. They ran, barely able to see straight in the lashing rain that hit them like splinters of ice; by the time they reached the tiny crawl-way through the *Gloriana* they were both drenched. Fenn pushed Comfort inside and again the rats squirmed away into their nests in fright. Tikki wriggled in the rucksack, eager to go and hunt, but Fenn had tied it tightly. He wasn't taking any chances; no one was getting left behind.

"Up here!" Fenn whispered, clambering over the slimy green floor and jostling Comfort up the iron staircase. The icy wind blew across the open deck and shavings of brittle snow had already started to settle inside. They squatted down out of sight underneath a rotting awning. From this vantage point Fenn could see anyone approaching in the alley and also the comings and goings on Lord's barge. Logan and Owen were sitting on deck to keep watch, huddled around a glowing brazier. They had rigged up a ramshackle shelter over their heads.

Fenn and Comfort didn't have long to wait before they heard a scuffling by the hole and the sound of rats squealing as they were kicked out of the way. Candlelight flickered in the shadows below as Fathom and Amber scrambled across the cabin. Fenn whistled down to them.

They climbed up the stairs. Fathom immediately knelt by Comfort's side and gave her a hug, rubbing her arms to warm her up.

"Gulper?" Fenn whispered to Amber. She shook her head. "He wouldn't believe me."

"But he promised not to tell," Fathom explained.

"I'm going back for him," Fenn said, but Fathom grabbed his arm hard and pulled him back.

"No, you're not," he hissed. "He's made his choice. You'll just wreck our chances of getting off. If we don't get on this boat, we might as well throw ourselves off the Shanties. It'll be quicker than starving."

"Fathom's right," Amber said. "Gulper will never leave those two. They're all he knows."

Fenn knew what they said was true; they had already gone too far by leaving the fort without Nile's permission. He would never take them back if he found out what they'd done.

Fathom peeped through a gap at the *Salamander*. "I know these barges. Worked on them in New Venice. I can get her started," he said. "But how do we get on board?"

"I..." began Fenn, hoping for inspiration. He peeped through the decaying struts in the barge's side. The watchmen below were now taking cupfuls of something from a pan on the brazier.

"I'll distract them," he said finally. The others looked at him sceptically and Amber opened her mouth to say something. Standing up briskly, Fenn cut in before she could speak. "Just be ready."

Amber smiled doubtfully, her fingers automatically reaching for her clover stud.

Fenn tiptoed down the stairs and wriggled out of the *Gloriana*'s side. No hiding this time. He felt sweat prickle on his back and goose-pimples stipple his arms. This was how escaping felt; this was what he'd been dreaming of for the past few weeks. Out of the blue, he remembered the first time Halflin showed him how to gut a pig – the pig Fenn had raised from birth. Fenn had been so scared of it: its deadness, its terrible stillness. He remembered being afraid of hurting it, which was ridiculous but true, and so instead of cutting, he feebly prodded the knife into the cold flesh. Halflin got angry and closed his hand around Fenn's to make him hold the knife confidently, in order to slice right through the pig's body, saying, "Stop pokin' it and have some respect; that pig died so you can live. If you're doin' somethin' do it proper."

If you're doin' somethin' do it proper.

Fenn steeled himself, thumped down heavily onto the jetty and jogged along far enough to ensure the two men saw him.

They immediately stood up and walked towards the barge rail, gazing silently as Fenn hastily approached, pretending to be out of breath.

"Is this Lord's barge?"

"Who wants to know?" asked Owen guardedly as he sipped his coffee. Steam blew in front of his face. He winced at the heat on his tongue.

"He sent me to get you," Fenn gabbled. Owen sniffed, wiped his cuff over the flecks of coffee stippling his beard and put his cup on the barge rail to cool. Something distracted him and he looked in the direction of the *Gloriana*. Fenn prayed that Fathom had extinguished the candle he'd been carrying.

"He needs help straightaway. Some of the other kids are getting suspicious," Fenn added.

In the shadows behind him, Amber and Comfort lightly tiptoed across the jetty, slipping over the rail.

"That's Nile's problem," Logan said, coming to stand with Owen. He rubbed his hand over his grimy face, scratching his salt-and-pepper stubble.

Fenn shook his head.

"Too many of them. He said to come quick. Help settle things down."

Owen gave him a sharp look, then tilted his head once more towards the *Gloriana*. Fathom had his leg out of the hole and froze. He was clearly visible to Fenn's sharp eyes but Owen didn't seem to notice, distracted by an increasingly loud thrumming noise in the distance. He turned to Logan.

"Can you hear that?" he said.

Logan ignored him, already swinging his legs over the rail, puffing with the strain.

"Are they all at Nile's?"

Fenn nodded, feeling sick to his stomach as he realised something wasn't sitting right with Owen, who was peering along the jetty. He needed to distract him. He quickly hitched the rucksack off his shoulders.

"Don't s'pose you've got a bit of bread to spare have you?" he asked, as he loosened the rucksack's final cord. Tikki bounded out of the bag then scampered up to Fenn's shoulders, where he curled around his neck. He nuzzled against Fenn's ear and Logan laughed in childlike delight, clapping his hands.

"A mongoose!" he said. "Ain't seen one of them for years! Can we give it some bread, Owen?" Owen shook his head dourly and cast his beady eyes over Tikki.

If he couldn't distract Owen, he could at least amuse Logan. Fenn made a special fuss of Tikki, making him run up and down his arms, desperately trying to keep the two men looking his way. Logan giggled with unbridled joy, nudging Owen. Taking his chance, Fathom ran lightly across the jetty and dropped over the side of the *Salamander*.

"Shouldn't keep the boss waiting," Fenn said. Logan looked back questioningly at Owen. Owen shook his head.

"Don't need two of us," he said and deliberately took his foot off the barge rail. But Logan shrugged his shoulders and stomped past Fenn down the jetty, heading towards the *Gloriana*.

One down, one to go, thought Fenn. He turned to look at Owen expectantly. "Lord wanted you both," he ventured.

Owen wasn't listening to Fenn. He had cocked his head again. Leaning over the barge rail, he looked out to sea.

"We never leave the boat," Owen muttered distrustfully, frowning. "Who are you anyway? I don't remember your face."

"I work for Nile," Fenn said breezily. His heart was thumping so hard in his chest now it felt like it was going to pop right out and bounce along the jetty all by itself like a ball. "I can keep an eye on the boat." He was hardly breathing now and he was sure his voice sounded squeaky and insincere.

"I bet," Owen said with a sarcastic smile as he reached for his mug on the rail. As he did, he frowned and peered closer, staring hard at the coffee – the surface was trembling. A deep boom sounded in the distance and the whole jetty shook.

"What the…?" started Owen, looking at Fenn, perplexed.

Before he had a chance to say more, a net was dropped over his head and Fathom and Amber yanked him down to his knees, binding the net tightly around him with ropes.

But Owen was stronger than he looked and thrashed wildly, immediately breaking free.

Fenn grabbed the handful of ash and salt from his pocket and chucked it hard in Owen's face, blinding him. He howled in pain. Fenn leapt over the barge rail, followed by Tikki, and helped Fathom grab Owen beneath his armpits and swing him over the rail onto the jetty, where he lay sprawled, clawing at his streaming eyes. Amber and Fathom hurried to the barge's bridge. Another thunderous boom sounded across the Shanties and Fenn turned to see where it was coming from, but at the same moment he was distracted by a figure stumbling out of the *Gloriana*'s side and then racing down the jetty towards the *Salamander* as if his life depended on it. It was Gulper.

As he got closer, Fenn could see that one of his eyes was bloody and puffed up, purple as a plum. He was gasping for breath and sobbing as he ran. Behind him, Fenn noticed a strange glow from across the Shanties. The thrumming was getting much louder now. He thought he recognised the sound and craned to see beyond the *Gloriana*.

Amber was frantically fiddling with the controls until Fathom pushed her aside. He flicked a few switches and the barge shuddered into life. Amber grinned at him in delight. Gulper staggered towards the barge, wheezing so badly he couldn't speak.

"Quick, get on board!" Fenn shouted. But Gulper ignored Fenn's outstretched hand, looking back over his shoulder, his eyes darting in fear. The humming was becoming deafening; something huge and mechanical-sounding was getting closer.

"I didn't tell! I swear," he gasped. "But Nile woke up! He's coming!"

Fenn looked at the *Gloriana*; lights were flickering inside her and behind the ship the distant glow had grown to a large orange cloud. The wind carried a smell of burning; the Shanties were on fire. His worst fears were realised: the sound he'd heard was a Fearzero's engine.

"Fathom! Let's go!" shouted Fenn, starting to untie the moorings. Fathom revved up the barge's engine.

Suddenly, in the distance, there was a terrible ripping sound of splintering wood and tearing metal, followed by screams and shouting. A hissing filled the air and the fog over the furthest barges thickened with steam from extinguished fires. An angry shout came from nearby, close to the end of the jetty. Gulper spun around.

Nile's head dangled down out of the hole in the *Gloriana*'s side, his hands only just touching the planks of the jetty. The long strands of hair he used to disguise his baldness were flapping and his kimono had snagged on the broken timbers as he tried to climb through. The entire hulk was

247

shaking, starting to crumble down around him.

"Gulper, help me!" he shouted, as he flailed around. Behind him, lost in the depths of the *Gloriana*, they could hear Mrs Leach wailing as the *Gloriana*'s sides collapsed inwards.

"Wait for me. Wait!"

Gulper looked at Fenn then back at Nile, who was thrashing about as powerlessly as the gulls they trapped. He took a step towards Nile, changed his mind, and took a step back towards Fenn. Tears of confusion fell from his eyes. Huddled on the *Salamander*'s bridge, Comfort sat rocking, holding her hands over her ears. Amber was shouting desperately at Fenn to cast off, but instead he held his hand out to Gulper.

"Jump!" He shouted.

Fathom revved the engine again. As Gulper dithered, Fenn heard a different sound approaching; a kind of whispering which, if they hadn't been at sea, he would have mistaken for the sound of the wind blowing through masses of leaves. He peered into the darkness, unable to identify it, but just at that moment Nile broke free, tumbling onto the jetty as Mrs Leach popped out behind him.

In a flash they were up and running towards the barge, but as they ran, the gangplanks behind them seemed to be lifting and falling like an undulating wave. A hissing and squealing tide of squirming fur, thick tails and fangs was heading towards them. Rats; hundreds of them, spewing out of every crevice in the *Gloriana*'s side.

"Gulper! C'mon!" shouted Fenn, loosening the final mooring rope, but Gulper was frozen in fear. Transfixed, he watched as the *Gloriana* was lit up by a vermillion blaze, roaring flames shooting up behind and through her. "Gulper!" Fenn yelled desperately, leaning as far over the rail towards him as he could without falling, wriggling his fingertips to try and catch Gulper's hand.

Nile staggered down the jetty, shoeless, Mrs Leach hot on his heels. Behind them rolled the carpet of rats, in their thousands now, running terrified from the wall of fire pursuing them. The wave caught up with Nile and began biting at his ankles and clawing up his kimono. He toppled for a few steps but then the weight of the rats on his back forced him over, instantly engulfing and flooding over him.

Mrs Leach was kicking at the rats, dancing about to try to stop them running up her dress, but in seconds the rats were swarming over and past them both, like water forks around rocks in a river, heading instinctively for the safety of the barge. Fenn still reached for Gulper, straining, holding out his hand.

"I'm coming!" Gulper shouted, moving at last.

But not to Fenn. He tried to run back towards Nile and

Mrs Leach, now both pillows of squirming grey. But it was hopeless; the wall of vermin hit him before he'd gone a yard. He thrashed about, kicking and sweeping his ratting stick through the rats as if scything corn, but the weight of them was unstoppable. Gulper was forced backwards, tumbling over the rail and falling onto the boat's deck just as Fenn untied the last rope. Fathom slammed the boat's controls forward and the barge jumped away from the jetty. Gulper was back on his feet in a heartbeat, trying to clamber over the rail to Mrs Leach, but Fenn held him back.

"It's too late..." he said. "You can't save them."

Gulper wailed, and as they looked back, they saw Mrs Leach had managed to stagger to her feet and pull Nile towards the water. Arms around each other, they pitched over the edge of the jetty and disappeared beneath the waves.

They were in the nick of time. The whole jetty suddenly crumbled into the sea; the massive weight of rats sinking down with it. The strongest, fastest rats hurled themselves through the air, hit the barge rail and fell back into the water. Hundreds more followed. The air was thick with the sound of splashing and squeals; the water between the barge and the sinking jetty began to jump and spit as if it had been brought to the boil. Rats started to clamber up the bodies of others and onto the side of the barge. Fenn grabbed an oar and he and Amber whacked at them mercilessly. One massive rat, with a thick, ragged tail like a rope managed to cling to the oar, despite Fenn shaking it, and clawed up towards his arm, so Fenn had no choice but to hurl the oar into the water. As the boat slid away, Gulper leant on the rail, trying to see if he could catch a glimpse of Nile and Mrs Leach resurfacing. Tears were rolling down his face.

Everything was vibrating now as the leaden humming sound was almost on top of them, unbearably loud. Through the darkness and fog, Fenn could just make out the sight of the outermost barges and boats buckling up. Something vast was ramming them from behind; their helms were being thrust into the air and dropped down again, smashing on the water and shattering into pieces. Looming out of the haze came a huge wall of steel and iron. Suddenly the Fearzero came into sharp focus; ploughing straight into the Shanties, knocking through the forts and destroying everything in its path. The *Salamander* rocked violently as Fathom locked the wheel hard to the right and accelerated through the huge wash.

Behind them came a grinding sound; the Fearzero had just snapped one of the fort's concrete legs like it was a matchstick; nothing could stand in its way. The blade of reinforced steel on its bow scythed through the barges and boats; even the heaviest vessels were breaking like toys in its path.

As the *Salamander* picked up more speed, heading out of the narrow inlet, a carnage of drowned rats and sinking boats was left in their wake. A deep, shuddering groan sounded as the struts of the first fort began to crumple and the whole edifice started to collapse. It sagged sideways first, knocking the next fort and then the third, like a colossal game of dominoes. All three plummeted into the churning sea below, their weight displacing so much water that a huge wave immediately bulged up and outwards. With the force of this rushing at its back, the *Salamander* was propelled out of the mouth of the congested channel like a cork popping from a bottle. Bathed in an orange rain of smouldering ashes, it surged into open water, riding at a dangerous angle on the crest of the driving wave. They all clung to whatever they could, praying the battered boat would withstand the strain.

20

Finally the waves began to subside and the *Salamander* eased down into calmer water. They were now a good distance away from the remains of the Shanties and Fathom slowed the engine as Fenn raced to douse the brazier on deck with a bucket of water. He didn't want to take any chances. As they looked back, they saw the vast black shape of the Fearzero blotting the illuminated horizon, crushing everything to smithereens. In its wake it left high banks of broken-up barges still spinning on the wash that swept out from its bow. Fenn could see it was going dead slow, on a deliberate course, gradually arcing around to destroy the forts that remained standing.

"We have to go back to help," Fenn said, grabbing the wheel, but Fathom held on tightly.

"Not unless you want to end up in a Mission or dead.

The Fearzero will pick up any survivors."

Fenn felt guilt weigh like a millstone around his neck. He guessed Chilstone's spies had reported a sighting and when Chilstone didn't find him amongst the boys rounded up, he'd ordered that the Shanties be destroyed. He remembered the Terra's words: Chilstone was a madman, chasing a ghost.

They sailed away from the light of the burning Shanties and into the night; empty, black and strangely silent. The Shanties had never been quiet; too many people, the constant squawks of street hawkers and gulls, the clanging of metal. Fenn could remember the stillness of the marsh when it was blanketed in snow, but the others, dislodged from their noisy world, looked scared. Amber and Comfort huddled in a corner of the deck between two huge coils of rope. Gulper slumped down beside them, weeping and shaking his head in bewilderment. Amber put her arm around him.

"Gulper … we've made it, we're free," she said, gently wiping the blood off his cheek with the palm of her hand. Gulper turned to look at her, white track-marks of tears streaking his filthy cheeks. His young face had become haggard with the nervous twitches that a life of pain and poverty had dealt him.

"Free?" he asked, his eyes searching her face and his lips trembling.

Fenn crouched down next to them. He shrugged

Halflin's coat off and wrapped it around Gulper, then he put his hands on his shoulders; to steady him, like Halflin had readied him to leave East Point. Tikki crept close, his eyes wide and alert to the sound of Gulper's whimpering, tentatively putting a paw up on his knee, sniffing the air.

"Free to go where?" Gulper whispered.

Amber and Comfort looked at Fenn expectantly.

"As far away from here as possible," he said. "East Marsh first, then maybe on to West Isle?"

The Shanties were a blister of yellow on the black horizon. While Fathom steered, Fenn got the others to check the barge for seaworthiness. He wondered if there were any crew hidden on the barge but every cabin was empty. Before any of them had a chance to see inside the secret cabin, Fenn boarded over the door; he guessed something like this had been Nami's fate. There was no point in his friends guessing that too.

Even though flakes of snow drifted in wintry flurries, mottling them with petals of ice, no one wanted to sleep below. Instead they rigged a tent across the deck and brought up blankets from one of the cabins. Fenn had found a nailed-up cupboard in the kitchen, inside which were hundreds of wads of neat rectangular pieces of paper, each printed with the words "TWENTY POUNDS" which, they scrunched up to relight the brazier.

They brought up any provisions from the kitchen that

could be useful: bags of rice and dried beans, rope, water purification tablets, boots, water bottles and knives. They found that the *Salamander* was well stocked with lamps, candles, paraffin and matches, and there were enough clothes to keep them all warm; although Fenn preferred Halflin's battered old garments to anything the Salamander's crew might have worn.

Amber, who had a nose for such things, added an ancient book to the growing pyramid of items; it was at least one hundred years old with two large yellow A's on it. It was some kind of atlas; water warped, its paper puffy with damp and frilled like the underside of a mushroom, but salvageable. Fenn peeled apart the pages that showed the old coast, long before East Marsh ever existed, and realised there had once been a lighthouse, fifteen miles south-west from the hill the Punchlock was now built on. Once dozens of lighthouses had dotted the shores, but since the Rising they'd all been submerged.

Amongst the food, Amber found a box of beans that looked like coffee but didn't smell like it. She nibbled on the corner of one and pulled a face, passing one to Gulper to try, but as she did so Comfort put her hand out, took it off her and licked the edge. She smiled, put the bean between her two hands and nodded, grinding her palms together.

"Guess it's OK to eat!" Gulper said.

Comfort pulled a log from the pile they were feeding into the brazier and knocked the bark off so she was left with a smooth, roundish cylinder of wood. She then piled the beans into a piece of cotton and began rolling and beating it until she had a fine powder. She mixed it in a tin jug with a spoonful of sugar then added hot water to it, making a velvety sweet drink that warmed their hearts with its lovely flavour. They'd never had chocolate before.

As they sat around the brazier drinking, Fenn remembered the evenings when Halflin had sat with him after a hard day at the Punchlock and how his grandad would try to distract them both with a story or strange fact; like how giant squids have the largest eyes of any creature, bigger than a plate; or how a tiger shark eats its brothers and sisters before it's born. But as he looked around at their dejected faces, he realised this wasn't the time for distractions. His friends needed dreams.

"What would you do if you got into West Isle?" he asked Fathom instead.

"Eat!" Fathom answered, laughing. Amber's eyes lit up.

"Me too. Then I'm building a house. For me and Comfort," she said, giving Comfort a squeeze.

"What do you know about carpentry?" Fathom asked teasingly.

"I'll use peat. The house I lived in when I was little was

made of it. Until it got flooded and washed away."

"You need to build on stilts. Like the houses of New Venice. They know how to build on water there. They're beautiful too," Fathom said wistfully.

"Nope, whatever you build needs to float," Gulper insisted. Fenn nodded.

"My grandad said the next Rising could be huge," he said quietly. "Even bigger than the Great Rising."

"Why are we talking like we're not going to get behind the Wall?" Amber said, exasperated. "We might!"

"Chances are, we won't," Fathom said. "Or one of us won't."

"It'll be me," Gulper said. "I don't look so good." Fathom smiled at him.

"You're unique," he said kindly.

"Let's make a deal," Amber said. "Either we all get in or we all stay out."

They all nodded.

"Let's have a toast then," said Amber.

But as Fenn watched Amber pouring out more of the sweet drink, he was really thinking about Halflin and where he would fit in all their plans. He looked up at the sky and felt a chill at the thought that Chilstone might be looking at the same stars at that very moment. Fenn suddenly realised he could never be part of a family, not with his friends, nor with Halflin: Chilstone would never let him because he'd never stop hunting him. Anyone that got in his way would get hurt, whether it was the Sargassons, or the people on the Shanties. This was Fenn's fight and one he had to fight alone. The others were now clanking their mugs together to toast their future. As Amber's mug rattled against Fenn's he was jolted out of his thoughts and felt a cold shiver of loneliness.

As the night wore on, they took turns at the helm. By the time it was Fenn's shift the sky to the west was still freckled with lingering stars sparkling against the inky night, but the sky to the east was fading. Amber appeared beside him.

"So we're heading for East Marsh right?" she said.

Fenn didn't seem to hear her, but carried on staring at the sea. The crumbling storm clouds were mottling to the colour of apricots as the sun crawled up over the horizon.

"Fenn?"

Amber's voice was barely above a whisper and her face was tense and white; she'd been up all night, too exhausted to sleep. She reached out for his hand and squeezed it tightly, as Fenn turned to look at her. He didn't know what to say. He'd got his friends out on the open sea and, if the Terras caught them, who knew what would happen. They could be killed and it would be all his fault. He felt scared and guilty but at the same time he knew that whatever he felt didn't matter right now; he had to say something. It was a shock to find the weight of his friends' hope was heavier than his own fears had ever been.

"My grandad will help us." He said.

Since he'd left all he'd wanted to do was get back to Halflin, to make sure he was all right, to do ordinary things again. But after the Sweep something had changed in Fenn. Halflin would be fifty-six next spring; it was time for Fenn to take his turn protecting him from the Terra Firma.

He imagined the dangers that lay ahead. What was it Halflin had said? There were four ways to stay alive: kill, fight, run or hide. He'd kept alive by doing the last two, but that wasn't the same as *living*. Whatever he did, he wasn't going to put his friends at risk the way he'd put Halflin in danger. He needed to get them to safety.

"Will it be safe to hide there?" Amber asked.

In his mind's eye Fenn focused on the geography of East Marsh. From his hours gazing through his telescope, he knew the tributaries and inlets as well as he knew the purple veins that knotted Halflin's gnarled hands. He would dock the *Salamander* where the *Panimengro* had hidden, deep in the marsh, down beyond the dead snags where the herons liked to fish. Halflin could sort out permits and give the others enough food for them to journey on to West Isle. Then Fenn would think of a way to get Halflin and Lundy to safety. Maybe they could go with his friends? After their safety was guaranteed he'd make contact with whatever was left of the Resistance on East Marsh. If there was no one then he'd get word out. He had to find people as tired of running as he was, and as ready to fight. He couldn't be the only one.

At last light burst over the horizon and the sun's shafts splintered out. Copper sunbeams striped the ocean like a bridge, showing the exact route to the east. He knew he was right to let her go, but even so, as he let Amber's hand drop away from his, a sharp pang of regret twisted deep inside. She stared at him, still waiting for his answer.

"I'm not going back to hide," he said. "I'm going back to fight."

21

After five days the fuel had run out and they relied on the sails. Food was also low and there was still no land in sight. For the last two nights Tikki had scrabbled up from hunting rats in the hold and eagerly bounded up to Fenn, empty-mouthed. Fathom had managed to land a couple of fish and Fenn had thought to collect and pack the snow that had fallen for the first three days so they had an icebox and a little water. But it wasn't enough; there were five of them and the hard work of sailing a ship meant they were all hungrier than ever.

So when dawn broke on the sixteenth day at sea, revealing a granite-grey strip on the horizon, they yelled with relief and danced around the deck. Still in jubilant spirits, they spotted the early sunrays slanting across the water, glimmering on something a mile or so to the north. As the

Salamander sailed closer they saw it was the lighthouse Fenn had found on the map.

It was low tide so the old lantern room just projected above the waves; a tiny glinting chamber. The panes of glass around it had long been smashed out of their lead glazing bars by the buffeting waves, but the thick, shatterproof lens remained, catching and refracting the early morning sun.

Fenn decided it was too dangerous to take a direct route across the valley estuary to the Punchlock, so instead he navigated the *Salamander* through the maze of inlets that looked tattered and lacy on the coastline map. After a few hours he found the spot some miles south of the Punchlock. They lowered the *Salamander*'s red sails and slowly punted upriver.

"We need to find somewhere to moor," Fathom said to Amber. But she wasn't listening. She was peering through the reedbeds, scrunching up her face as she tried to see.

"Is that East Isle's Wall?" she asked, lifting Comfort higher so she could see over the barge's sides. Fenn nodded, while Fathom and Gulper followed her gaze, squinting through the glaring white light across the marsh. None of them had ever seen a horizon where land met sky, or if they had they'd long forgotten it. In the far distance they could just make out the vast shadow of the Wall; the two ends had been joined at the foundations, but a huge section was still empty and looked like a square bite mark.

"There's nowhere to hide here," said Gulper, shrinking from the vastness of the marsh, his eyes wide and round. He wrapped his coat tighter and clamped his hands in his armpits. "I don't like it."

Fenn knew he had been right to be cautious; the *Salamander* would be too obvious if they moored it here in broad daylight.

He climbed up onto the pilot room roof to get a better sense of direction and swung his telescope over the landscape. At last he spotted the stack of a chimney poking out. "Bear right," he shouted down. Within a few minutes the jetty came into view in the distance, but before they reached it they saw another channel, only just wide enough for the *Salamander* to pass through. Fenn glimpsed an iron sign with faded letters: "Hill Farm".

"I know where we are!" he shouted. "Up there." He pointed. They punted the *Salamander* up the narrow creek, skimming over the silvery tassel weeds glinting in the clear frosty water.

It was hard work and the sun was high above them by the time they reached the farmhouse. Only the joists of the roof remained above water but its barns and outbuildings were further up the hill, half-submerged. The whole place had been abandoned years earlier, before Halflin's grand-parents were alive, when the land got too waterlogged to farm. Almost everyone in the coastal districts had moved upland after the First Risings, when they were certain there was no hope of ever returning to their farms and houses.

The main barn was as big as a church and made a good hiding place for the barge. Its weatherboards had faded to the soft gleaming silver of birch trees and, like the house, its tiles had been looted, leaving only a few mouldy roof joists, as delicately balanced as a house of cards. Although there was no roof on the barn, ivy had grown up over the far end of the building, dripping down in a thick curtain and giving cover from prying eyes. Autumn leaves, blown from the marsh elder further up the slope, fluttered through the naked rafters and drifted on the water like wet flames, banking against the barn's rotting walls in fiery, sodden mounds. The children punted the barge inside until they felt the bump as it grounded on the stone floor.

Once the barge was stowed they tore branches off the marsh elder and draped them over the vessel to camouflage it further. Although it had no fuel left, they knew they'd need it again.

"Will your grandad have fuel?" Fathom asked as he wove the leafy fronds together and hung them from the bow.

"Enough to get to West Isle." Fenn nodded. "He's been stockpiling for a generator."

Then they parcelled up the essentials for the journey to

Halflin's and waded through the freezing water up to the higher ground. As they walked, Fenn scanned the horizon: puffy clouds were already scudding across the sky and he noticed white crystals forming on the base of bulrush heads. Halflin used to say, *If rush grows a beard, snow's ter be feared.* They needed to be quick – they could freeze to death if they were caught out on the marsh in snow.

But it wasn't just the cold Fenn was worried about. On the muddy shore, he had seen muntjac deer prints; far apart, which meant they had been running. The prints headed deep into the reeds where they could get tangled in knotweed and drown. They wouldn't risk drowning unless something more frightening was behind them.

"Hurry up," he said sharply, tucking Tikki deep down inside his Guernsey to keep warm. "We need to get there before dusk."

"Which way?" Gulper asked.

"Follow the river. It flows to the Punchlock," Fenn answered.

They had been walking for three hours and Fenn still wasn't sure he was heading in the right direction. Snowfall began speckling the empty marshlands and the air became still; not even the sound of reed warblers broke the peace. Dusk was starting to fall on the snowy landscape and they were all frozen. They trudged on, taking turns to carry

Comfort, so small she kept getting stuck in the glutinous mud. Ahead, Fenn saw a river with a line of ash trees growing along it, meaning it was one of the older rivers.

"We're lost aren't we?" Amber snapped.

"No, I'm just not sure where we are yet," Fenn said calmly. He wasn't going to let her panic add to his own. "This way."

It was harder than he had expected. There was no path, only the line of the reeds, which were so thick and lush it was hard to see the river at all unless they kept close enough. Their boots kept being sucked off in the deep boggy mud, and they were soaked through.

Dusk fell further, turning the sky violet. The first star pricked out, like a needle piercing cloth. They lit the lanterns, tying them into sticks that Fenn had cut clefts into. He was more worried now; a slight wind had picked up, blowing inland from the sea and taking their scent with it.

"We should find somewhere to shelter," Fathom said.

"I hate this place," Amber said. "How much longer till we get there?"

"If I could get up higher I'd get a better view of the marsh, maybe see the Punchlock," Fenn said.

There was a soft rise ahead, a little hillock, breaking the monotonous reeds that grew around it. They headed towards it quickly, but as they climbed up, Fenn knew something wasn't quite right. He knew higher bits of land should have bushes growing on them, but apart from some short tufts of malnourished grass and yellow lichen, the mound was bare. Ahead of them, Gulper called over his shoulder.

"I can see for miles…"

Then he'd gone. One second he was there, silhouetted against the plum-coloured sky, the next – nothing. Amber screamed.

"Gulper!" Her voice was higher than the boys' and it smacked the surrounding water like a knife on a glass. Fenn clapped his hand over her mouth.

"Shh!" he hissed. "Lie flat. Spread your weight out."

Immediately they all lay down as Fenn edged towards the hole Gulper had fallen through. He peered down but it was pitch black inside.

"I think it's a house!" Gulper called up.

Fenn realised they must be on the roof and quickly threaded a rope through the lamp handle and lowered it down. Below, Gulper was in a room of some kind, half-filled with oozing mud.

Night had nearly fallen and, but for the toads croaking, the marsh was quiet as a grave. From somewhere far off in the distance, faint but distinct, a long, lonely howl spiralled upwards into the night.

22

They tied a rope around one of the roof joists that looked sound and climbed down. As soon as Fenn reached the floor he let Tikki out, but instead of running off to explore, Tikki scampered up and coiled himself nervously around Fenn's neck. The room was almost completely filled with slimy mud sloping up to the corners of the ceiling. It must have oozed in through the windows as the marsh had grown up around it. From somewhere in the darkness a faint dripping echoed.

"Look around," whispered Fenn. "Check it's safe."

He gave the door a push but it wouldn't budge. There were panes of glass in it, semi-frosted, with clear pieces of glass etched in a flowery pattern, but it was covered with grime so he couldn't see through. Fenn turned his back to the door and, using his elbow, he punched the glass. He put his hand through the smashed pane and twisted the handle, but it still wouldn't open. There was mud banked up against the other side.

Fathom put his shoulder next to Fenn's and they pushed together. After a couple of shunts they'd nudged it open enough to all squeeze through.

They were in a big panelled hall that had several doors leading off it. Slabs of plaster had fallen away from the walls, leaving patches of wattle and daub, hundreds of years old. It had obviously once been a grand house. Every door they tried was either locked or blocked up with mud on the other side, until they reached one so rotten that it fell off its hinges as it swung open, revealing a short corridor. The walls were covered in embossed wallpaper, which was peeling away from the plaster and now hung in folding drapes. There were pictures of smiling people hanging on the walls; family groups, children being pushed in a tyre hung from a rope, a toddler blowing out miniature candles stuck in a cake. The children were mystified; none of them had seen images like this before and even if they had, none of the scenes bore any resemblance to their own lives.

"D'you think that's what life's like behind the Wall?" asked Amber, rubbing her thumb through the dirt on one picture to reveal a pretty girl leaning against a horse whose harness was pinned with a red satin rosette. But

Fathom wasn't going to waste time on dreaming now. He was hungry.

"C'mon," he said. "I bet there are supplies."

The others followed him, but Fenn hesitated; he didn't like how Tikki clung tight to his neck. Something wasn't right.

They emerged onto a huge landing where the remains of a few banisters wrapped around a sweeping staircase led into a pit of swampy water with algae as thick as custard. Gulper picked up a piece of broken picture frame on the floor and idly chucked it in. It landed with a plop and a few bubbles popped on the surface. The air filled with the putrefying smell of dead water.

"That's disgusting!" Amber said, holding her nose. Gulper shrugged.

"I've smelt worse."

Fenn was staring at the floor; mud caked the highest treads of the staircase and Fenn noticed a few animal prints, but apart from that, there was no sign of life.

"We need to find somewhere dry for the night and light a fire. Look out for stuff we can burn," said Fenn.

"In here?" said Fathom, creeping forward with Gulper close behind, followed by Amber who had hitched Comfort onto her back. Fenn brought up the rear, looking over his shoulder at the long dark corridor. Fathom pushed a pair of double doors that opened into an enormous bedroom.

Opposite was a bank of mud that had seeped in between the ceiling joists and the roof, just like in the first room; the whole house was gradually being devoured by the marsh. Carpets still lined the floor, so soggy they were spongy to walk on, and all the way up from the skirting boards to the ceiling were outcrops of fungi, billowing out from the loose plaster, as flat and white as stepping stones. To the right, deep in shadow, was a four-poster bed with deep velvet drapes still drawn around it. In its pelmet a colony of bats clustered together, nestled tight as mussels in the folds of cloth. Opposite the bed a huge stone fireplace took up one wall, with a fancy gilt mirror over the top. The faint light from the lamp barely reached the corners of the room, but they could just make out the enormous cobwebs hanging in dusty swags from a chandelier, soft as wedding veils. Inside, black thick-legged spiders skulked motionless.

It looked like someone had tried to carry on living there; moving their possessions upstairs when the lower rooms got too waterlogged. In the corner stood a few crates and hanging from the wall was a sort of manger, still full of dry sticks and logs. A few tins of food lay on their sides amidst the shredded remains of food packets spoilt by animals. A rusted camping stove had been lodged inside the fireplace and close by a bamboo bookcase slumped drunkenly to the side, its shelves bowing under the weight of mouldering books. Some pages lay scattered around the hearth; the remnants of books that had been used to make fires. There was a smell of rot hanging in the air. Fathom immediately began rifling through the crates, searching for something to eat.

Gulper and Amber had been distracted by the mirror, laughing at how scruffy and filthy they looked. Comfort craned to see and stared at her reflection, then hid her face in confusion only to peep out at herself and smile. Gulper lit a second lamp, which he stood on top of the mantelpiece. The mirror glass reflected the light back into the room, showing a wardrobe on the far side of the bed.

"Look at my hair!" Amber shrieked. She tried to flatten it down, but red tufts kept springing back up.

"What about me?" asked Gulper, pulling back his lips and examining the remains of his teeth. He stared morosely at his reflection. "I didn't realise I was so ugly," he said sadly.

"We all are," Amber said kindly, giving him a friendly slap. She turned to Fenn to smile.

"I've found beans … and more beans," said Fathom laughing, weighing two tins in his hands. But Fenn was silent. Tikki had started trembling.

In the middle of the room Fenn saw a patch of moss growing on the floor in a perfect rectangle. Tikki suddenly slipped down off his shoulders and disappeared into his rucksack, making a mewing sound. The bats shuffled in their sleep, wrapping their ink-black wings closer around themselves, like mackintoshes pulled tight against the rain.

"It's freezing in here; we'll need some blankets," Gulper said, walking towards the wardrobe.

Fenn still didn't reply. He was thinking about how moss could only grow if there was some daylight coming in. He looked at the steep bank of mud and clambered slowly up. Just as he thought; mud had poured in through a window. The top of it was still visible, but the panes had been broken down by the pressure of the marsh. Fenn could easily crawl out, which meant animals could just as easily get in. That would need blocking up for them to be safe, he thought. He was just about to call down to Fathom to ask him to pass up some wood, when he heard a crack and looked back at the fireplace. It was Comfort. She had slapped her hand against the mirror, and was staring beyond her own reflection, into the room. Her mouth was stretched wide, circling the scream she couldn't make.

Somebody – or something – was stirring in the bed.

Fenn's throat went dry with fear. He held his lamp higher so the light from it would reach.

From the innermost black of the bed a ragged shadow was rising up, as if the sheets had come alive. Whatever it was lumbered down onto the floor, landing cumbersomely, caught up in the curtains. Fenn watched as it dragged itself up to its full height, inching out from the rotting blanket that clung to its hunched back. A sickly stench drifted out as it shambled out of the gloom and a raw, throaty snarl curdled in the dark. Suddenly two slits of yellow-green reflected the light as it opened its sleepy eyes.

It was a wolf.

Fenn slid back down the mound of earth to get to the others. As he landed at the bottom, his foot hit something hard – a wooden curtain pole, knocked from the window as the mud pushed in. He grabbed it and held it out like a sword. As Amber's scream broke free from her frozen throat, the bats loosened their grip on the pelmet's fringe and swooped down into the room, scything spirals around the chandelier.

"Get behind me but don't turn your back on it," Fenn whispered. He knew if they ran the wolf would see prey, not predators.

It was old and ill, though it had once been a giant; the alpha in the pack. Now it limped slowly forward into the ring of lantern light, watching them hungrily, and Fenn noticed its paws were splayed wide and its claws had grown so long they corkscrewed beneath its pads from lack of use. Its haunches sagged from muscle waste and its matted fur clung down his back. As it gazed at them it hung its mangy head, almost as if it was ashamed at what age had reduced it to, but deep inside its throat a low menacing growl still rumbled on. It may have been old and skinny, but its teeth were as long and sharp as they'd ever been and Fenn knew a hungry wolf was far more dangerous than a fed one. As the last piece of fabric slipped off its back the bones of a muntjac tumbled out. With sickening dread, Fenn realised that if it wasn't hunting for itself, then the rest of the pack had to be nearby.

"Gulper! Back up here slowly. Don't show you're scared," Fenn said.

"But I am!" Gulper managed to croak.

The wolf was looking at Fenn now; instinct telling it that Fenn was the leader. It growled deeper and sniffed the air, looking for his scent. Fenn brandished the pole, but the wolf stood its ground. It now turned its huge head in a low menacing sweep away from Fenn to Comfort as Amber pushed her up the mound of earth towards the window. It lowered its head and dropped a little on its front paws, preparing to pounce.

Comfort was now safely through the window. Fenn glanced quickly over his shoulder and saw Amber disappear through the hole too. The wolf watched them go, still growling. It took another step forward, challenging Fenn.

"Go!" Fenn shouted. He swung the pole back and forth in an arc to give Gulper and Fathom time to scramble up the mound.

The wolf continued to pad forwards, but still it didn't spring. It was too old, too weak to fight with all of them, but now there was just the one. Fenn swung the pole, catching the wolf on its snout as it nosed forward. The wolf yelped and stumbled sideways, watching Fathom disappear through the window; then it lifted its head and let out a long howl. Fenn's blood ran cold; the wolf was calling the pack back. Instantly Fenn caught the sound of another howl from out on the marsh. In the dark, from all around, the air filled with low moans and answering whines.

"Don't run!" Fenn shouted as he edged up the slope, half on his back. As he tried to haul himself through the window, he saw the wolf lower its front legs, preparing to leap. He hurled the lantern down the mound of earth and as it fell the paraffin leaked out, spraying the room with fire and setting Fenn's pole alight. The wolf ran snarling and snapping into the dark, shying away from the tumbling flames. Seizing his chance Fenn scrambled through the hole.

"Don't run!" Fenn yelled again to the others as he stumbled out onto the pitch black marsh.

But it was too late; they were all sprinting for the cover of the nearest reedbeds.

Fenn ran after them, holding the burning pole, stumbling over clumps of sedge as he lurched towards the tall grasses. Fear had plugged their ears and panic blinded their eyes. Fenn was the only one to see the flashing green in the dark; the pack was already in the reedbeds, separating out and making a net ready to encircle them. There was nothing for it; they had to stay together, so Fenn ran towards the wet black of the bulrushes. Suddenly the snarling and panting sounded much closer.

"Stop!" Fenn yelled.

By the time he found them, they were huddled together, terrified. The wolves were all around but still not showing themselves.

"Form a circle! Face outwards!" Fenn shouted.

He swung the burning pole in a circle around them, then wrenched up some rushes and quickly twisted them together. He lit the end and threw them to Fathom, who then lit a second clump of rushes he'd torn up. Soon they were all clutching burning brands of reeds. But even the fiery lights didn't deter the pack. The wolves grew bolder, slipping in and out of the reeds, sizing up the gaps between the children and working out a way to separate them. They were eyeing up the smallest and weakest: Comfort. Suddenly one of them saw a chance and launched itself at her.

Fenn threw himself in front of Comfort and waited for

the wolf to tear into him. Instead there was a twang and the wolf yelped and twisted mid-leap, falling lifelessly into the mud beside them. A few seconds later another larger wolf suddenly stopped in its tracks and began whining and sniffing the air. A gleam of silver streaked through the reeds like an arrow. Then there came a sharp bark and a rushing sound from above. In an instant the second wolf fell beneath the snarling jaws of a huge white wolfhound. It was Gelert, Lundy's faithful hound. A second later another twang sounded and a wolf yowled in the darkness, then they heard a dull thud as it fell down onto the soaking earth. A third wolf shot past Fenn, savagely thrashing its jaws from side-to-side as it skimmed past his legs. Two more wolves, their muzzles stretched back across their teeth, sprang just a few inches beyond Amber, with Gelert bounding after them, snapping at their hind legs as he chased them off. Fenn listened as more wolves started snarling in the darkness nearby, followed by Gelert's tormented bark. Then he heard a cry.

Suddenly the entire pack melted back into the whispering reeds and the marsh fell oddly silent. Fenn stumbled through muddy water to find Gelert whimpering. He had a cut down the side of his leg, but instead of licking it clean he was tugging at something lying on the ground. As Fenn ran up his heart flipped, thinking it was Halflin. He knelt down and pushed the tangle of crushed reeds away.

It was Lundy.

He tried to pull her upright. His hands were immediately covered in blood. A terrible gash ran across her collarbone and she was bleeding heavily.

"Help! Over here!" he shouted. The others rushed over and together they gently lifted Lundy up and carried her onto drier land.

"Quick! Get round me!" Fenn ordered. "Make a circle. The wolves are afraid of the flames." He took his jacket off and pushed it under Lundy as best he could, then ripped off his jumper and pressed it hard against the wound.

"Fenn," Lundy whispered, rasping for air.

"Shh," he said, gently taking her hand and pressing his other hand down hard on the jumper. He'd seen too many animals dying to not recognise the look in her eyes. Gelert whimpered loudly. He knew too.

"You weren't meant to come back," Lundy whispered.

"It's all right," he answered, tucking the coat tightly around her. "My friends are with me." Lundy tried to shake her head, but she was too weak.

"You have to leave! Now! All of you," she managed at last.

Fenn stroked her arm, trying to reassure her.

"We'll get you home. Halflin will know…"

Lundy gripped Fenn's wrist with surprising strength.

"He's gone," she sighed heavily. A wolf growled somewhere nearby and Fenn was distracted for a second. He shook his head; he couldn't have heard properly.

"Gone?" he repeated, frowning. Halflin couldn't leave the Punchlock. Hadn't he always said he could never leave? "Where?" he asked. Lundy closed her eyes.

"Dead," she said, her voice feeble as thistledown.

Lundy's words looped in his mind, making no sense. It was as though he had lost his footing and was falling through air. Like the time he missed a tread climbing back down from the loft, and had pitched head first towards the floor, certain in that split second that he was going to die. But Halflin had lunged across the kitchen and just caught him, so Fenn was bruised but not broken. Now his catcher was dead and Fenn was dropping into emptiness, with nothing to break his fall. He felt like he'd been winded and would never breathe again. Fenn shook his head; he'd only been gone seven weeks, people don't just die. If his grandad had died, he would have known. He would have felt it. Wouldn't he?

At last he took a breath. The air ripped thornily down his throat and filled his lungs with a cruel coldness, as if he was drowning. Nothing ordinary could ever be ordinary again, not even breathing.

"How?" he asked, staring blankly. Pain was balling up in

his lungs like it had when he'd swum through the sinking boat the night of the Sweep.

"Chilstone. Tried to get word to you," Lundy answered. She began to cough, clutching at Fenn's arm with the last of her strength, pulling him nearer. "Your parents..." Lundy was trying to talk quickly, desperate to jam everything vital into her final breaths, using up the last dregs of her life on him.

"They had nothing to do with that attack on Chilstone's ship. They were coming to light the Punchlock – it's the signal to start the revolution. It wasn't just about revenge; Chilstone killed them to stop the Seaborns rising up – to kill our last hope." Her voice was becoming inaudible and her eyelids flickered. Fenn knelt closer so she wouldn't have to struggle so hard to be heard.

"There's a key..."

"A key?" he asked.

"The Demaris'..." Lundy tightened her grip around Fenn's wrist until her fingers pinched. She was losing her hold on life so was keeping a hold of him. "It proves who you are but Halflin hid it, to protect you..."

Fenn felt her fingers loosen, like a rope slipping its knot.

"Lundy..." he began, but her face was blurry as tears filled his eyes; he wanted to thank her. He'd never thanked her, and now it was too late.

He put his ear a few millimetres from her barely moving lips to hear her last words, but whatever she was trying to say, he couldn't hear. Instead she smiled slightly as Gelert licked her hand, then she closed her eyes.

23

They buried Lundy by the *Ionia* that night under the scattering snow. While Fenn and Fathom cut away the turf for the grave, Fenn finally decided he'd have to trust Fathom with the truth and told him what he was going to do, and why. Meanwhile, Gulper helped Comfort pick a few celandines and the two of them made a posy with these and a sprig of mistletoe, which they tucked between Lundy's folded hands. Amber unhooked a sail from where it had been hung to dry and made a shroud for Lundy's body; no one wanted to place her in the cold earth without some cover. Then they lay the clods of turf over her, and on top of this piled the big flat stones she'd collected for this sole purpose; she'd always known the earth would be too wet to dig a deep grave when the time came. Fenn scratched her name on a piece of slate with a shard of flint, then all five children piled the wet, black earth up against the rough stone and silently said farewell, wiping their hands clean on their clothes.

While they worked, Gelert lay quietly, but when Lundy's body was covered he circled the stones again and again, whining. Finally he lay down on the grave and rested his head on his massive paws, and no cajoling could make him move.

It was time to go. As the children took what they needed from the *Ionia*, replenishing their meagre supplies of food and clean water, Amber found Lundy's cat hiding. She carried it out with it purring in her arms; two kindred spirits.

"I'm taking the cat," she said.

"Put it in the catch basket then," Fenn answered, barely looking up. He whistled to Tikki, who had scampered up onto Amber's shoulder, trying to tease the old tom cat, and Tikki ran to Fenn, squeaking with excitement and anger. Amber waited for Fenn to say more, but he simply draped Tikki around his neck and silently packed his rucksack. She had tried to ask him about Halflin as they carried Lundy back to the *Ionia*, but he wouldn't say anything except that they had to get off East Marsh. The night was fading to mauve, but Gelert still refused to move, growling when Fathom tried to drag him away by his collar.

"Leave him," Fenn snapped.

He knew Gelert was never going to leave Lundy and wished he'd had the same tenacity with Halflin. Then he forced himself to stop thinking like that. Now was not the time. All he needed to think about was getting his friends off the marsh and to safety. That was all that mattered. Fenn pulled out two rabbits from the meat safe that Lundy must have caught the day before and dropped them by Gelert. He didn't so much as glance at them.

"Ready?" Fenn said to the others as he hitched his bag onto his back. He set off without another word. He wanted to get to the Punchlock before dawn properly broke, then, if there were still boats there, they could catch the early tide.

They trudged on, the marsh waking up around them, the light fresh and bright. The wind scattered the clouds, shaking meagre flurries of snow that instantly dissolved in the warming sun. None of it mattered to Fenn and he couldn't find a single word to say to anything Amber asked or pointed out. An hour passed in silence, save for the meowing from Amber's cat, when suddenly Fathom pointed through the reeds.

"What's that?" he asked.

From where they stood the tethering post of the Punchlock looked like a gallows; a high post with an arm at a right angle to it, from which an iron chain dangled and creaked in the icy breeze. Amber shuddered. Winter winds had stripped the trees of their leaves and through the scribble of branches Fenn caught sight of the snowy roofline of his old house.

"The Punchlock," Fenn answered. He hardly bothered to look. The sight of Halflin's prison made him sick with anger and now was the time for clear, cold thinking.

Fenn led them up the secret path he and Halflin had escaped along the morning he'd seen the *Warspite*. When he got to the old oak tree the path forked, and he pointed out the way that led through the gorse bushes down to the Punchlock. It was foggy over the water but he could make out the shapes of the boats that had been waiting to be sunk the morning he and Halflin had run to Lundy's. They were still tethered, awaiting their fate, except it had turned out to be Halflin's last day, not theirs. Fenn took a deep breath to quell the dizzying hatred he felt for Chilstone. He knew he had to keep his head; his heart was broken, but not his spirit.

"Guess there's no need to go back for the *Salamander*," Fathom said, following his gaze.

"Which one should we take?" Amber asked.

"You should take the old Gleaner," Fenn answered brúsquely. "Barges get picked up more and Gleaners are lighter; get through less fuel."

"*You*?" Amber said, sharp as a whip crack.

Fenn ignored her.

"The fuel's in the work shed. If it's locked there's a key on top of the lintel. Keep your eyes open. Nicking boats from a Punchlock carries an automatic death sentence."

Amber stared at him intently.

"I'll see if there's anything there we can use back at..." He nodded his head towards the hut, but he wasn't going to call it home. Home meant Halflin. The others disappeared down the path.

Fenn slowly crept up between the gorse bushes and silverwort until he reached the garden at the back of the hut, then he slipped up into the woodshed. The chicken perch was bare and the pigsties were silent. The old sow had gone. A breath caught in Fenn's throat. He hadn't expected to miss the pig. He tiptoed out and slipped behind the sails Halflin had been mending, which still hung, stiff with a starch of frost. Using the sails as cover he ran towards the hut.

The back door was hanging open and banged in the breeze. For one happy second Fenn had the strongest sensation Halflin was still alive, as if he'd just come in and slammed the door behind him, and before he knew it, Fenn had an excuse ready for why he was outside the hut. But then the door swung open again, showing the lightless interior. There was no one there. No one to tell him off any more, no one to make excuses to.

He crept inside. The place had been ransacked; the table

and chairs knocked over and the shelves swept clean of their belongings, which lay broken and ground into the floorboards. Leaves had blown in over the kitchen floor, there were bird droppings on the shelves and a confusion of prints that showed animals had sheltered there.

Tikki jumped down and started sniffing the floor nervously; he could smell Fenn, but there were other dangerous scents here. Wolves had been in, looking for food, marking their territory, seeing if the hut would make a good den.

Most of the bottle glazing had been smashed out from the windows and the sackcloth curtains ripped away. Halflin's drying rack had been pulled down, leaving leaves and seed heads scattered all over the ground. Behind the cold stove, a mound of something white and soft lifted and scattered in the draft from the open door, catching Fenn's eye. He knelt down and gathered up the mass of feathers spread around the shrivelled remains of the old gull. It must have starved.

He didn't cry. He didn't even feel like crying. Instead he cradled its desiccated body for just a moment before gently wrapping it in some sackcloth and laying it back in the shadows.

As he straightened up Fenn saw the rug had been kicked out of the way, revealing Halflin's secret stash-hole. He rushed to it and looked in. Darkness stared back at him but then he cast his mind back, remembering the second cubby hole behind the first. He gently pushed his finger into the missing knot of wood and pulled the panel out. There was a tin. Tikki came and nosed at his hand as Fenn lifted it out and opened it.

Inside was Halflin's medicine, a few pieces of jewellery, a compass and a wallet of fake sea-permits. Four of them were pristine, never used. Fenn sighed with relief; his friends were safe. He was just stuffing the tin in his rucksack when he saw something lying in the thick dust of the secret hole. He reached down and lifted it up. It was a key, dulled with age, dangling on a tarnished chain. The grip was gold, shaped like rope and fashioned into a D, with a twisted design like a mooring knot around it. Fenn held it up, staring as it spun back and forth, gleaming softly in the early morning sunlight. Such a tiny thing, but Halflin considered it dangerous enough to be hidden for thirteen years. Fenn gritted his teeth; it had been dangerous without it so he might as well be reunited with the tiny object. He looped the key around his neck.

As he stood up, a little pouch fell on the floor, which must have fallen from the tin. He picked it up and pulled the two cords open. Inside were five or six curls of what he guessed was his jet-black baby hair, tied with tiny pieces of thread. They had been saved by Halflin, as treasured and secret as everything else in the tin. Fenn yanked the cords to close it again and dropped it back in the dark. Then he, put the panel back, scuffed the rug back over, hooked Tikki under his arm and hurried out.

The others were already waiting by the Gleaner by the time Fenn got back, and small pillows of blue smoke were puffing out from its soot-speckled funnel. Gulper dragged the last barrel of diesel from the work shed, up to the vessel's side.

"Think that's enough?" he asked as he rolled it onto the deck. Fenn nodded.

"Find anything?" Fathom asked. Fenn read the Gleaner's name.

"The *Madeleine*," he said. "Good name for a boat."

He handed the wallet with the permits over to Fathom.

"These will get you anywhere," he said quietly. "Look after them; one for each of you."

"Where's yours?" Amber asked suspiciously.

"I'm not coming. Not yet." There was a tone in his voice they'd never heard before: rigid and immovable. They all stared at him.

Amber looked at Fathom to see if this was a joke. He wasn't smiling. She looked at Gulper, who was as confused as she was.

"We have to stick together!" Gulper said.

"I'll follow on soon," said Fenn. Amber glared at him, the

old flinty look back in her eyes.

"Why?"

"Fathom knows. He'll explain it all when you're safe away from here."

Fathom nodded.

"Knows what? What do you know?" Amber snapped, staring at Fathom first then back to Fenn.

"That it's not safe for you lot to stay with me." Fenn tried to smile. He nodded at Amber's clover earring. "You'll have more luck without me."

"You can't stay here alone," Gulper said.

"No, he can't. Tell him Fathom." Amber looked at Fathom for support but when she found none, she fell silent and tears ran down her cheeks.

"I'll be fine. I've got Tikki," Fenn said. Amber suddenly threw her arms around Fenn's neck and sobbed aloud. Fenn tried to disentangle himself but before he could get free, Amber let go anyway, almost shoving him away. She fumbled with her scarf for a second before she closed his fingers around something hard and sharp. Then she ran back along the gangplank and disappeared below deck.

"Better get going before you miss the tide," Fenn said to Fathom.

He gave Comfort a kiss. Then Fathom and Gulper hugged him briefly before following Comfort onto the boat.

Fathom pulled back the gangplank and Fenn dropped the moor line off the bollard. Gulper hoisted the line back over the gunwale.

"See you in West Isle," Fenn called.

The *Madeleine* chugged away and the soft swell from her wash slopped against the jetty. As the ship surged across the estuary towards open sea, Amber appeared by the rail, trying to catch one last glimpse of him.

Fenn was already halfway up the rise towards the hut before he dared open his hand, still clenched around the object Amber had pushed into it. He knew what it was before he looked; in the centre of his palm lay Amber's lucky brass clover. He was going to need it and, as he pinned it through the cloth in his shirt pocket, his heart started pounding so hard that it felt like it would crash through his ribs. He wanted to turn around, to wave, to run back and go with his friends. Instead he continued to walk on, doggedly. From over the estuary, he just caught Amber shouting with all her might.

"Fenn!"

But Fenn refused to turn around or stop; it would do no good for her to see him weeping. There was no place for tears in this world.

Fenn went back to the hut and bolted the doors. He hadn't

slept for days and was exhausted. He hung sacking over the gaping windows then wrapped himself in any blankets he could find, tucked Tikki down by his feet and curled up on Halflin's bed, burying his face deep in the pillow and breathing in the sweet smell of dry bulrush and pipe smoke. He fell into a deep sleep and didn't wake until it was nearly dusk.

It was time; he knew what to do.

He washed under the kitchen pump, rubbed his hair dry with a blanket, then went outside. He found what he was looking for in the woodshed, hidden behind the rusting generator: a large jerrycan full of kerosene that Halflin filled the lamps from, and a tin of engine oil. Next he salvaged a few glass jars from the hut's windows, tore down the sheets that divided the rooms and ripped the blankets off the bed. He piled all these in a barrow and wheeled it to the Punchlock.

In the lowering light he filled each of the jars with the kerosene, a layer of oil, then stuffed a piece of torn blanket in the top. Into this he shoved a plaited scrap of sheet to make a wick. When he had made four of them he stopped and rested, sharing a can of corn he'd found with Tikki, as they watched dusk fall over the estuary. The wind had fallen and the sky was clear, except for one dark cloud; a flock of starlings, moving swiftly and changing shape constantly like a shoal of airborne fish. Fenn remembered Halflin explaining how the birds waltzed on the breeze to protect themselves from predators.

As darkness arrived, Fenn locked Tikki in the work shed so he wouldn't follow him, laid the jars carefully in a catch basket, hitched the jerrycan onto his back and walked down the thin gangway that Halflin had used to do maintenance work on the Punchlock. When he got there he shimmied up the post, gripping it with his knees and ankles like a monkey.

The wood was blackened by years of bitumen painted to stop the salt erosion and it stained Fenn's hands and clothes. At the top, three thick iron straps secured the T-shaped bar from which the tethering chain creaked gently. Balancing carefully, Fenn crawled out onto the arm, pouring kerosene along it and splashing more down the mast. Finally he slid back down and did the same all around the lock. Then, walking backwards, he poured the last of the kerosene along the gangway. The whole thing took no more than ten minutes. Breathing hard, Fenn picked up the first jar, lit the rag, took a run up and flung it at the Punchlock with all his might.

It flew like a comet, leaving splinters of fire in a tail behind it, but his aim was out and it missed completely, landing in the water. He lit a second. This time his aim was true and it smashed in a satisfying rosette of flame against the Punchlock post. For a second the flame sagged, like a curtain, then it flashed upwards like a bird taking flight and fluttered along the post. He lit a third and threw it so that it shattered on the lock itself. Now the entire structure was alight. Gold, rose and emerald licks of fire twisted and flicked their way across the post and dropped down like tears, fizzing as they hit the water. The starlings scattered in fright.

The Punchlock post began to bubble and blister as the tar melted in the heat. Bitumen oozed out of the wood and a bright tongue of flame licked out from the top of the post where the tethering arm was fixed, as sparks twirled up into the air and the flames ate into the old oak. The heat was so intense that the iron straps supporting the arm started to melt, dripping and sliding down the post in molten red streams. After a few minutes there was a splintering sound as the arm of the Punchlock started to collapse. The embers of the burning wood blazed high into the sky, illuminating the whole estuary. Suddenly the beam crashed down, smashing the edge of the gangway, where the fire buckled and flicked out.

Fenn carefully packed the remaining bottle into his rucksack and went back to unlock the work shed. Tikki was hiding under Halflin's bench, his eyes wide with fear at the smell of fire and the strange flickering light. As soon as he saw Fenn he scampered up. Fenn cuddled him close, carefully tucking him down into his reefer jacket to keep him safe. Then he shut the door and clambered quickly back up the hill, away from the searing heat.

Fenn followed the low wall in front of the hut and skirted around it until he reached the scrubby, stony land that sloped down towards a small cliff. From there he could see the world clearly; to his left the estuary swelled out towards the sea, to his right the river and streams glistened like mercury between the dense reeds. He flattened out a tussock of dry moss, sat down and put Tikki on his lap, stroking him gently as he watched the jetty and Punchlock burn and slowly collapse into the sea. Only its mast still stood, blazing like a beacon in the dark, the black smoke drifting like a stain across the water.

A damp breeze suddenly swept up from the estuary, bringing ash fluttering over the entire hill, snowing down on him and making his eyes stream. He shivered as he stared out at the huge sea, the Whale's Acre, then he held Tikki against his chest and lay back on the ground, gazing up at the starless sky.

No more hiding in the darkness. A fire like this would be seen for hundreds of miles.

Coming soon…

FENN HALFLIN AND THE RISING OF THE SEABORN

Hunted by the brutal Terra Firma, Fenn
Halflin's survival now depends on finding
the last of a rumoured resistance group.
His journey will take him deep into a
treacherous marsh, but as the water levels
continue to rise, the fight to get the Seaborns
behind the Wall has never been more desperate.

Read more great adventures...

Timothée de Fombelle
Vango Book One: Between Sky and Earth

Fleeing from the police and more sinister forces on his trail, Vango must race against time to prove his innocence – a journey that will take him to the farthest reaches of distant lands. Can Vango uncover the secrets of his past before everything is lost?

"Exciting, unusual and beautifully written." *David Almond*

Vango Book Two: A Prince Without a Kingdom

Vango has spent his life abandoning his loved ones to protect them from the demons of his past. But the mystery of his identity has started to unravel, and in the shadows of war and persecution, the truth will finally come to light.

"A distinctive and atmospherically cinematic tale." *Independent*

Rob Lloyd Jones

WILD BOY

London, 1841. A boy covered in hair, raised as a monster, condemned to life in a travelling freak show. A boy with an extraordinary power of observation and detection. A boy accused of murder; on the run; hungry for the truth. Ladies and Gentlemen, take your seats. The show is about to begin!

"A pacey, atmospheric and thrilling adventure." *Metro*

WILD BOY AND THE BLACK TERROR

A new sensation grips London – a poisoner who strikes without a trace. Is there a cure for the black terror? To find out, Wild Boy and Clarissa must catch the killer. Their hunt will lead them from the city's vilest slums to its grandest palaces, and to a darkness at the heart of its very highest society.

"An exhilarating read with great characters."
The Bookbag

Amanda Mitchison
MISSION TELEMARK

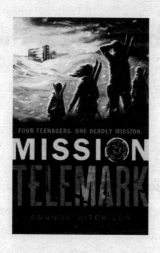

Norway, December 1942. The British government has become aware that Hitler is trying to find a way to make a nuclear weapon. Now the Allies' fate rests in the hands of four teenagers who must survive for weeks in freezing conditions before they launch a sabotage attempt that will decide the course of the war.

"A gripping, well-paced adventure." *The Daily Mail*

About the author

Francesca Armour-Chelu grew up by the Suffolk Coast. She studied English and Drama at Goldsmiths and went on to work in museum education and public libraries. Her experience of living on water meadows in an abandoned Edwardian railway carriage inspired her debut novel, *Fenn Halflin and the Fearzero*, which was short-listed for the Mslexia Children's Novel Competition 2012. Francesca lives in Suffolk.